APERTURE

SURFACE AND ILLUSION: TEN PORTFOLIOS

The poet Charles Baudelaire, in a scathing review of the 1859 Salon in Paris, wrote, "If photography is allowed to stand in for art in some of its functions it will soon supplant or corrupt it completely thanks to the natural support it will find in the stupidity of the multitude. It must return to its real task, which is to be the servant of the sciences and of the arts, but the very humble servant, like printing and shorthand which have neither created nor supplanted literature."

It was in 1859 that photography was shown for the first time at the Salon along with painting, sculpture, and other works of art—though it was relegated to a side room of its own. Still, this was a controversial turn of events, for the inherent "realism" of photography both threatened and secretly aided painters in the second half of the nineteenth century. For instance, it is known that Courbet, Delacroix, and Degas all painted from photographs, but only Delacroix openly celebrated the promise of the medium. Most painters of their generation refused to regard photographs as potentially artistic material in their own right.

Of course time has proven that photography, no less than painting (or sculpture, or lithography, or, for that matter, poetry) can, in the rights hands, be a conduit for meaningful artistic expression. We now take this for granted, and understand that its uses are many and varied, its meanings now encoded within a broader discourse of twentieth-century art.

"Surface and Illusion" presents ten portfolios of photographic work by artists we do not necessarily think of as photographers. Drawing primarily on the disciplines of painting, sculpture, and film, this issue seeks to explore the intersection of two-dimensional and three-dimensional representation—the link between the *built* and the *imaged*—as well as the ways in which time, memory, and narrative function between films and still photographs. Many artists could have been included (and indeed were considered) for this issue. Robert Rauschenberg and David Hockney have both, in their omnivorous approach to artmaking, often incorporated photographic techniques and materials, as have Anselm Kiefer, Eric Fischl, Barbara Kruger, and countless others, many of whom have been featured in the pages of *Aperture*. Ultimately, the selection was based on a desire to present work by an unexpected collection of artists who have undertaken serious investigations into the representational potential of the photographic medium.

From Picasso's near-Cubist experiments in photographic technique, explored here by Anne Baldassari, curator of the Picasso Museum in Paris, this issue travels to Charles Hagen's meditation on the hauntingly self-reflective photography of Norwegian painter Edvard Munch. David Frankel looks at historical and contemporary approaches to photography by two of the twentieth century's most influential—and divergent—sculptors, Constantin Brancusi and Kiki Smith, while photographs and journal entries by abstract painter Richard Pousette-Dart reveal his little-known, aesthetically rich forays into the photographic medium. Sculptor Petah Coyne, known for her gothic wax creations, turns to photography to make equally suggestive images of monks in motion and Mexican piñatas, sketched in charcoal-y streaks of gelatin silver.

Turning traditional distinctions between media inside out are the photographs of Louise Lawler, whose conceptual project it has been for many years to use photography to question and to recontextualize works of art, along with the public, the collectors, the museums, and the auction houses who consume and traffic in them. Rosalind Krauss looks into Lawler's imagery—and especially her paperweights—in this issue.

The German painter Gerhard Richter has actively explored the relationship between painting and photography throughout his career, making hyperrealistic paintings, or paintings of blurred motion that suggest photographic imagery without employing photographic technique, or alternately painting directly on top of photographs. The intensity of his explorations is echoed in his often contradictory remarks about the function of art, some of which are printed here. The explorations in photography by fellow German Sigmar Polke span his career in painting and mixed media, and, as Paul Schimmel writes in his essay here, correspond to some degree with his travels and experiments with mind-altering drugs, often resulting in works of transcendent beauty.

Two innovative filmmakers—Wim Wenders and Chris Marker—have in different ways given much thought to the relationship between the still and the moving photographic image. For Wenders the still image is suggestive of entire narratives in the wealth of its visual information—the gestures, the clothes, the texture of light in a landscape. For Marker still images, like films, are inextricably linked with the workings of human memory. They are touchstones in our individual and collective sense of the past.

It is our hope that "Surface and Illusion" will serve for many as a bridge, not only between photography and other forms of contemporary artistic practice, but also between and across a variety of media. For media, in this light, are nothing more nor less than different means of representing the external world and exploring the interior world of the mind.

THE EDITORS

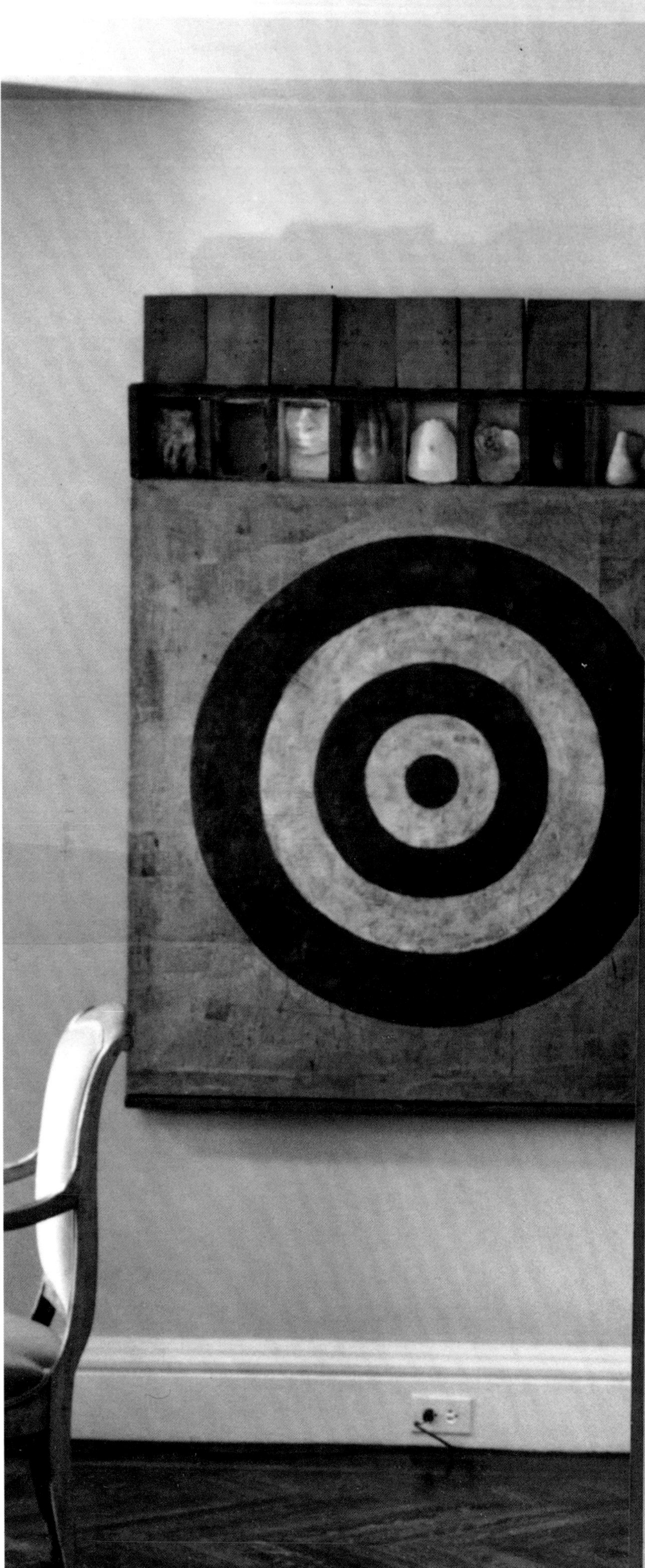

Louise Lawler, *From Here to There*, 1990

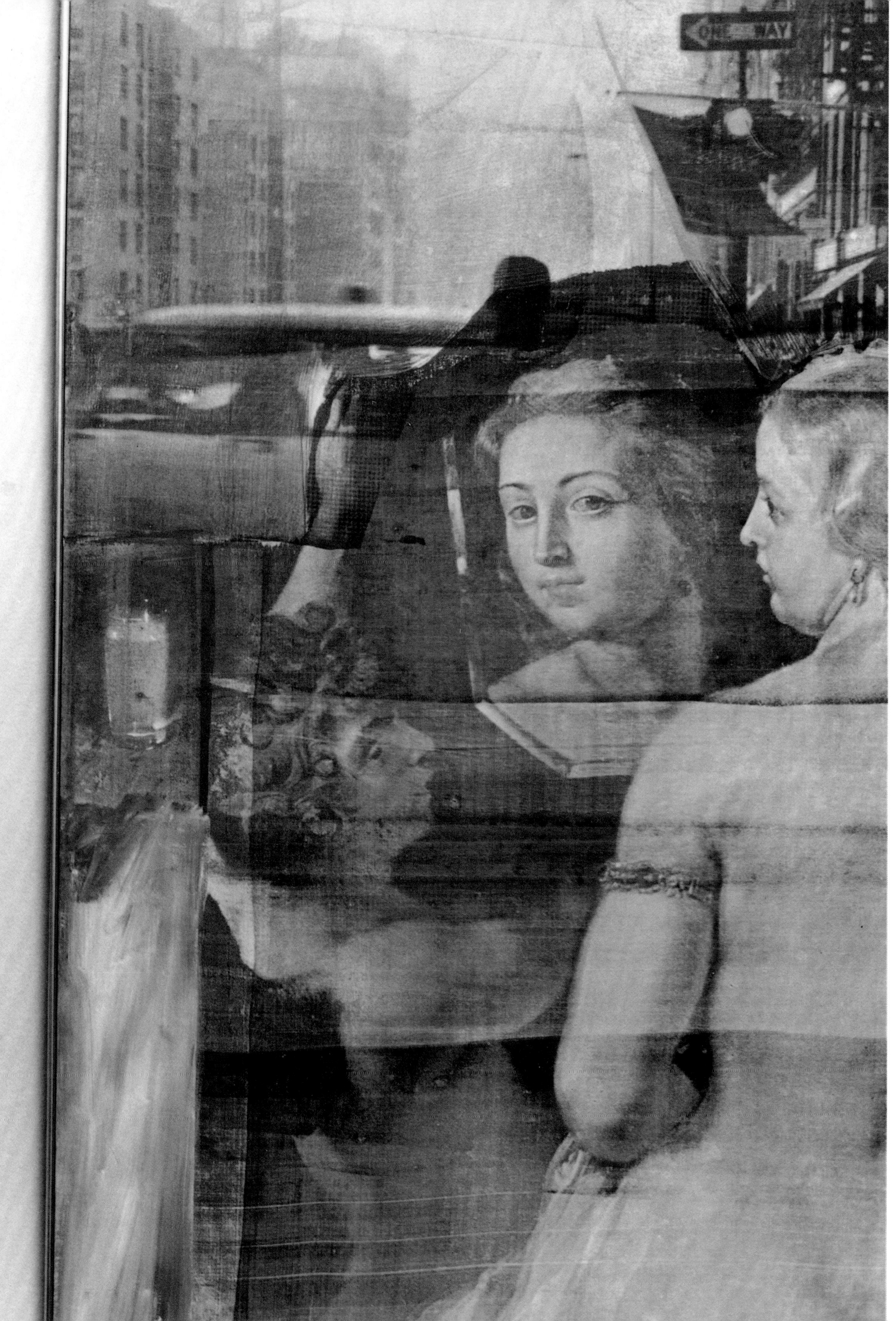
ONE WAY

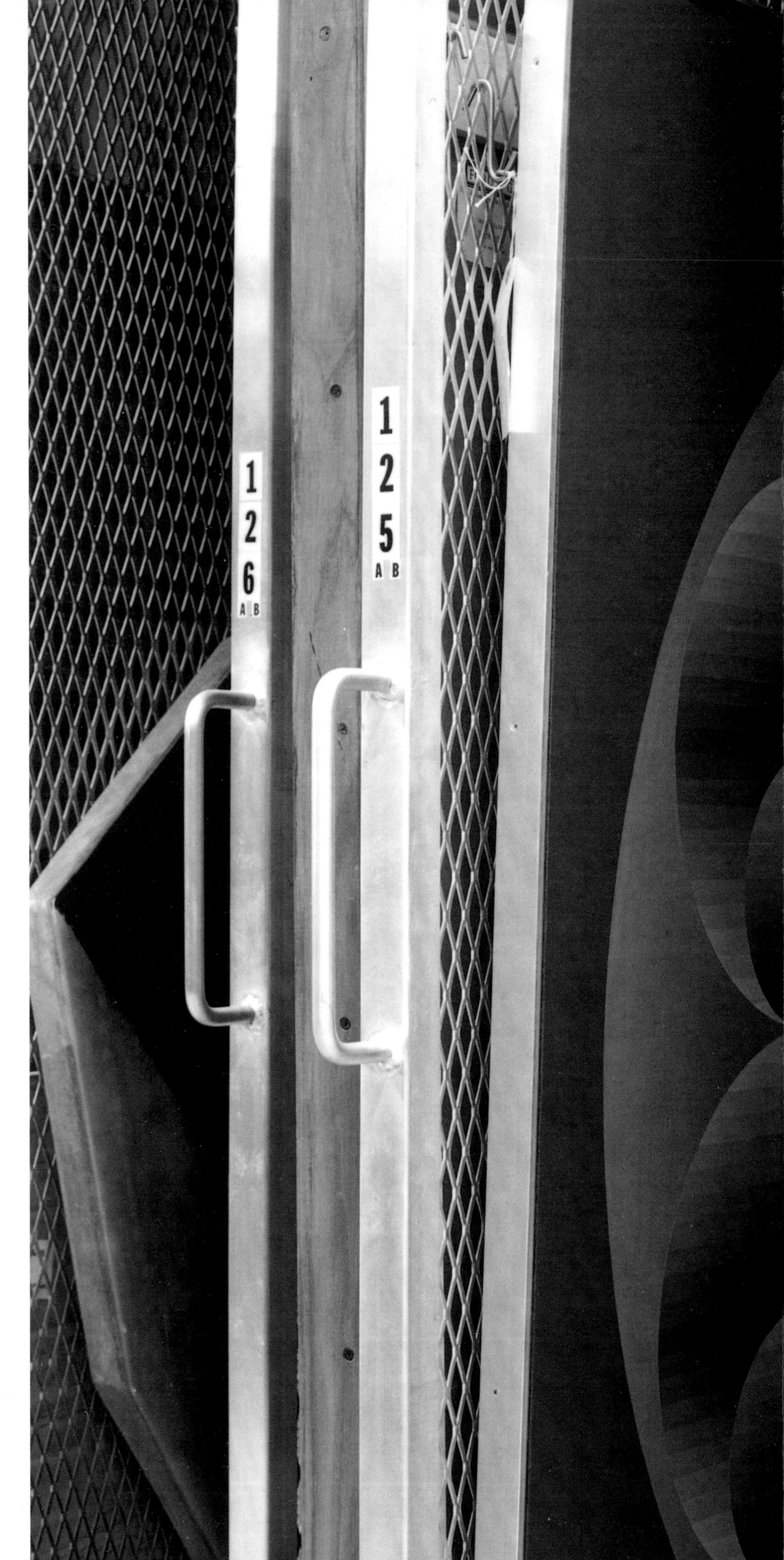

Louise Lawler, *Sargent*, 1990

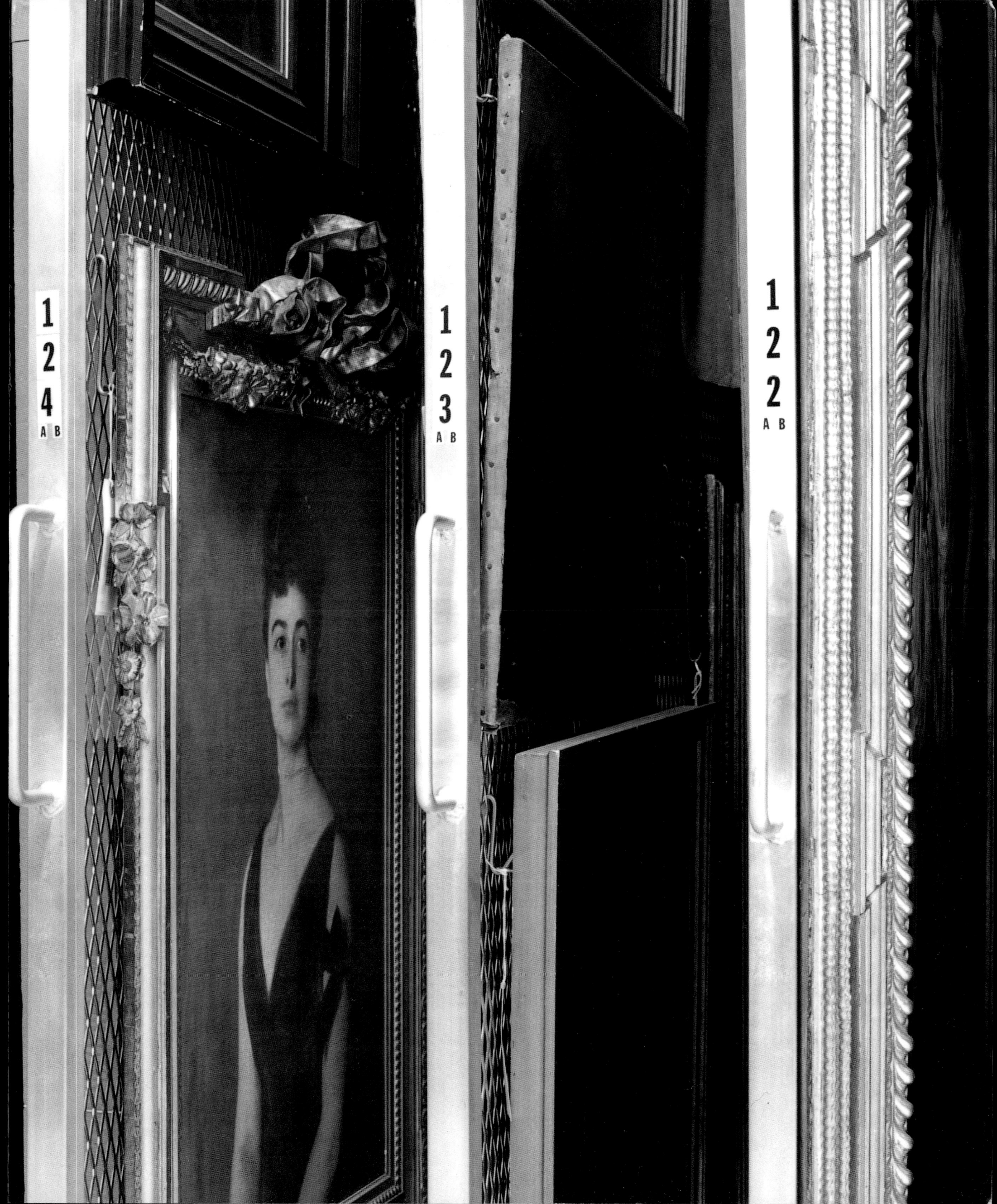

124
A B
123
A B
122
A B

PICASSO THE PHOTOGRAPHER: BEYOND APPEARANCES

The curator of the Picasso Museum in Paris investigates the artist's little-known photographic work.

BY ANNE BALDASSARI

A survey of Pablo Picasso's personal archives has made it possible to appreciate the true extent of his interest in photography. Composed of more than 15,000 works and documents, this collection reveals an artist curious about a wide range of images (*carte-de-visite* portraits, stereoscopic views, and postcards) and a vigilant keeper of his own life's mementos. Bearing the signatures of Man Ray, Dora Maar, Brassaï, Lee Miller, Robert Capa, Henri Cartier-Bresson, Robert Doisneau, David Douglas Duncan, Edward Quinn, and others, these prints represent an exceptional catalog of twentieth-century photography. The archives also provide evidence of Picasso's research within the plastic resources that the photographic medium offers[1]: works combining photography, etching, graffiti, cutouts, the recording of his ephemeral sculptures by Brassaï or Gjon Mili, and photogram experiments conducted with André Villers. Unpublished documents have also made it possible to identify several instances where Picasso used photography as a direct source for his painting. In this regard, an analysis of his work from the period 1915–1923, which is too often simplified as an academic retreat, should now give greater consideration to the influence of the photographic idiom: the tonal scale, distortions of perspective, and effects of framing.[2]

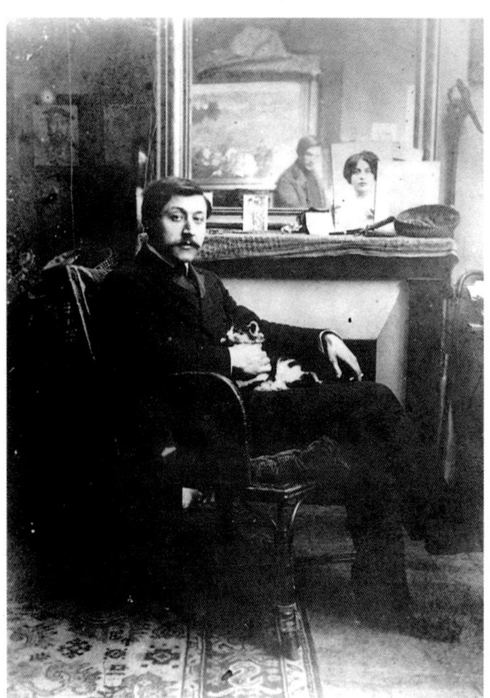

The most valuable component of the archives is by far the hundred or so negatives and original prints that form the basis of the exhibition "Picasso photographe, 1901–1916" [Picasso: Photographer].[3] It is now an established fact that Picasso began taking photographs and developing his own prints from the beginning of the century. This activity is symbolized in the photographic portrait of the painter Ricardo Canals: the picture can also be seen as a self-portrait of Picasso, who is reflected in the center of the mirror holding his camera (left).These photographic experiments by Picasso show a remarkable assurance in composition and great technical inventiveness. They are all the more meaningful in light of the formal upheavals that were occurring in the painter's work at the time: in turn, photography gives new impetus to his research in painting. The few examples presented here demonstrate some of the means the artist used in his attempt to transcend the rules of perspective that govern the images of the camera obscura: changing or splitting the viewpoint, superimposing images, and numerous other devices that serve to shatter mimesis, and to take the medium beyond its own limits.

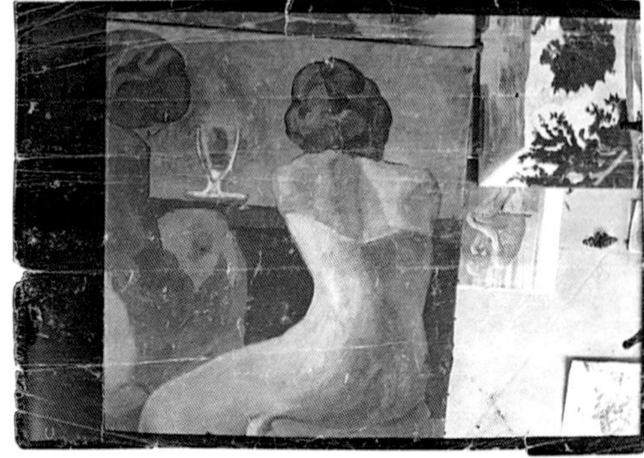

Above: Pablo Picasso, *View of the Studio.*
Bottom left: Pablo Picasso, *Portrait of Ricardo Canals*, Paris, 1904
Opposite: Pablo Picasso, *Self-Portrait in the Studio*, Paris, 1901–1902

The course was set with the first photographic print (1901) that is attributed to Picasso, *Autoportrait dans l'atelier* [Self-portrait in the studio] (opposite). Superimposition of two negatives or the outcome of a deliberately short pose in front of the lens? The image reveals the silhouette of the painter, wearing a top hat and wing collar. On the thin layer of gelatin, the ghostly presence of the painter appears to float out from the wall. On the back of the photo Picasso has written in Spanish: "This photograph could be titled: 'The strongest walls open for me to pass. Behold!'." He paraphrases a line from Lautréamont's "The Songs of Maldoror," in which the author depicts the Creator as he tears through the site of his debaucheries, leaving his victim behind, flayed from head to toe. The metaphor could describe both the position of the artist on the threshold of a

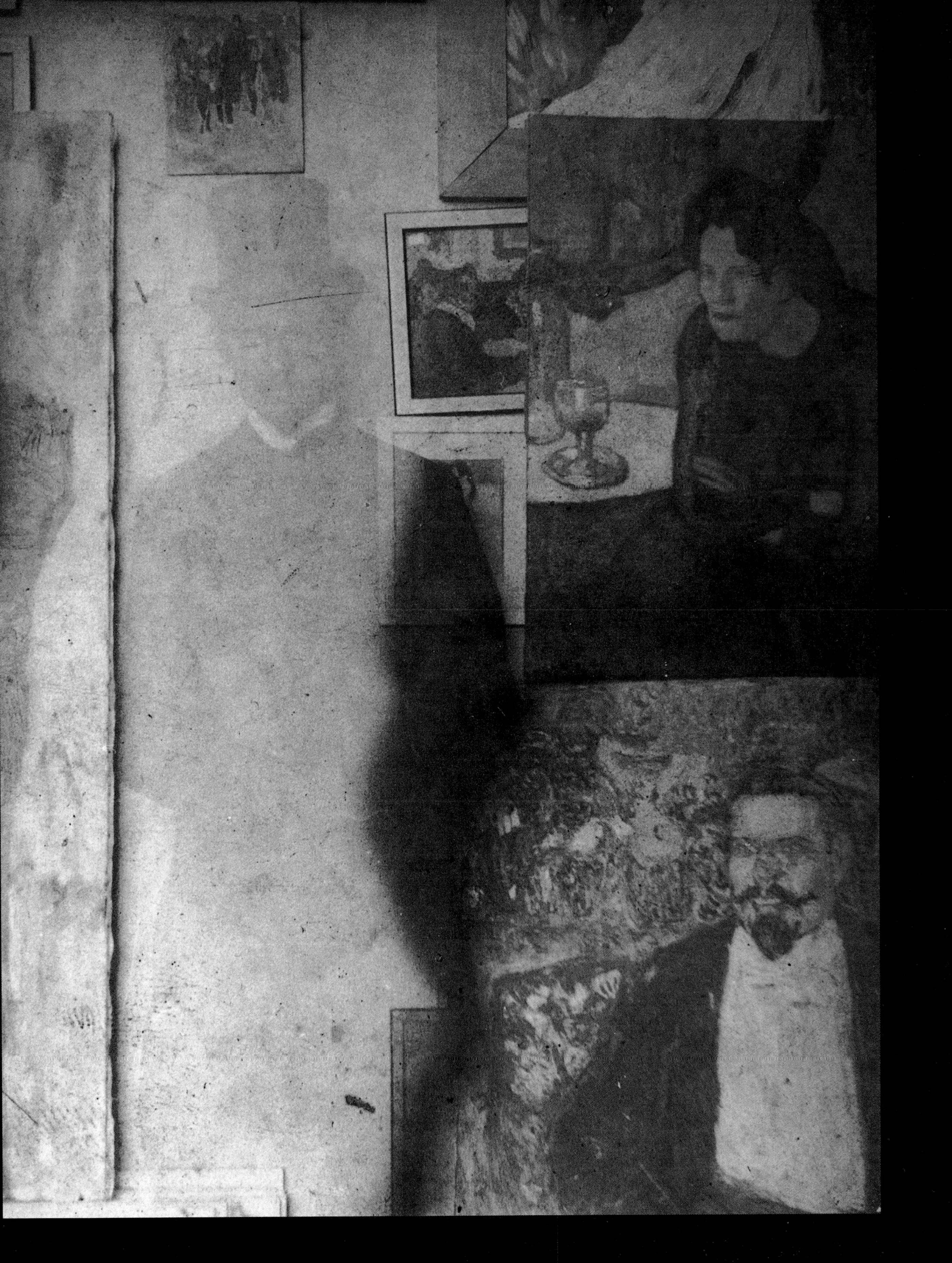

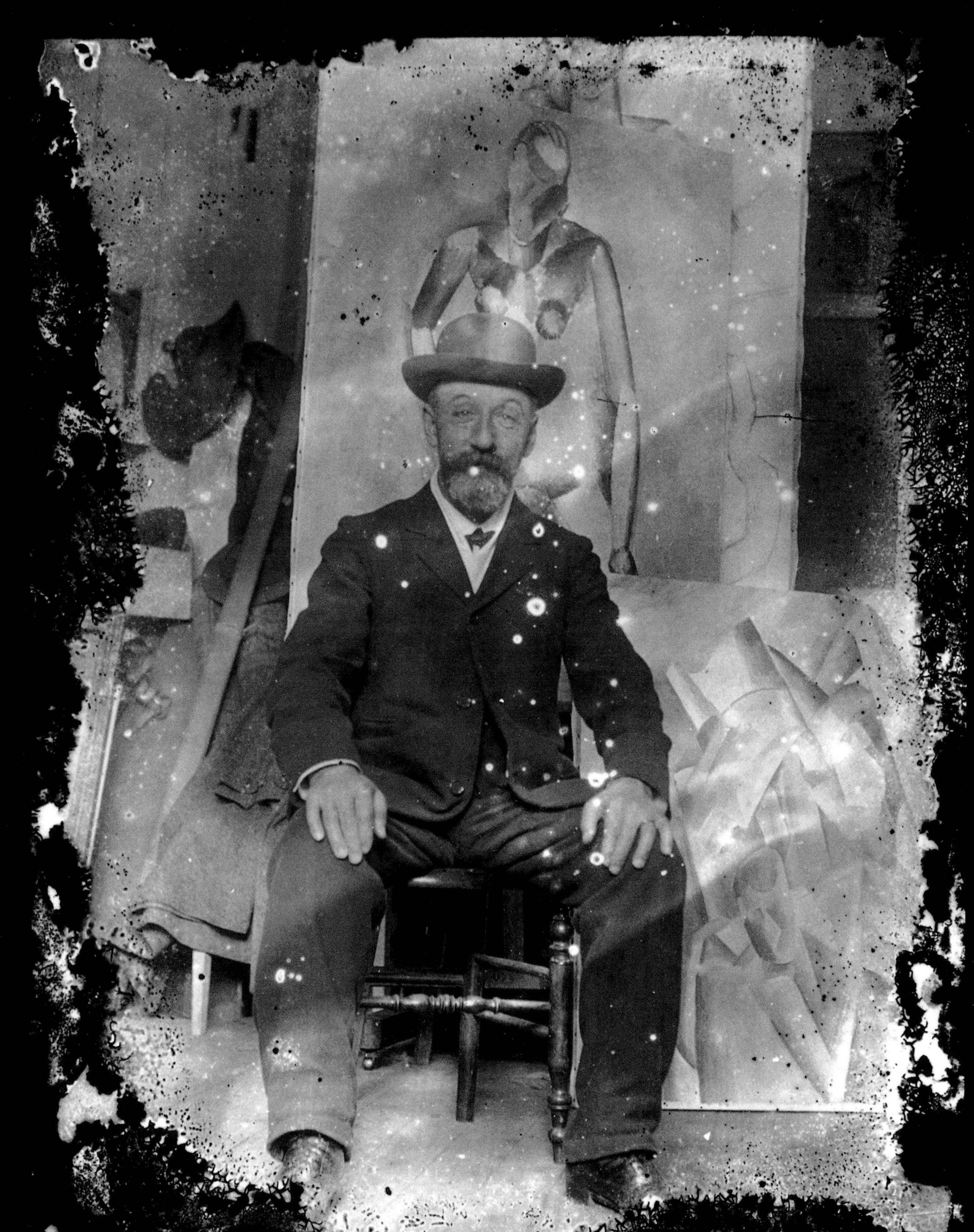

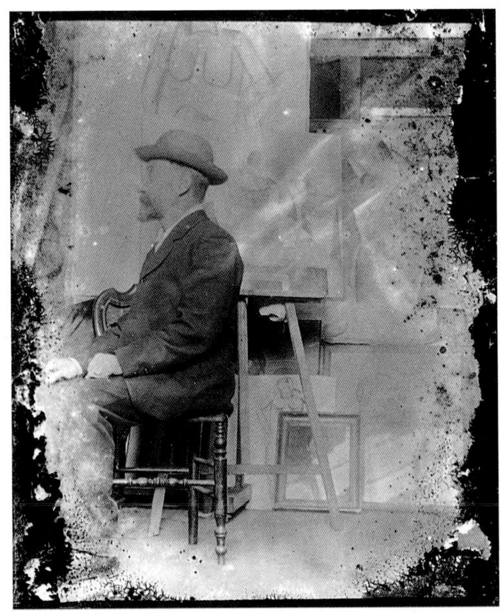

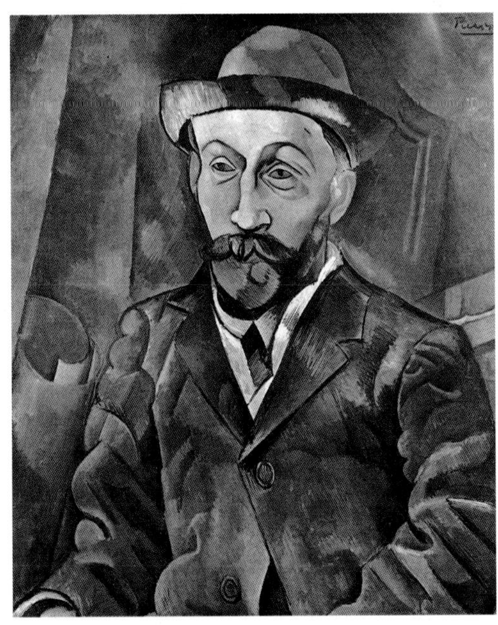

Opposite: Pablo Picasso, *Portrait of Clovis Sagot, frontal view*, Paris, 1909
Above top: Pablo Picasso, *Portrait of Clovis Sagot, profile*, Paris, 1909
Above bottom: Pablo Picasso, *Portrait of Clovis Sagot*, Paris, 1909
Right: Pablo Picasso, *Portrait of Le Douanier Rousseau*, Paris, 1910
Far right: Pablo Picasso, *Portrait of Le Douanier Rousseau*, Paris, 1910

merciless battle with painting and the revolution of appearances, like the skin of the subject folded back on itself, to follow. As in another image, *Vue d'Atelier* [View of the studio] (page 6, right), each of the paintings is cut off to produce an entirely new structure, an arbitrary mosaic of values and signs. Thus photography points to the initial stages of what would develop nearly ten years later into the *papiers collés* (pasted papers) approach: partial motifs overlap and uncover each other, delivering or concealing their message. Cutouts, off-centering, transparent subjects, uncertainties of the physical surface, *Autoportrait dans l'atelier* includes, on recto and verso, superimpression and subscription, two sides of the same ambiguity.

In the spring of 1909, Picasso painted a portrait of his dealer, Clovis Sagot, one of the more remarkable paintings of the period called "Cézannian" (left). Two photographs, taken in the Bateau-lavoir studio, one frontal view and the other in profile, show the model seated in front of a hanging of the work in progress (top left and opposite). This system of dual effigy is clearly reminiscent of police mug shots, which had been perfected in France by Alphonse Bertillon several years earlier. From this ambivalent identity of the subject—the accused?—the painting seems to draw out an almost classic bourgeois three-quarter portrait, midway between the harshness of the face-to-face and the eccentricity of the profile. Yet this photographic study also serves to revive volumetric treatment. The same body that Cézanne sought to reduce to a cylinder is seen here as an optical fusion of heterogeneous front/profile planes, which distend the figural link to achieve the single structure of the subject.

The final break would come several months later, in Horta, a Spanish village, during the summer of 1909, which remains the turning point in the creation of Cubism. Picasso engaged in intense photographic activity during this trip. The writer Gertrude Stein, with whom he corresponded regu-

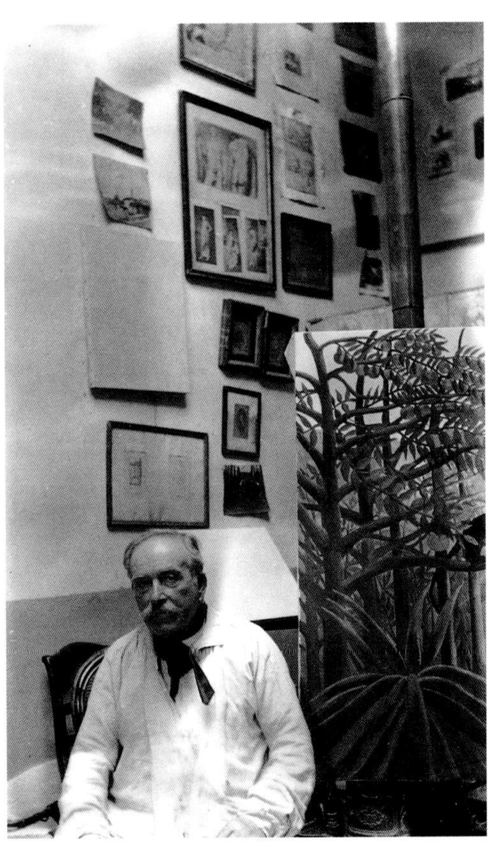

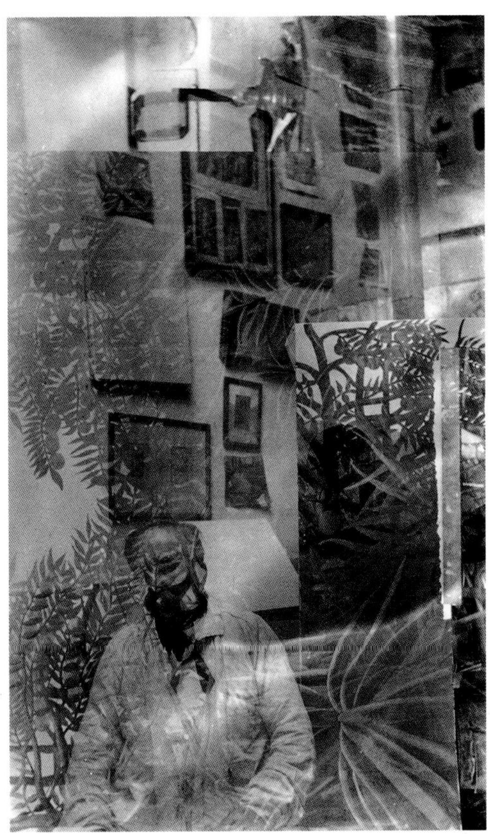

larly at that time, compared the landscape photographs to paintings such as *Le réservoir à Horta* [The reservoir at Horta] or *Maisons sur la Colline* [Houses on the hill]. There are also photographs of the studio which record the portraits that the artist painted of his companion, Fernande Olivier. Studies and canvases, hung on walls or set on the floor, follow. Often the paintings are shown in twos. These variations on a theme illustrate, with almost stereoscopic relief, how the pictorial art of the illusion is deconstructed. The photographic experiment would be taken further still: in one photograph Picasso superimposed the images of three negatives and six canvases. Without completely dissolving their identity, this fusion arouses an intense optical vibration, creating a parallel to Cubism in painting.

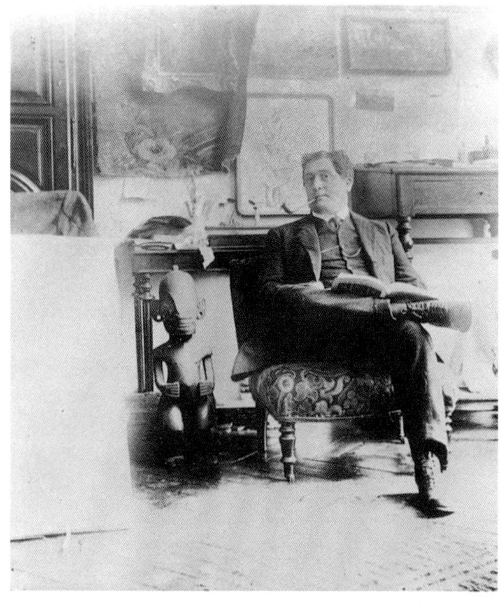

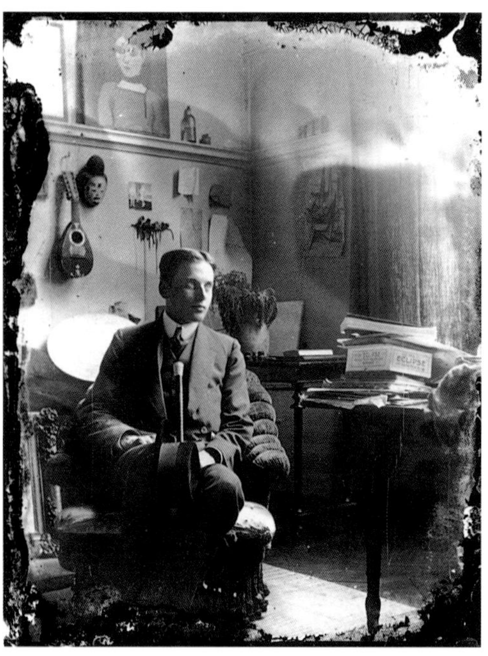

Picasso also resorted to photographic superimpression of images in an astonishing portrait of Le Douanier Rousseau (page 9). Taken in 1910, a few months before the model's death, this portrait has survived thanks to two recently discovered twin negatives. One of them shows the artist in his studio, in front of his final work, *Singes dans la forêt vierge* [Monkeys in the virgin forest]. The other contains an identical composition but superimposes onto it a second image that is a reproduction of the same painting, framed horizontally. The effect of this unusual superimposition is formally very similar to that of several important paintings completed in 1910–1911: individual portraits, such as that of Daniel-Henry Kahnweiler (top right), or generic subjects such as *Homme à la pipe* [Man with a pipe] or *Le Poète* [The Poet].

Pulverizing the shape into a multiplicity of planes and facets, analytical Cubism diffuses figurative "annotations" on the surface of the canvas. There are just as many visual indices in which it is possible to identify several characteristic traits or emblematic elements recorded in a series of photographs that Picasso took in his studio on Boulevard Clichy—of himself and of several of his friends, including Guillaume Apollinaire and Frank Burty Haviland (left). A similar technique of visual diffraction and condensing is used in the photographic *Portrait du Douanier Rousseau* [Portrait of Le Douanier Rousseau]. This time, however, Picasso is working *de visu*, without a canvas or a brush. He gives himself over to the mechanical, "objective" power of the camera. As if scrambled, saturated with signs, the image announces its two levels of reading at the same time that synthesis evokes a new entity. The geometric grid of the wall and frames creates an optical trap where the vegetal network of an imaginary jungle is inscribed. Like an African mask, a monkey covers the painter's face. With this semi-figurative, semi-abstract hermetic puzzle, Picasso uses photography as a process to experiment with and gauge visual material, and once again to look at what lies beyond appearances.

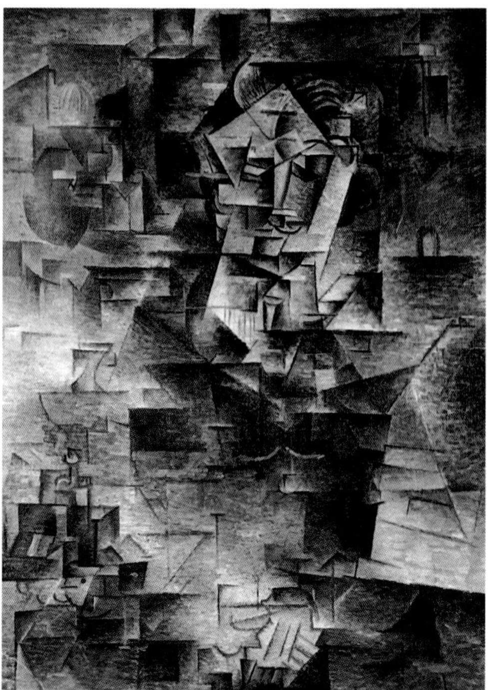

Above: Pablo Picasso, *Portrait of Daniel-Henry Kahnweiler*, Paris, 1910
Opposite: Pablo Picasso, *Portrait of Daniel-Henry Kahnweiler*, Paris, 1910
Top left: Pablo Picasso, *Portrait of Guillaume Apollinaire*, Paris, 1910
Bottom left: Pablo Picasso, *Portrait of Frank Burty Haviland*, Paris, 1911

Translated from the French by Karin Lundell.

1. This research was the subject of an exhibition in 1995 entitled "Picasso et la photographie, 'A plus grand vitesse que les images.'"

2. The exhibition, "Picasso, sources photographiques," scheduled for early 1997 at the Picasso Museum in Paris will be devoted to this topic.

3. Picasso Museum, Paris, 1994.

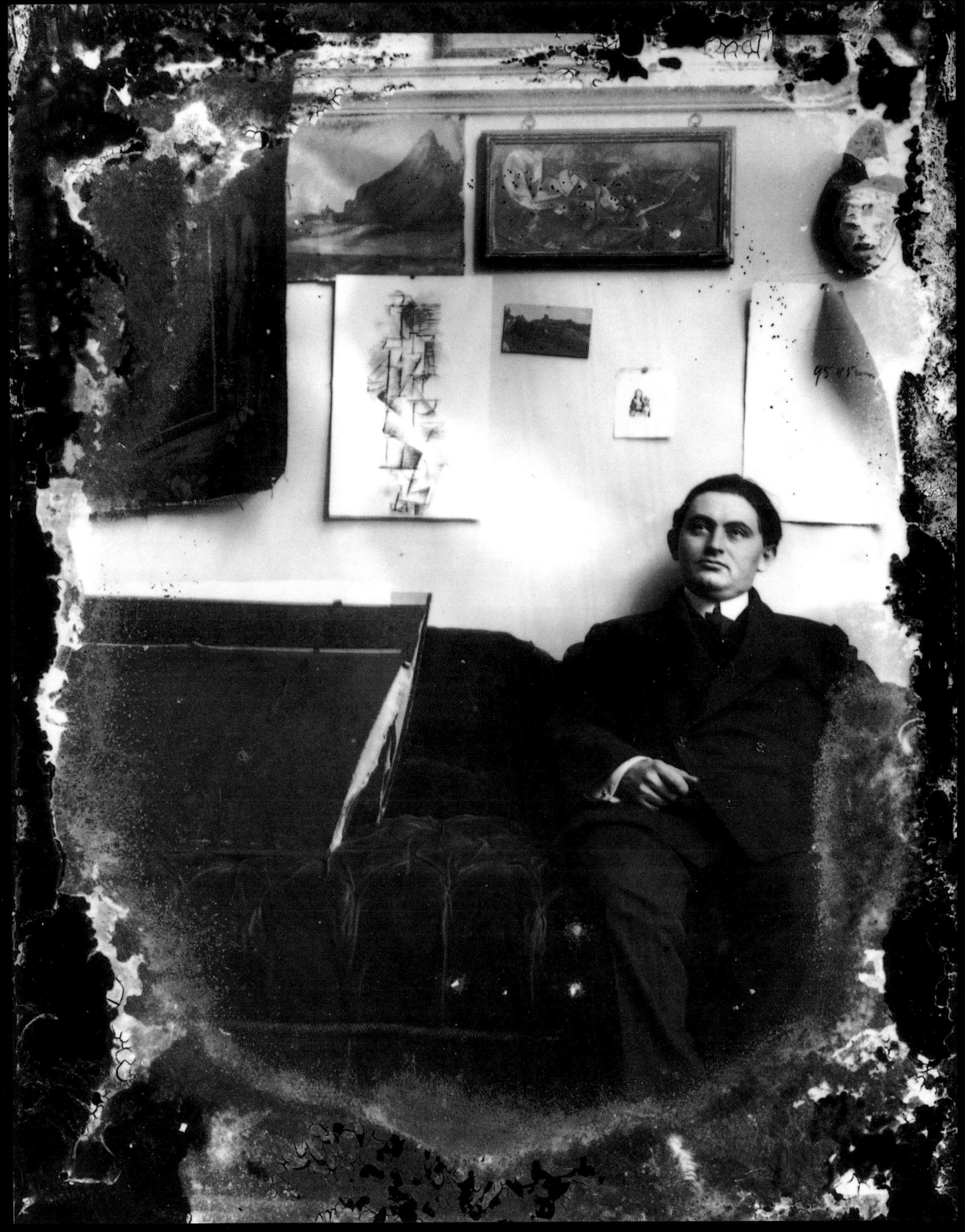

DARK MIRROR:
THE PHOTOGRAPHS OF EDVARD MUNCH

In Munch's photographs can be seen a freedom from the conventions of both painting and art photography, and a willingness to use the process of photography as a means of psychological exploration.

BY CHARLES HAGEN

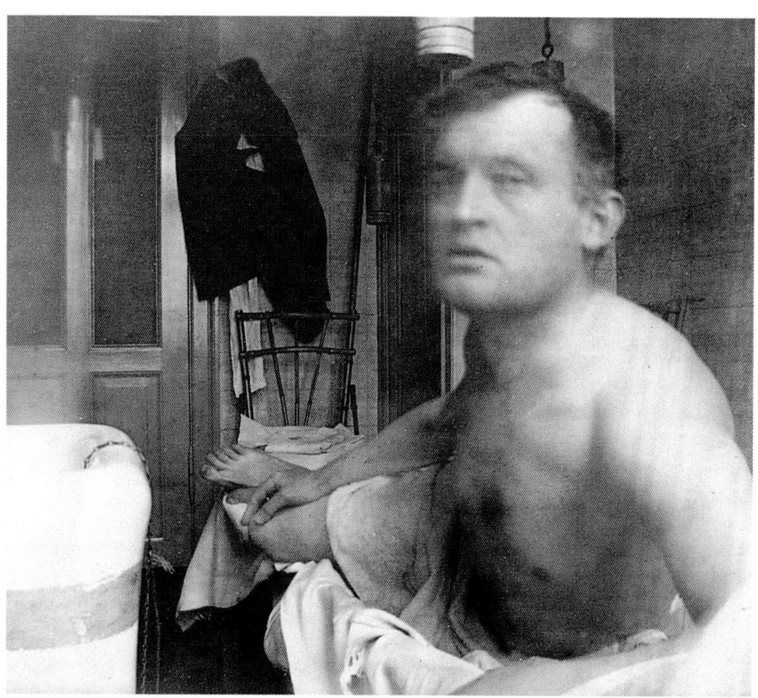

Edvard Munch, *Edvard Munch à la Marat at Dr. Jacobson's clinic in Copenhagen*, 1908–1909

The old man offers his profile to the camera. He looks first out of one side of the frame, then the other, his squarish jaw pointing now toward the sky, now to the ground. In some pictures he wears a dark coat and an elegant, broad-brimmed hat; in others he is bare-headed, his receding white hair testifying to his advanced age.

In still other photos the old man poses indoors, in front of paintings. In all of the images his face is slightly out of focus, and in some cases blurred. Whether these qualities are intentional isn't clear: to take many of the pictures the man has apparently held the camera at arm's length, and maybe the lack of sharpness simply reflects the inability of his lens to focus at such a short distance.

But the fuzziness of the man's figure is consistent in all of the pictures, even though they were taken on different occasions. And the haziness fits well with the mood of introspection and doubt that the self-portraits suggest as a group.

Offering further evidence that the pictures are more than just test shots with a new camera is that the pictures are all by Edvard Munch, the Norwegian artist whose best-known paintings are charged with an excruciating psychological intensity and a sense of profound neurotic anxiety. In their own way, the photographs share the disquiet that suffuses the paintings. Taken in 1930–31 when Munch, then nearing seventy, was recuperating from a burst blood vessel in his eye that had threatened to blind him, these tension-filled images can be seen as attempts by a man newly reminded of his mortality to explore his troubled psyche.

Only a year before, Munch had dismissed photography as incapable of plumbing emotional depths. "The camera cannot compete with brush and palette—as long as it cannot be used in Heaven or Hell," he wrote in a famous aphorism that he stewed over for years before finally publishing it in 1929. Despite this famous rejection, it has become apparent in recent years that Munch used photography throughout his life, as both an aid to his painting and a kind of mirror with which to contemplate his tormented being.

This new awareness of Munch's close relationship to photography comes in large part from the research of Arne Eggum, curator of the Munch Museum in Oslo, where Munch's photographs were recently shown as part of a traveling exhibition of photography by Nordic artists entitled "Art Noir." As Eggum points out in *Munch and Photography* (Yale University Press, 1989), Munch, like many other people in the late nineteenth century, was surrounded by photography. When he traveled, he posed in hotel lob-

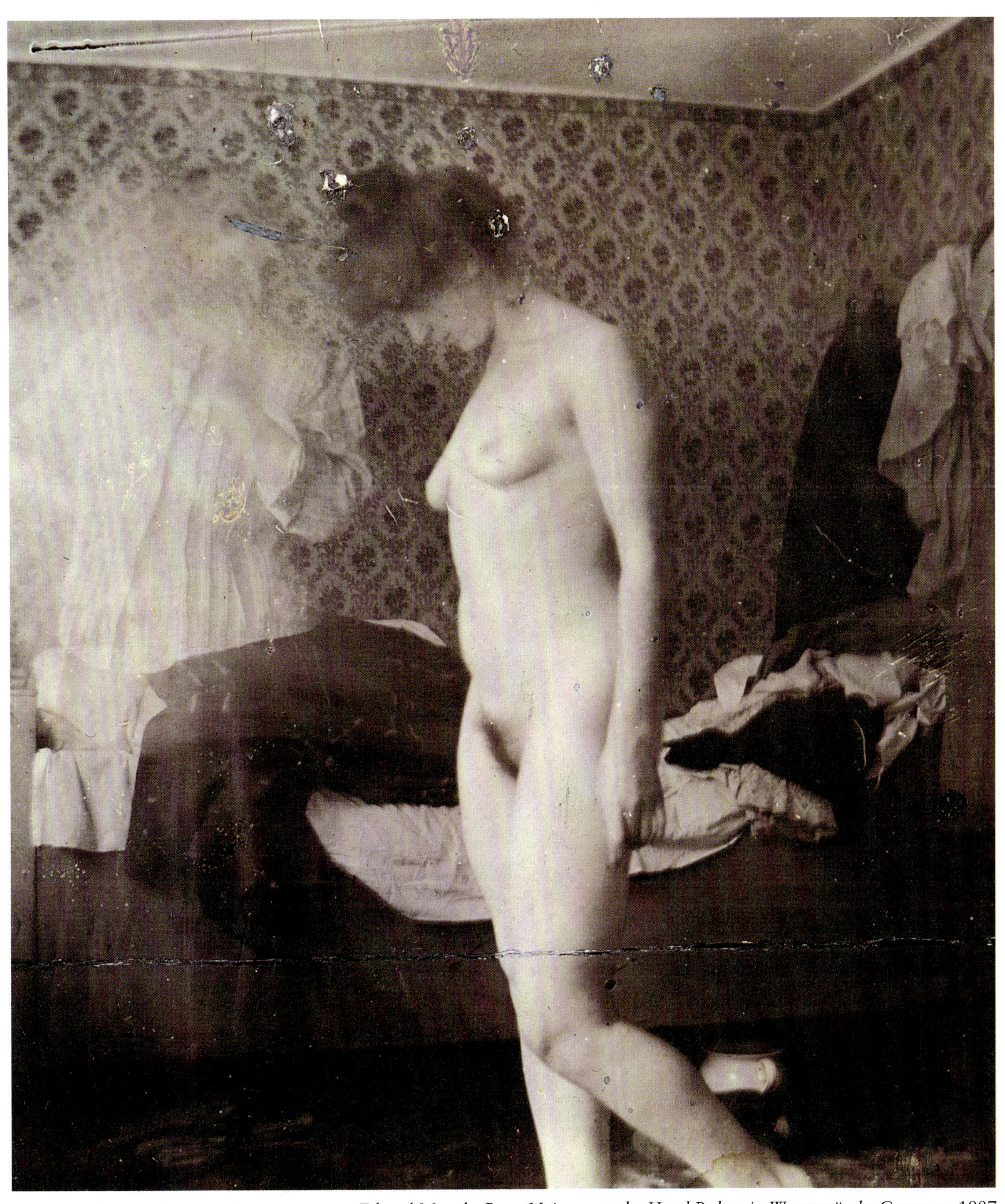

Edvard Munch, *Rosa Meissner at the Hotel Rohne in Warnemünde*, Germany, 1907

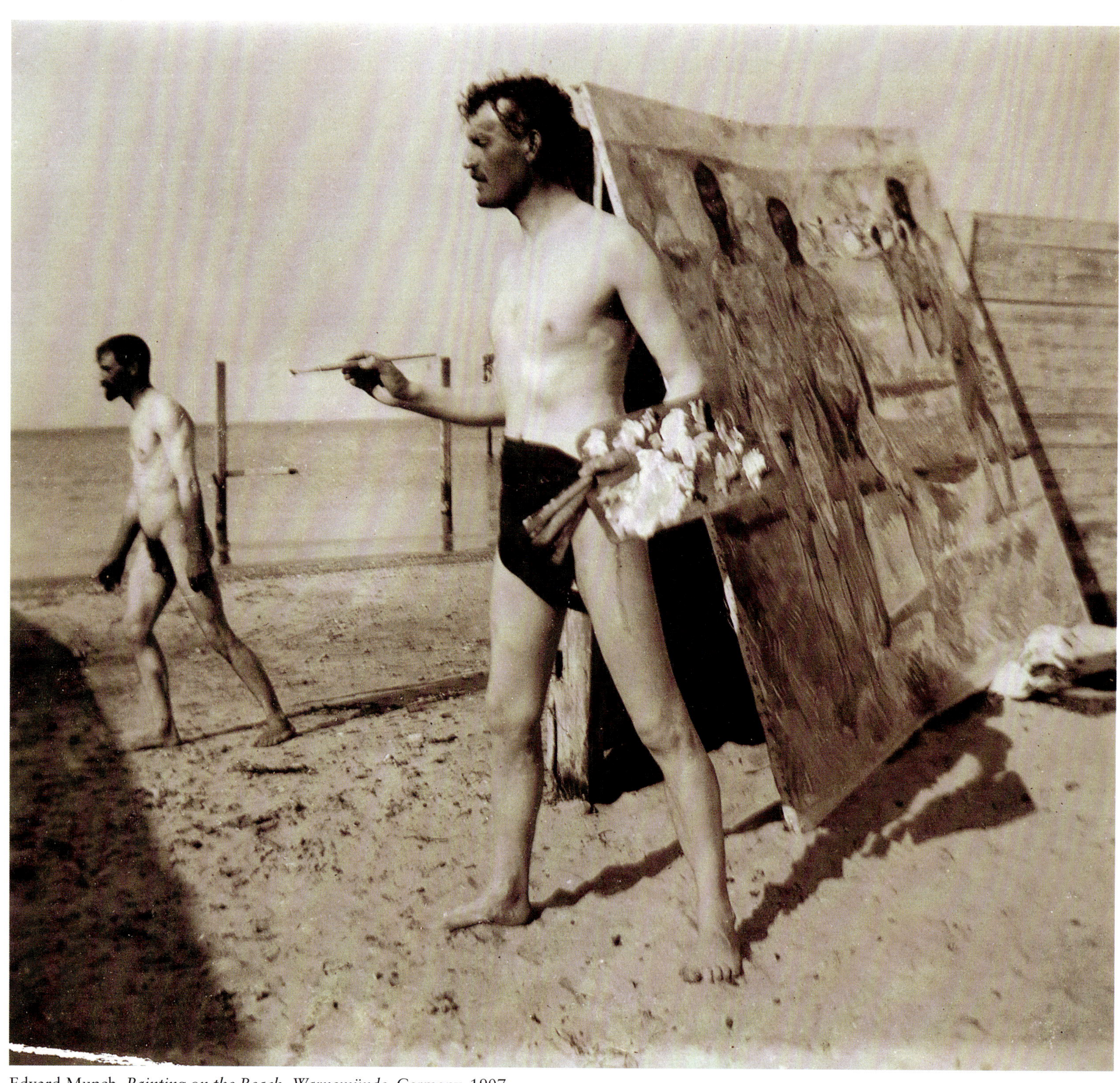

Edvard Munch, *Painting on the Beach, Warnemünde*, Germany, 1907

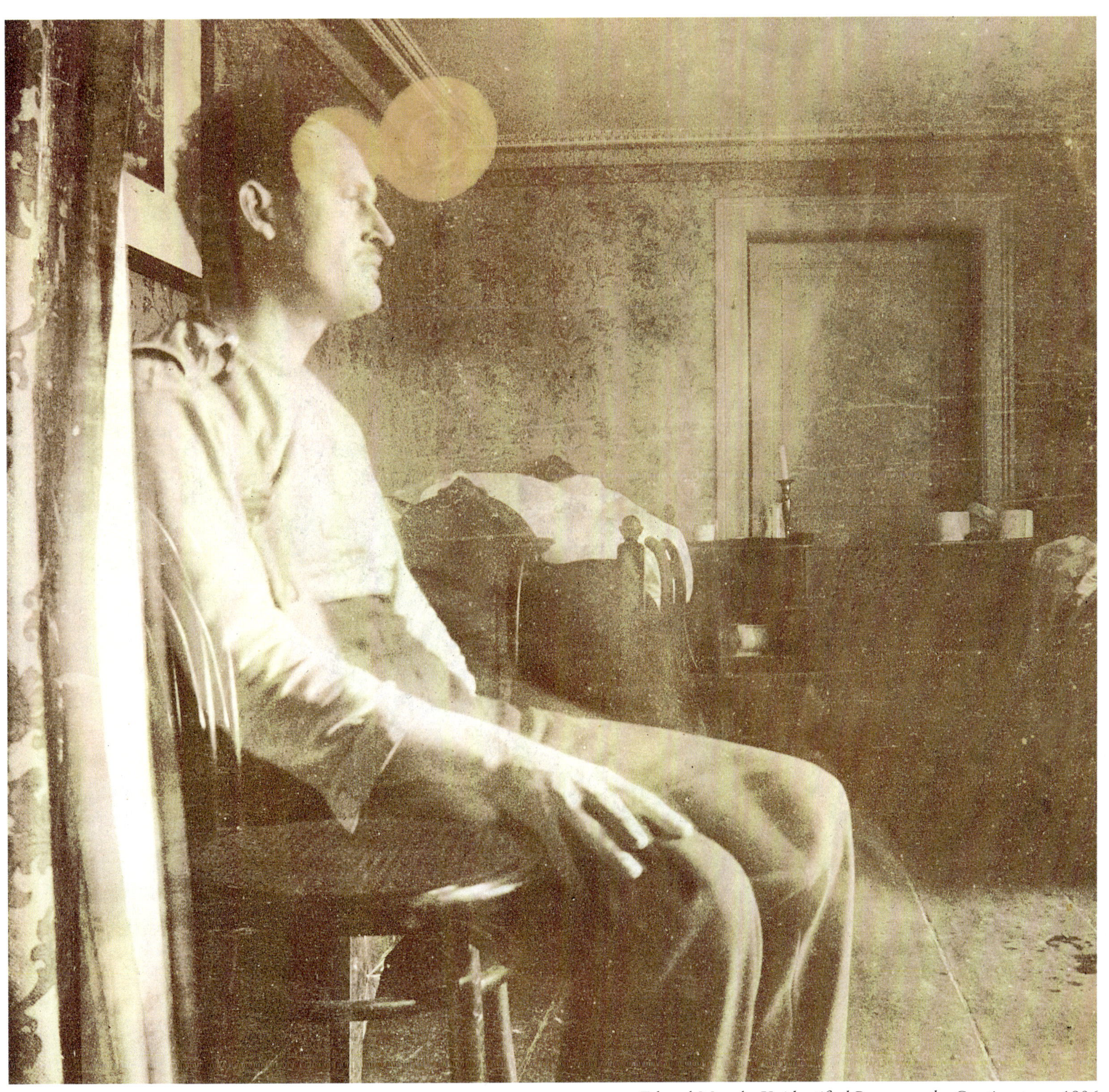

Edvard Munch, *Unidentified Room on the Continent*, ca. 1906

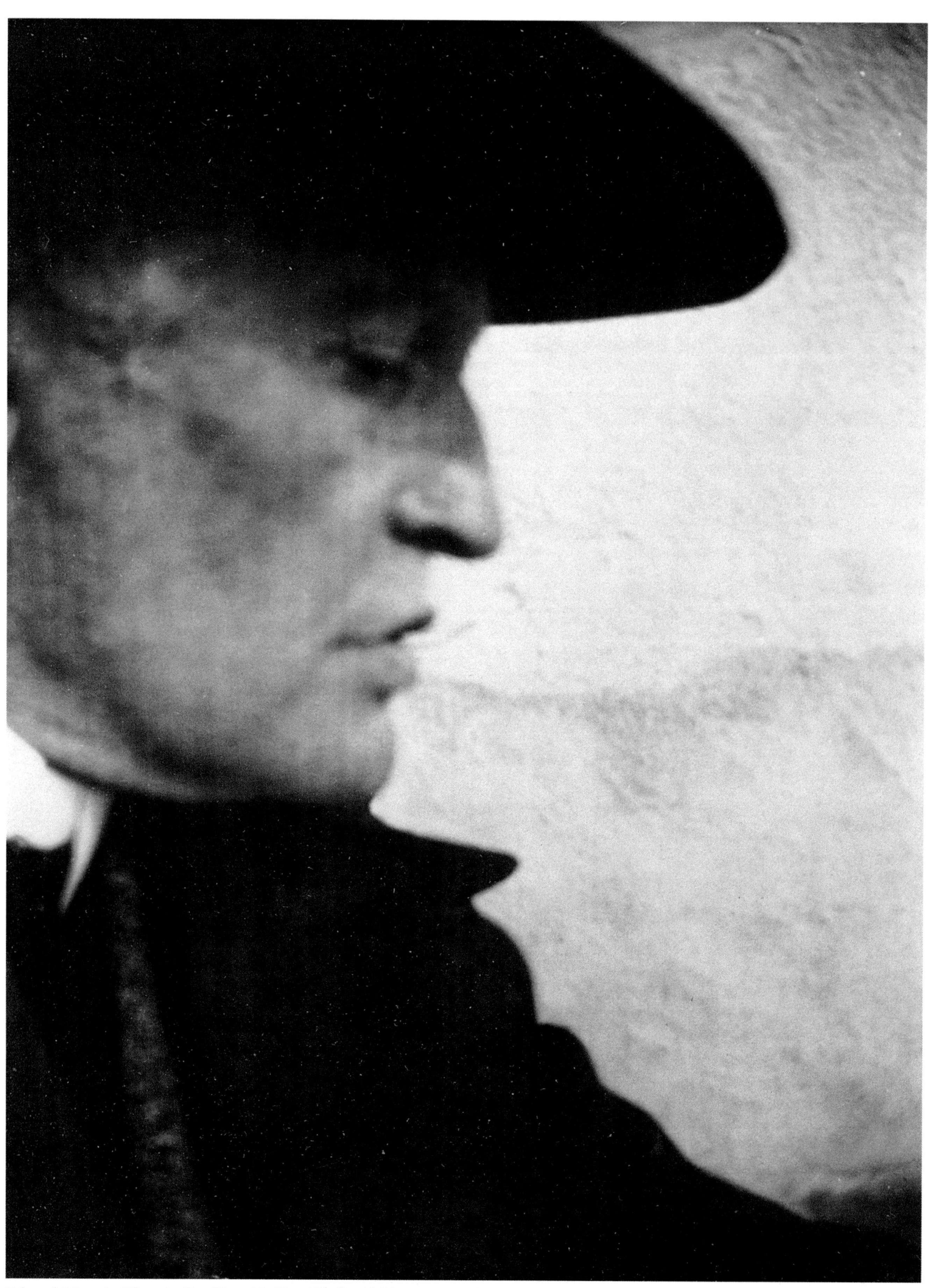

Edvard Munch, *View in Profile with Hat, Ekely*, 1930

bies for postcard portraits, or with friends for group portraits; beginning in 1902 he photographed family, friends, and visitors to his studio, working with a small Kodak camera and developing and contact-printing his own negatives. He used both commercial photographs and images he had taken himself as studies for paintings.

But by far the most interesting of Munch's photographs are his self-portraits. Between 1902 and 1908 he made an extended series of these images, in most of which he appears as a vague, ghost-like figure. In 1943 the eighty-year-old artist carefully labeled a portfolio of these pictures as the "Fatal Destiny photographs."

The period in which these haunting portraits were made was for Munch a time of great emotional stress. In these years he was living in Berlin, driven from Norway by its extreme provincialism. It was in the German capital, a kind of Paris to Northern European artists, that an exhibition of Munch's paintings in 1892 caused an uproar and led to the founding of the Berlin Sezession group; a decade later and an ocean away, Alfred Stieglitz would look to this event for a name for the circle of Pictorialist photographers he gathered around him.

But Munch had nothing to do with Pictorialism. One of the most refreshing aspects of his photographs is their freedom from notions of art. Munch obviously made them for his own purposes, and in their directness and lack of pretension they reflect the painful honesty of his own questioning of his identity. In them can be seen a freedom from the conventions of both painting and art photography, and a willingness to use the process of photography as a means of psychological exploration.

Other factors contributed to the deeply introspective tone of Munch's self-portraits from these years. The central trauma of his childhood, the deaths of his mother and favorite sister of consumption, continued to shape his stark view of existence, and to inflect his art. In 1902 his long relationship with his model and companion Tulla Larsen ended; in a fit of despair at this separation Munch shot himself in the hand.

In many of the self-portraits Munch's enervation and emotional distress are almost palpable. In several pictures, for example, he lies in his bed shrouded in shadows, afflicted by an illness more spiritual than physical.

In a series of images that may date from the summer of 1903, Munch photographed himself in his backyard, naked; one of these depictions seems to have served as a sketch for his 1903 painting *Self-Portrait in Hell*, in which he stares anxiously out of the canvas while red and yellow flames flicker around him. Several years later he photographed himself naked again, this time on the beach at Warnemünde; in one image he poses in the foreground, palette and brushes in hand, while a nude male model in the background seems about to run away. These pictures, too, appear to have been used in a painting, *Bathing Men*, from 1907.

Another group of photographs comes from the following year, when Munch was a patient at Dr. Daniel Jacobson's private clinic in Copenhagen, suffering from alcoholism and what Munch described as "a complete mental collapse." A few pictures are snapshots of nurses in the clinic, but others are self-portraits in which Munch presents himself either in profile or gazing out at the camera, a worried expression on his face, his figure reduced to an ectoplasmic blur. In one particularly striking image he is shown barechested, lying next to a bathtub, with his square head looming up in the foreground; on the back of this photo Munch later wrote "Marat in the bath."

After the nervous and physical breakdown that had caused him to check into Dr. Jacobson's clinic, Munch moved away from the anguished intensity of his earlier works and consciously adopted a more outgoing approach, painting brightly colored portraits and landscapes. Only at the end of his life, as he faced the prospect of his own death, did Munch's underlying anxiety and neurotic dread reappear in his art. It was in that period that he made his other series of photographic self-portraits, the close-ups of his aged face taken by simply holding the camera at arm's length.

Photography was always a secondary medium for Munch; he seems never to have had artistic ambitions for the works he produced in it. But that is an important source of his photographs' power. Freed of all pretensions to being anything other than themselves, they provide moving evidence of his own struggle to understand himself, and to throw light into the dark corners of his soul.

Edvard Munch, *Self-portrait in Hell*, 1903

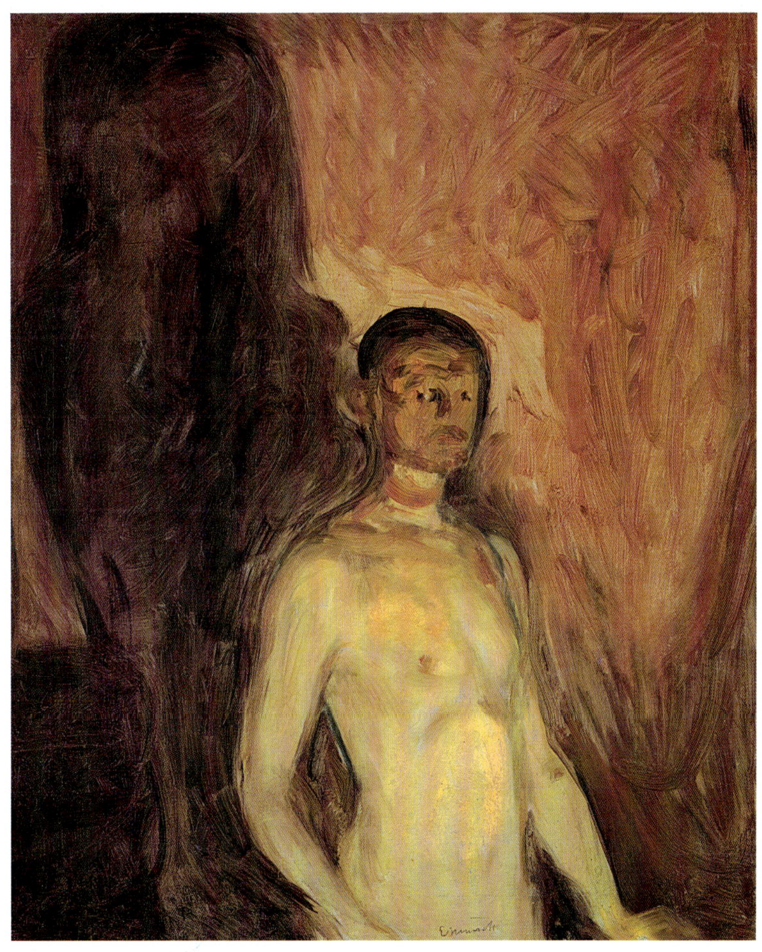

STUDIO POSES: PHOTOGRAPHS BY CONSTANTIN BRANCUSI AND KIKI SMITH

Photographic explorations by two of the century's most innovative sculptors of the human form.

BY DAVID FRANKEL

How many visitors to the large Brancusi show at the Philadelphia Museum of Art last fall, having made the trip for the sculpture's sake, surprised themselves by the length of time they spent with a less-known part of the artist's work—his photographs? Not Kiki Smith—and not because she bypassed the photographs, but because they were principally what she went to Philadelphia to see. The project of most of Brancusi's photography was to document his work in sculpture. Coincidentally, Smith herself had a show coming up that did just the same thing.

Smith has been taking photographs for a long time now, mainly, she told me, for her own pleasure. When she was spending time in Germany in the 1980s, "It looked different from here, so I took pictures of tons of things and made picture movies and sent them to people." Later, working at the Art Foundry in Santa Fe, New Mexico, she began photographing her sculpture in production, because she was fascinated by the disjunction between the finished metal and the various stages it went through in the making. These and a few shots of work installed in exhibition were the images that constituted her show at PaceWildensteinMacGill, New York, this winter.

What is most striking about these photographs is their fragmentation—they show no sculpture intact, or in any sort of context. "There's never any overview" in them, Smith allows; "you never get any distance. It's being inside the whole, inside the life." Shooting from close up, she swaps the totality for the detail; nor is she precise about focus. Smith's sculpture is body oriented, often messily or somberly so; acute to flesh's frailty, it moves from the microscopic, internal view (in glass enlargements of sperm, for example, or of teardrops) to figures with, often, a deeply melancholic undertone. The photographs, it seems to me, tend to emphasize the sculptures' morbidity, sometimes at the expense of their subtlety—of the multiplying emotions, meanings, and qualities suggested by its various surfaces, materials, and forms. Seen very close, a row of sculptural molars look like great rocks, a dental Stonehenge. A figure is cropped so that its shoulders, shadowed chest, and bowed head suggest the forehead and eye sockets of a skull.

It is the opposite approach to that of the usual, and useful, photography of art, and an exercise in frustration for anyone who simply wants a report of Smith's work. Smith has in effect confiscated the privilege of the viewer. In taking photographs, she says, "One of the great things is choice about paying attention." With

Kiki Smith, *Untitled*, 1995

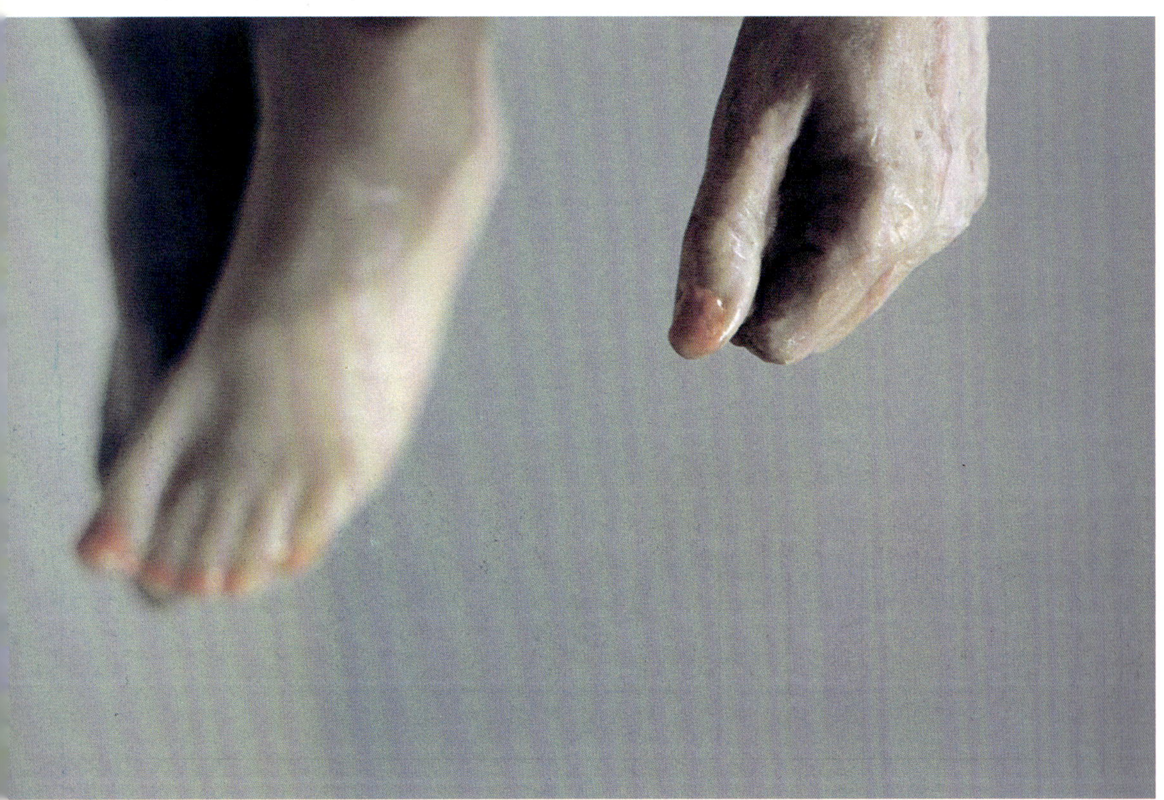

Opposite: Constantin Brancusi, View of the Studio with the *Écorché* after the *Antinous*, ca. 1901–02

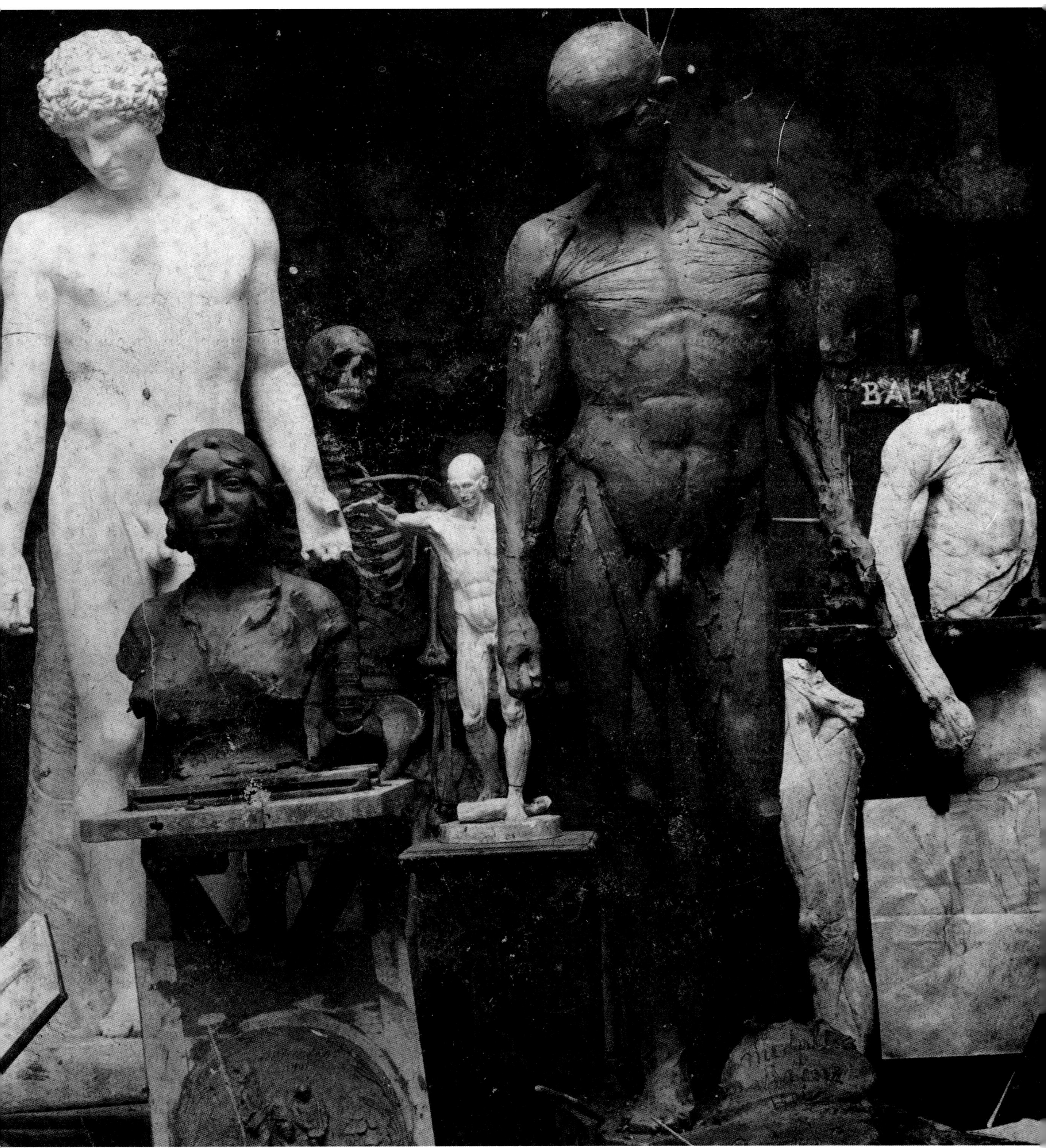

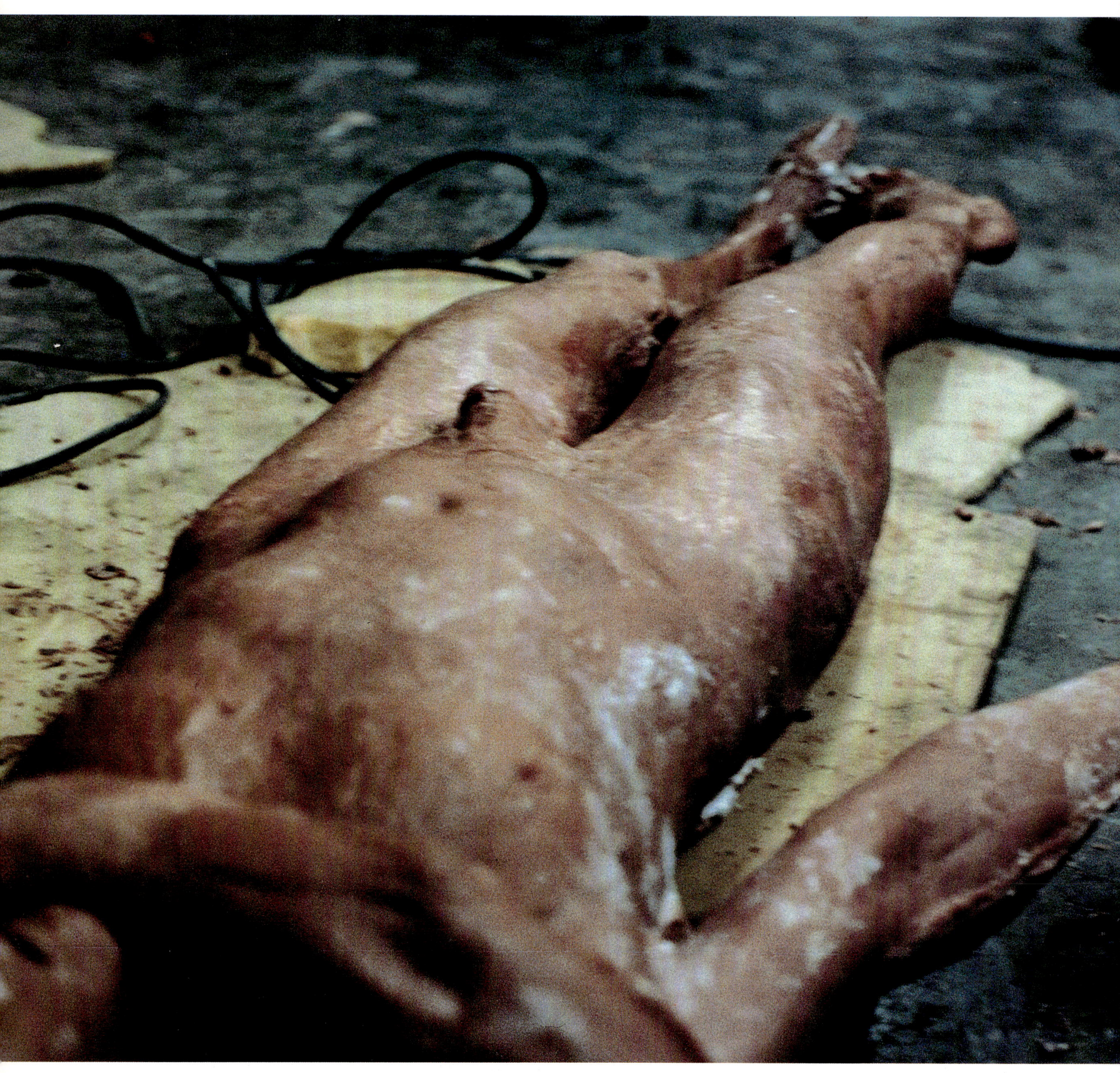

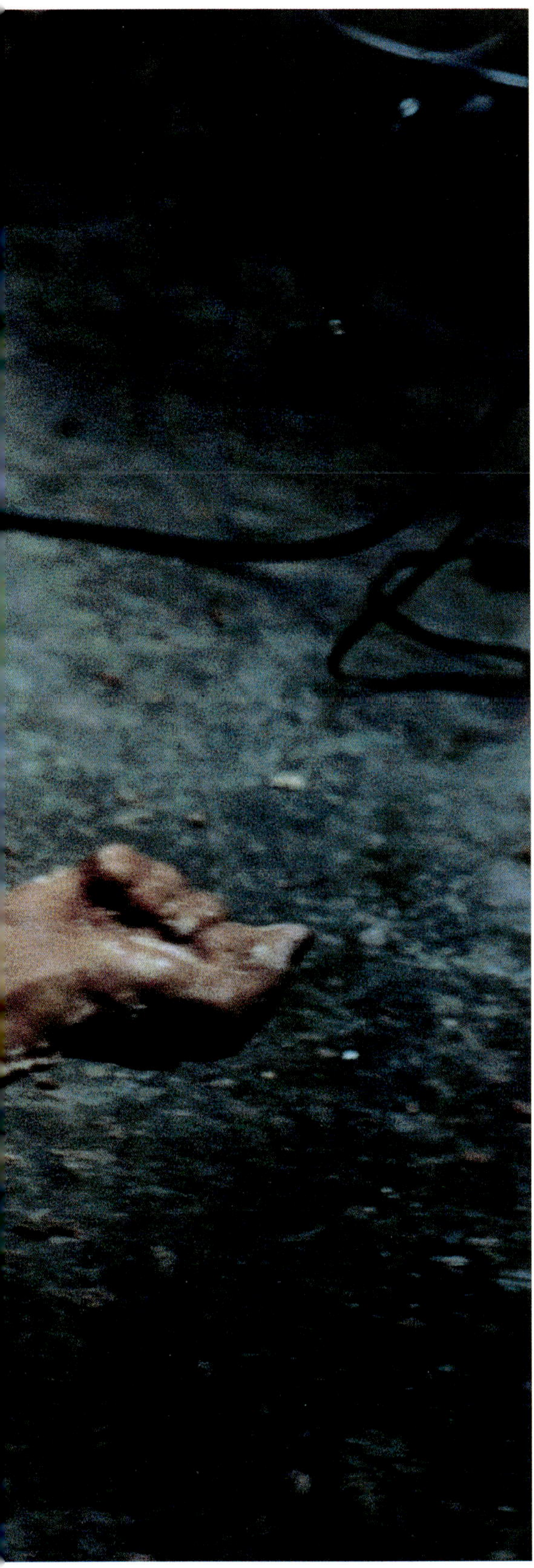

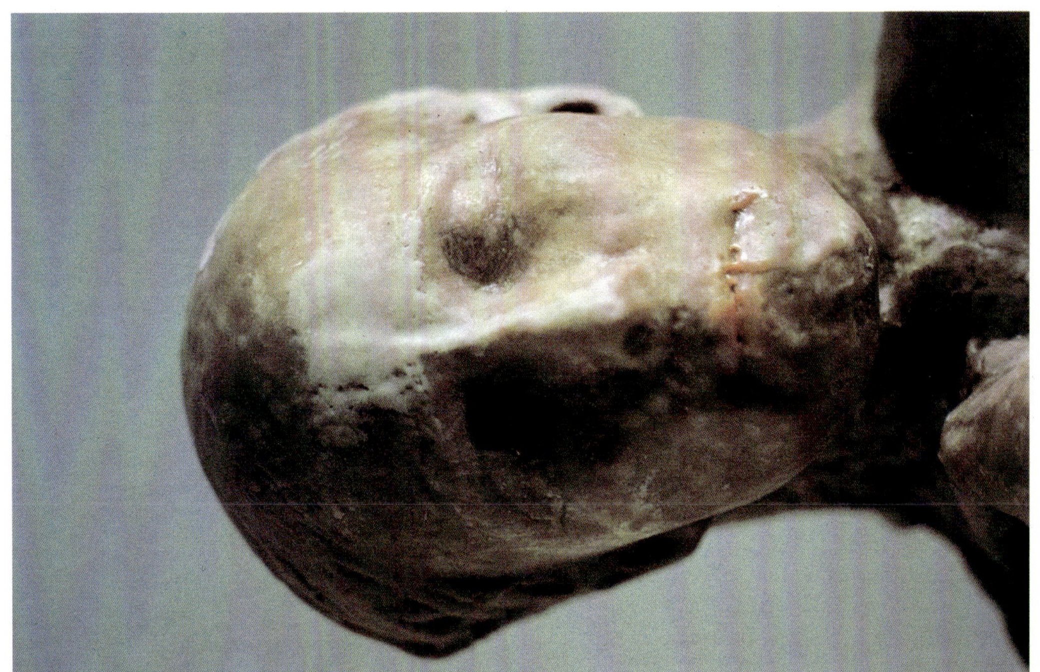

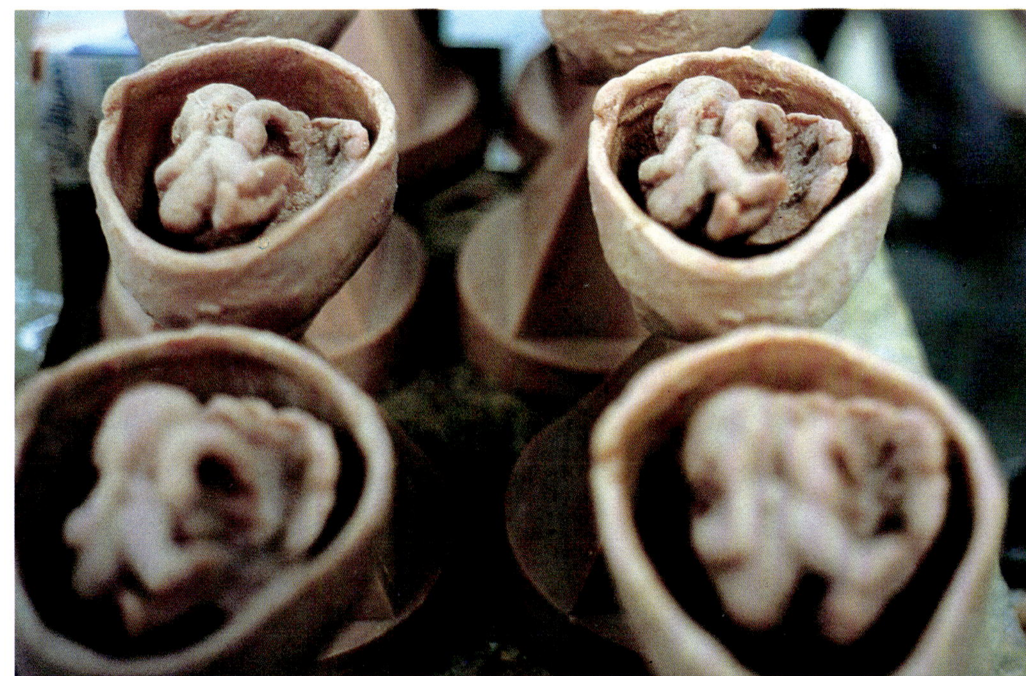

Photographs on pages 20, 21, 24, and 25 by Kiki Smith, *Untitled*, 1995

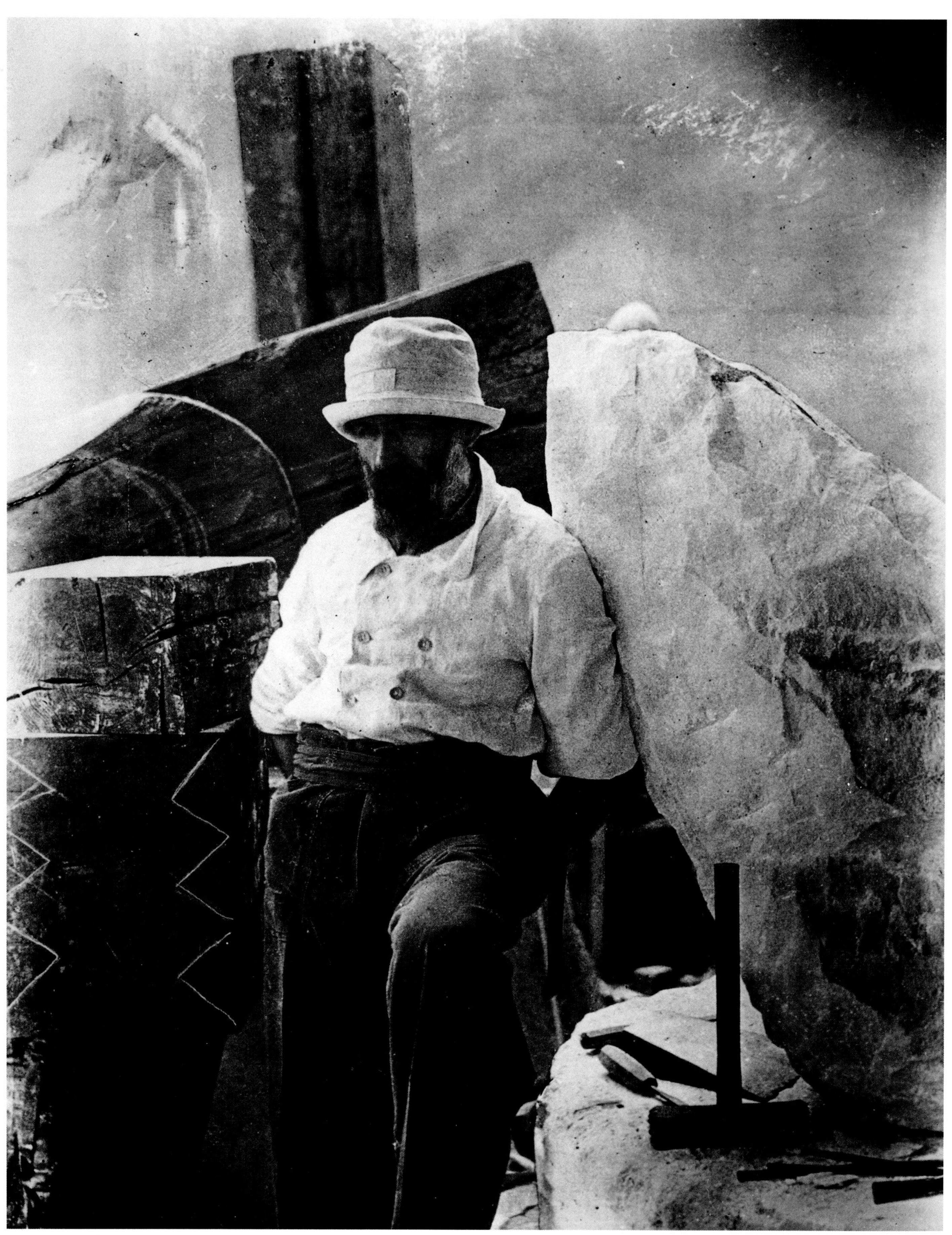

Constantin Brancusi, *Narcissus*, ca. 1914–16
Opposite: Constantin Brancusi, View of the Studio with an *Endless Column*, *Fish*, and *The Sorceress*, ca. 1925

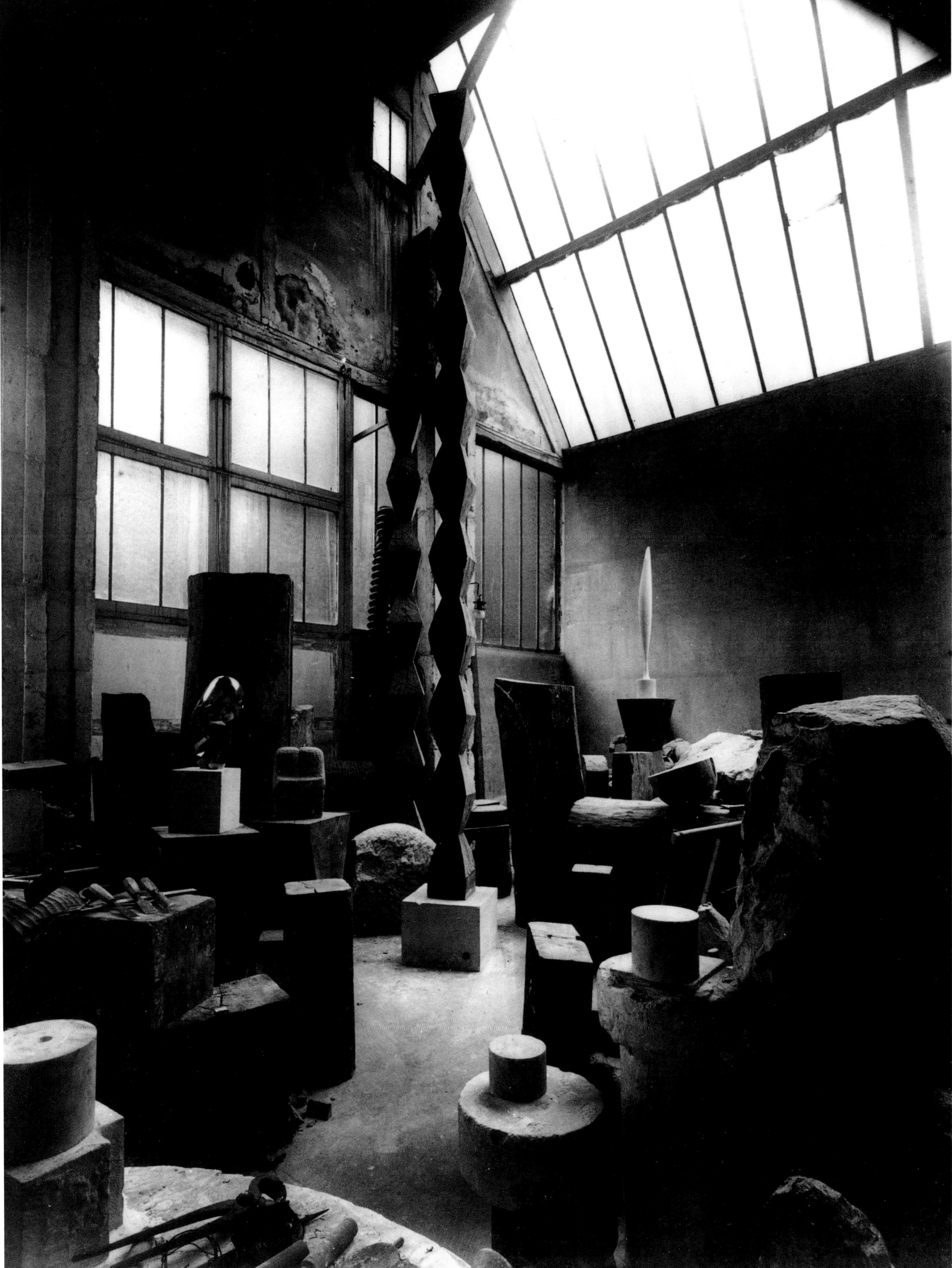

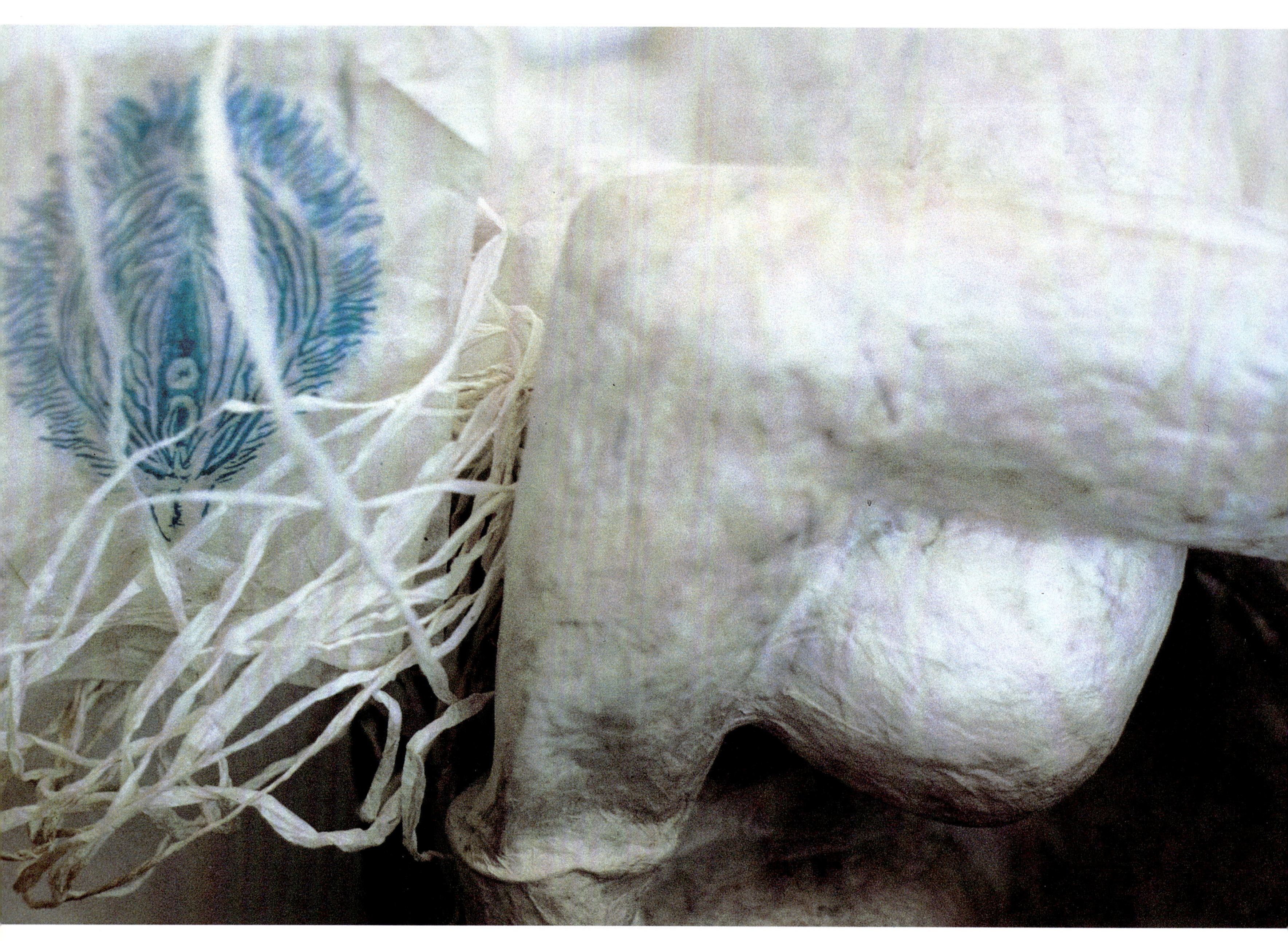

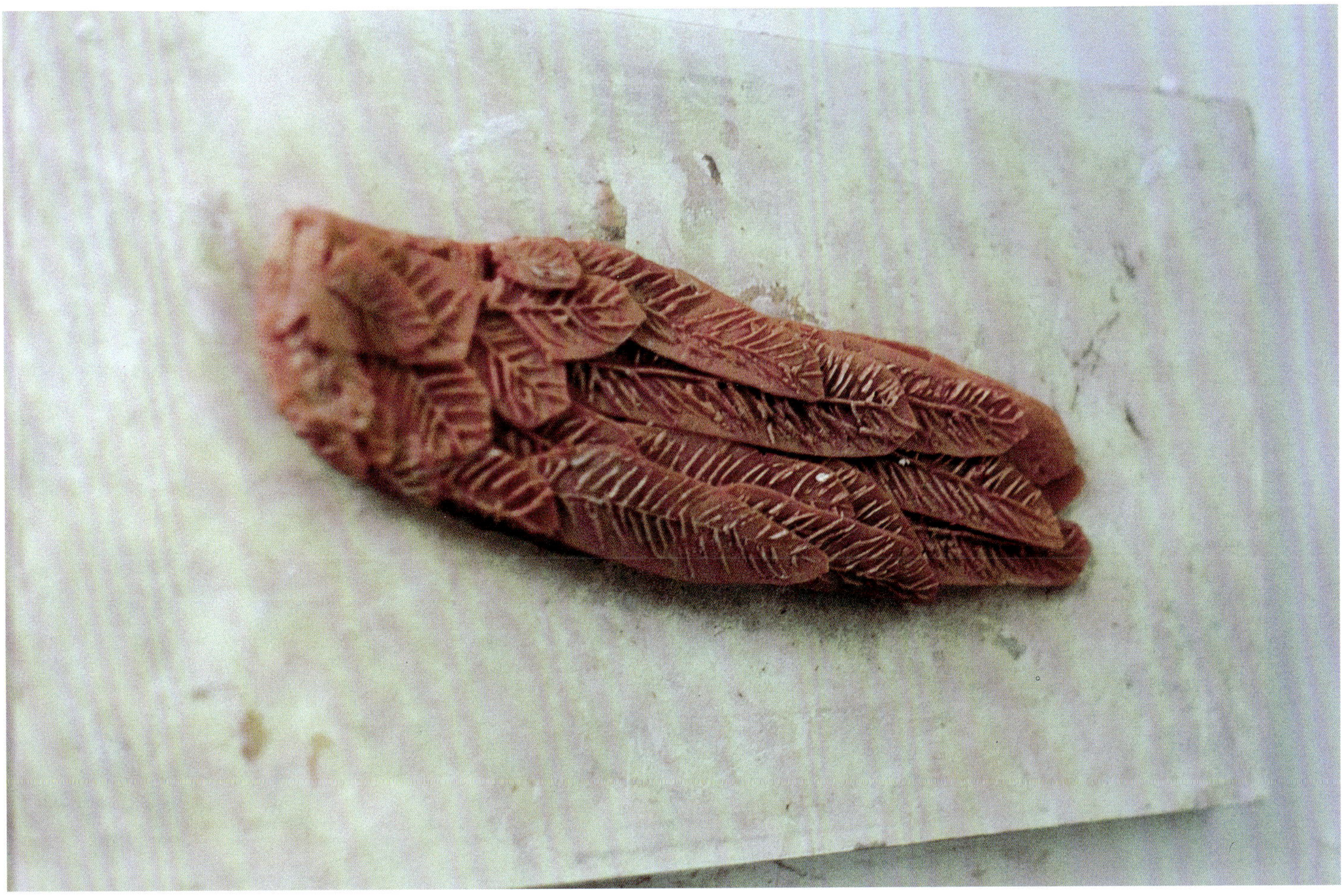

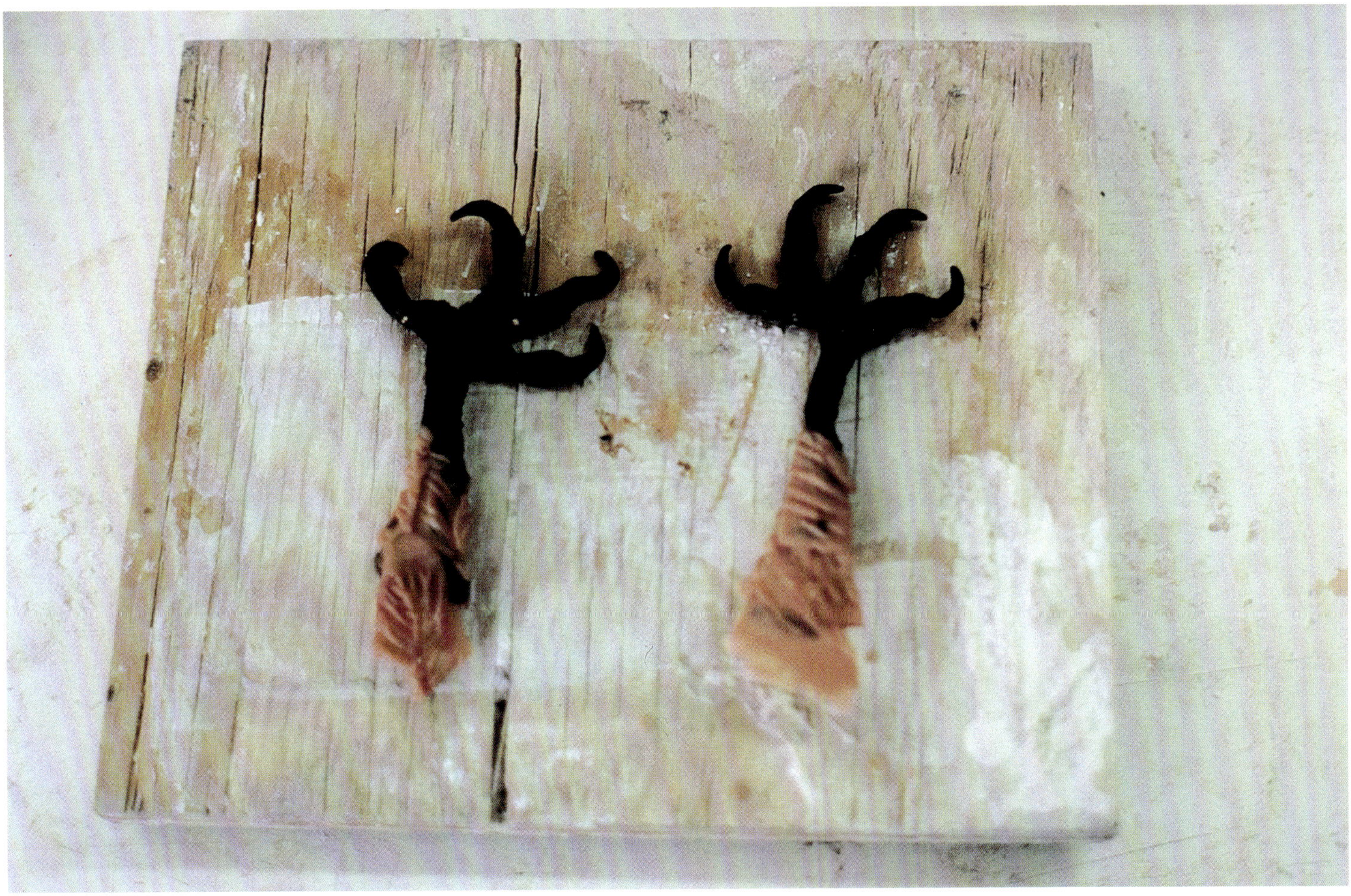

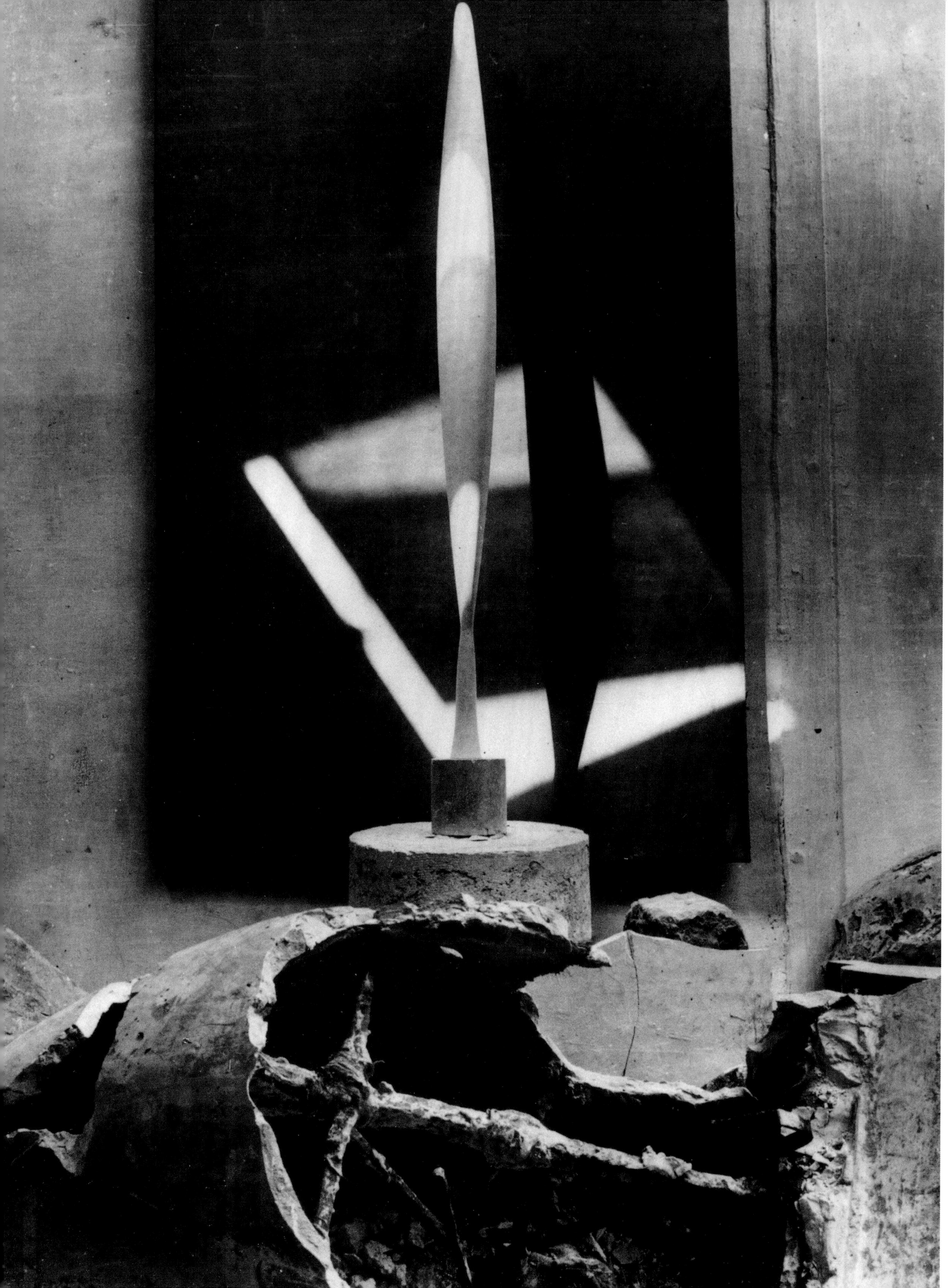

sculpture, though, that choice usually belongs to the spectator, who can walk about the work and pick any number of angles and distances from which to look. By photographing her sculpture, Smith takes that luxury away; she wants it for herself.

On this level Smith's and Brancusi's photographs operate similarly. In a catalog essay for the Philadelphia show (which was co-organized by the Centre Georges Pompidou, Paris), Friedrich Teja Bach firmly establishes the conceptual integrity of these images—the way Brancusi uses the photograph as a two-dimensional tool with which to analyze and explore his three-dimensional objects, and also to explain them, by framing them in controlled circumstances of context, position, and light that feed our understanding of the artist's thought. Looking at Brancusi's photographs, we may feel that we glimpse how he himself imagined the sculpture's life—that we are to some degree seeing the work as he saw it. Like Smith, he is directing our perception and our response.

. . . [Smith's] images, like Brancusi's, are analytic, if in a reflective kind of way that seems to obscure as much as clarify, worrying at and denying the effect the sculpture might have by itself, or in a group.

Overall, though, the idiosyncrasy of Smith's approach is only underlined by the comparison with Brancusi, and this is in part because, absorbed though Brancusi clearly was with the camera's aesthetic possibilities, the genesis of his photographs lay elsewhere: as Bach writes in the Philadelphia catalog, "Brancusi's photography began as a way of showing his work to interested persons who lived away from Paris." Elizabeth A. Brown, in her book on the subject, spells out more plainly what Bach means: "Most often Brancusi's reason for taking a photograph was market-driven: he needed a reproduction of a new piece for a potential buyer." Indeed, Brown adds, several of Brancusi's photographs "were printed on postcard stock, allowing the artist to send pictures to distant patrons with a minimum of fuss." Brown also understands how Brancusi used photography to disseminate an image of himself as artist: he "took and released several photographs of himself relaxing, often with a cigarette positioned rakishly in the corner of his mouth, the image of the sexy bohemian. He presents himself as a dashing outsider, like a character from a Hemingway novel. . . . The intention is . . . to influence the way an art audience would imagine his work and life."

So, where Smith literally takes her sculptures apart in her pictures, Brancusi evokes an encompassing gestalt. Carefully placing and lighting a work, he will shoot it in its entirety, making an image that stands as a neat conceptual package. He will also take broader but equally careful shots of stretches of his studio, and of the array of objects that pose there; and these photographs eloquently phrase that place in the cadences of a romance, a Modernist-artist fable. They seem, in other words, to demand a *Vanity Fair*–type caption about "Brancusi's legendary studio in Montparnasse." In one self-portrait showing Brancusi at work, he is brightly lit from below and to the side, so that tall shadows climb the walls, overtaking his upper body and the tops of the works clustered around him. The effect is dramatic, worthy of, say, the Josef von Sternberg of *The Scarlet Empress*. It's undercut some, though, by the fact that it throws the surface Brancusi is working on into an improbably and impractically deep gloom; which reminds me of watching a pop group playing, or rather, lip-synching, on TV once, and noticing that the guitarist was accidentally strumming his tie.

Brancusi's photographs are often convincingly grand, as when he shoots bronze and taller plaster versions of the *Cock*, all receding and reverberating with Himalayan distance and range, and all leaping in sheets of fine grays toward the light. His self-portraits, to their credit, can show a sly sense of humor: the famous one in which an *Endless Column* seems to grow out of his head is as funny as it is symbolic. There is, though, an element of calculation in these images—an alertness to commerce, and to the good opinion of Brancusi's public, and of posterity. That current in the work hardly cancels its aesthetic strength and its art-historical interest, but certainly coexists with them.

Smith, on the other hand, had no audience in mind when she took her photographs, which she calls a "secret hobby." Working, she says, by intuition, she photographs because "it's so pleasurable to do. It's nothing I think about that much." Yet her images, like Brancusi's, are analytic, if in a reflexive kind of way that seems to obscure as much as clarify, worrying at and denying the effect the sculpture might have by itself, or in a group. Photographing a pale wax figure, for example, Smith frames to crop the torso out completely; from the top of the picture, one hand and, more distantly, one foot hang down like stalactites. The method recalls the various surgeries of Surrealism, but where that work often has a streak of cruelty, this is more like commemorative or funerary art, and implies a sober sense of mortality. For Smith, images like this one "float between alive and dead, fake and natural." Yet their mourning quality is qualified by the coolness of the abstracting impulse by which she cuts up her work, and a body, this way.

Smith traces her taste for "looking at the details to make the whole" to her father, the sculptor Tony Smith, who, she points out, combined small components into larger works. But there's also an immediate charge: "There's something really sexy about removing things from life's space. It's fetishlike. You get to control it." Asked about her motive for taking photographs, Smith says she's "probably just cannibalizing" one set of works to develop another. Applied to sculpture that has the sense of physicality that Smith's does, the word has a certain resonance.

Opposite: Constantin Brancusi, *Bird in Space*, ca. 1929–30

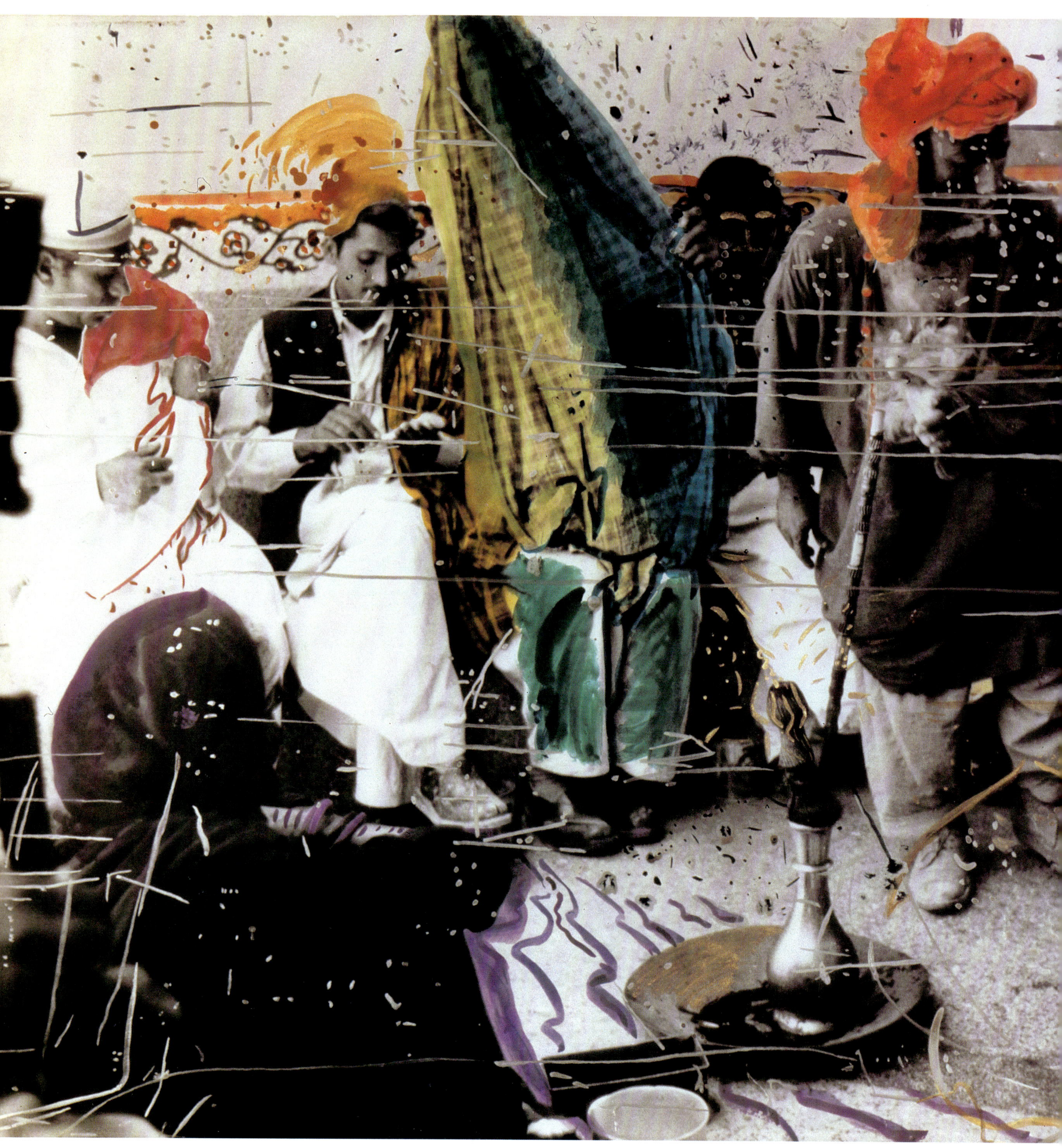

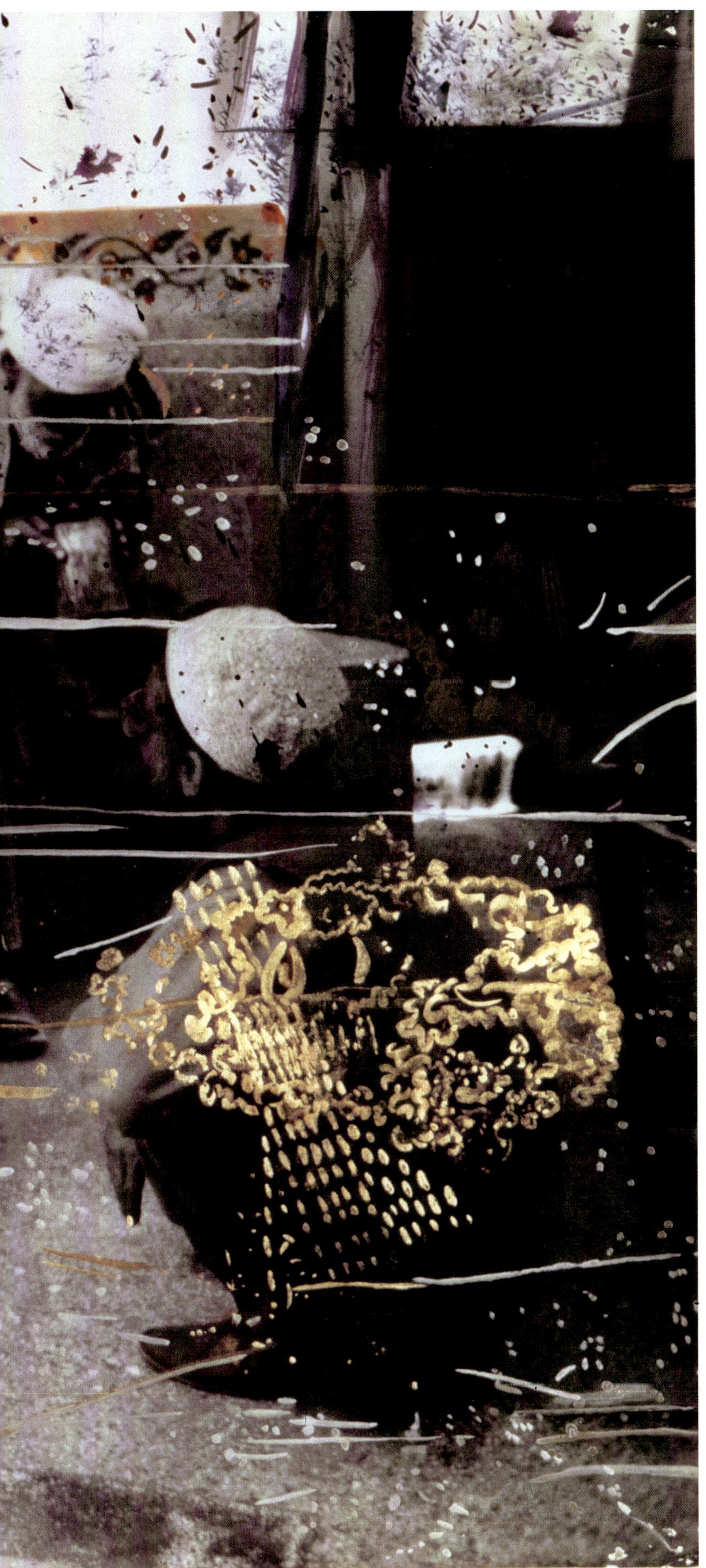
Sigmar Polke, *Untitled* (Quetta, Pakistan), ca. 1974/78

POLKOGRAPHY

German painter and multimedia artist Sigmar Polke makes use of photography to advance his search for an altered state of vision.

BY PAUL SCHIMMEL

For the past thirty years, Sigmar Polke's art has perplexed critics and public alike with its multiplicity of styles, subjects, and positions. Polke's paintings, drawings, photographs, and sculpture have variously been described as metaphysical and profound on one hand and jocular and deliberately dumb-witted on the other. Trying to hit Polke's moving target with the cannon of art historical apparatus is no easy task. His densely layered art, with its commitment to finding again and again an equivalency between subject and technique resists facile interpretation.

One key to understanding the complexities of Polke's art, however, is to appreciate the extent to which his personal life informs it. More than any other medium he uses, photography provides the most direct window into Polke's life. Beginning with the images of his family and friends and himself in his early conceptual photography (ca. 1964–69), continuing through the work made during his travels in the 1970s, and finally throughout his search for immortality in the Goya series and the experimental non-negative prints of the 1980s and 1990s, Polke's photography reveals the intersections of his life and art and informs all of his art with specific glimpses into the life of this very private artist.

The Paris series (1971) marks the beginning of a period in which Polke adventurously and almost recklessly experimented with the manipulation of prints to extend the representational possibilities of photography. It was also the first in a series of photographic suites based upon the artist's journeys around the world—specifically, to Paris, New York, São Paulo, Afghanistan, Pakistan, and Australia. These suites constituted the primary body of his work during the 1970s. For Polke, the world was full of unexplored wonders, and the camera was a magic box that helped preserve his memories of them.

With the Paris series, Polke began a new chapter in his artistic life, one in which painting and drawing took a backseat to his photographic activities. Shot during his first trip to the city, these photographs evoke the romantic spirit of a young man in love.

An image that appears in several of the photographs is that of a hand-held mirror that reflects a nude torso. (This image anticipates by a decade Polke's interest in Francisco Goya's painting of an old woman with a mirror, which he explores in the important Goya series.) Reflecting the artist's eye, Polke's mirror converts a three-dimensional world into two dimensions, and, like the camera, crops, defines, and flattens its subject.

Polke's use of intuition and the unconscious in the darkroom photographic experiments roughly parallels the more refined experiments of his Dada and Surrealist predecessors. Like these artists, Polke benefited from the painter's vision and liberated the medium from the central perspective of the objective lens. (One particularly relevant precedent is to be found in the work of Christian Schad, who created the first photogram. Schad's associations with the Zurich Dada group and his close friendship with Walter Schirner, the extraordinary fake journalist, perpetrator of crimes, duelist, and language counterfeiter, anticipated Polke's own interest in forgery, robbery, and *la vie dangereuse*.) Similarly, Polke's use of layering, overdrawing, found patterns, and nontraditional materials recalls the examples of Francis Picabia, whom he considers to be the last European painter.

After the Paris series, Polke began to manipulate his photographic prints extensively and introduced a motif that he would explore in great depth in the early 1970s: the magic mushroom. As he stated, "At this time I tried the mushroom. I ate them, and I smoked them as did many of my friends. It is something that belongs to the children and has the magical quality alluded to in *Alice in Wonderland*."[1] After having "imagined" the mushrooms into one of his photographic works through the application of ink, he began exploring the religious, spiritual, and mind-altering capacities of the fungus. For Polke and other artists of his generation in the early 1970s, hallucinogenic drugs opened up creative possibilities beyond the rationalistic structures of modern European culture—a promise of freedom that ultimately inspired him to travel to Central Asia and South America in 1974 and to participate, to the extent that he could as an outsider, in the lifestyles of the indigenous peoples he encountered.

In 1974 Polke's search for experiences of heightened emotional content took him to Afghanistan. While there, he made a separate trip to photograph and film a bear fight, a monthly ritual battle between a bear and dogs. This event provided the artist with a focused activity of intense conflict and became the subject of a sequence of fourteen photographs entitled *Der Bärenkampf* (The bear fight, 1974).

In addition to numerous photographs he made in Afghanistan, including images of menacing-looking soldiers and the unlikely shot of a surfboard atop a car crossing the Khyber Pass, on the same journey Polke photographed extensively in Quetta, Pakistan. There he obtained images that ultimately became some of most visually exquisite and most carefully crafted photographs in his entire oeuvre. He shot these images of opium dens in 1974, but it was not until three or four years later that he laboriously hand-colored the exquisite details of their imperfections, including handprints and scratches, to convey the mind-expanding experiences to be found there.

Polke made three different types of prints from these negatives. The first type comprises straight prints. In the second type, Polke made each print by printing a negative of an image of an opium den on top of one of an indeterminate subject of great density; this process endows the picture within a picture with a dark, mysterious atmosphere that conjures up the subject of the photographs themselves. The third type includes prints laboriously hand-colored with egg tempera inks and gold and silver paint, which Polke made several years after the photographs were originally shot. His alterations and manipulations so beautifully interfere with the negatives that the viewer becomes nearly as entranced and seduced by the hallucinogenic properties of the opium as were both the photographer and his subjects.

In these works Polke, with an unusual sense of craftsmanly detail, painted the architectural and figurative elements in tones of orange, red, blue, green, purple, and turquoise. However, the rich, otherworldly quality of these colors only forms a backdrop to their more dramatic aspects. Every scratch, fingerprint, and visual imperfection is carefully in-painted with silver and gold leaf, beginning with what was already in the negatives (as evidenced by looking at a set of the unretouched black-and-white photographs). Polke elaborated these imperfections to such a degree that they form a scrim of scratches, glitches, and dots between the viewer and the subject. In so doing, he created the visual equivalent of the "white noise"—the hum of murmuring voices—that both disrupts and ultimately informs the ritualized proceedings of the consumption of opium. Going a step further than the photographs of the Paris series, which were printed while "under the influence," these images materialize a sense of the experience produced by consuming the drug.

Polke's desire to read the invisible served as the impetus for his series of photographic works based on Goya's painting *The Old Women* (1812). Polke first became interested in this painting when he noticed, while looking at a postcard reproduction of it, that Goya had repainted a significant portion of the original composition and that the pentimento was apparent even in a commercial reproduction. In addition to the three large-scale "Goya" works, a number of smaller ones utilize collage, photogram, colorization, and chemical manipulation. The first works in the Goya series are a group of photocopies Polke made from photographs of the Goya painting on which he drew figures. Polke's articulation of phantom angels, warriors, jesters, mythological beings, and religious figures is proof of his interest in grappling with the invisible phantoms of life. Those very apparitions, phantoms, and unseen phenomena become the overwhelming objective of his photographic work following the Goya series.

To understand the quasi-religious nature of Polke's investigation into Goya's picture, it is important to know that his initial interest in it was precipitated by his vision of its underpainting. This vision catalyzed both his photographic investigations and his hand-drawn alterations. After he had come to appreciate that which was visible in the painting and to envision that which was not, Polke began to "collaborate" with it in his systematic application of various Polkean techniques. After seeing an actual X-ray of the painting, he was able to appreciate fully the complexity of the underpainting he had previously seen only as pentimento.

In contrast to his paintings of the late 1980s and early 1990s, which switch between abstraction and representation, Polke's pho-

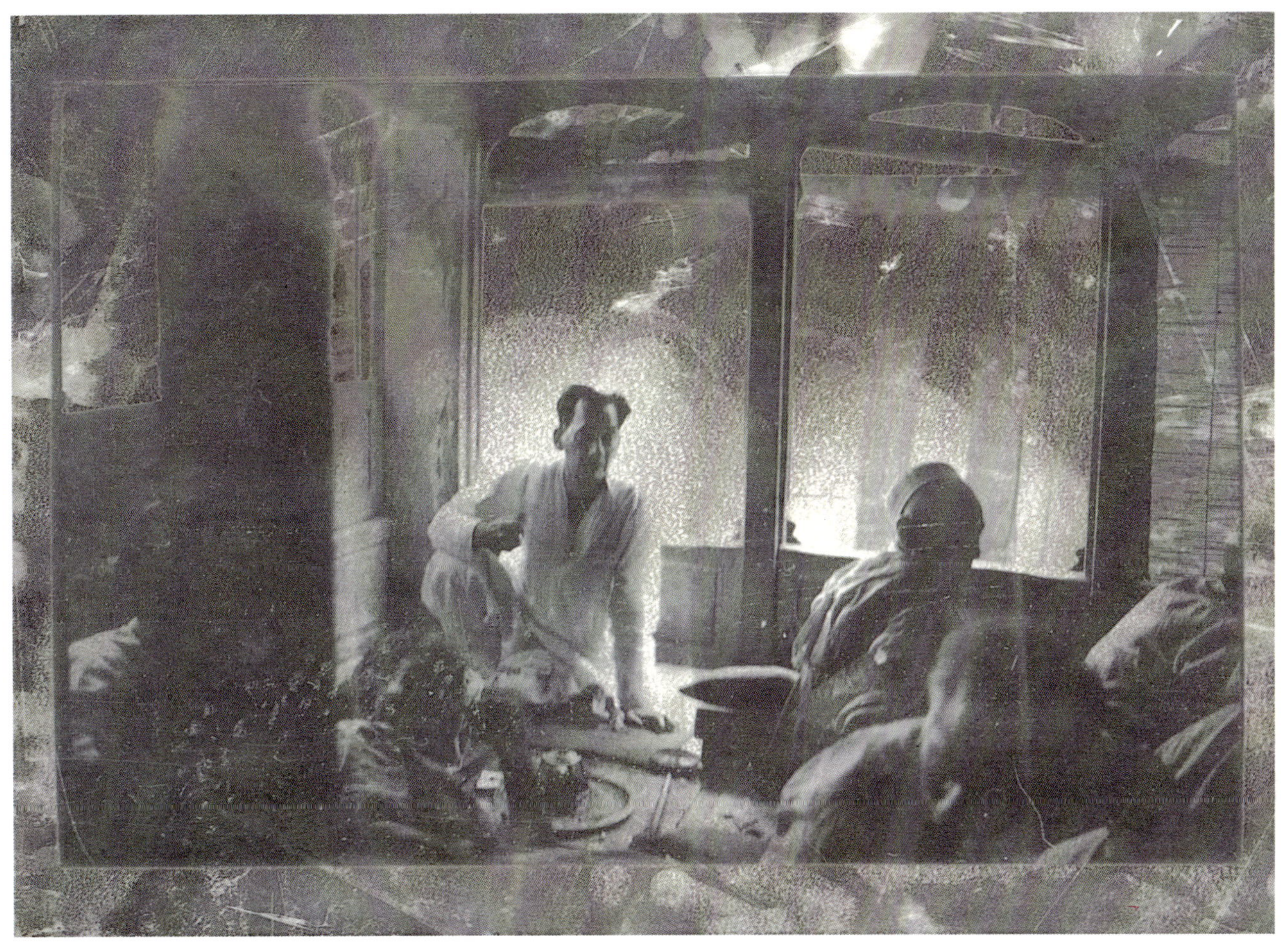

Above: Sigmar Polke, *Opiumhöhle* (Opium den), ca. 1974

Below: Sigmar Polke, *Quetta, Pakistan*, 1974/78

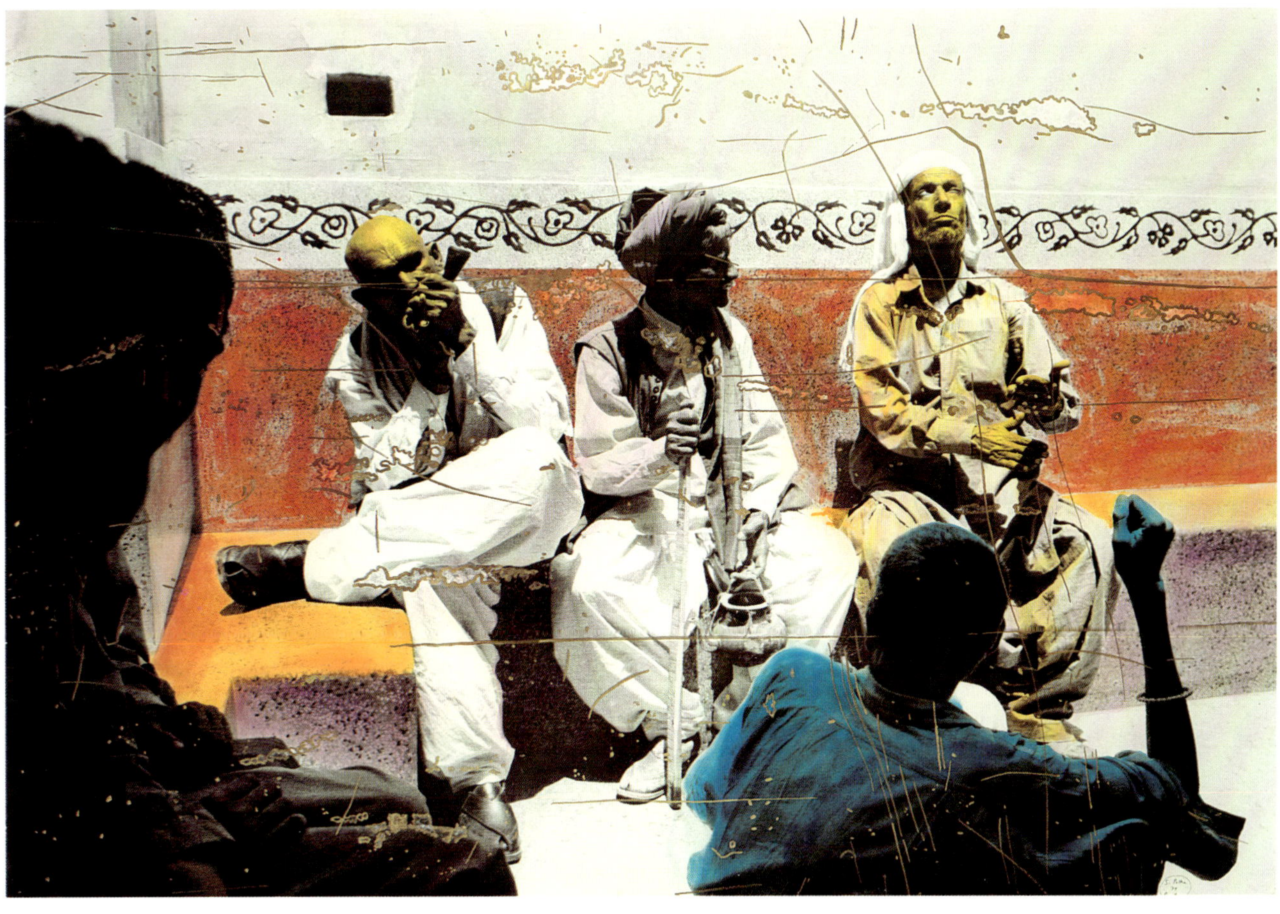

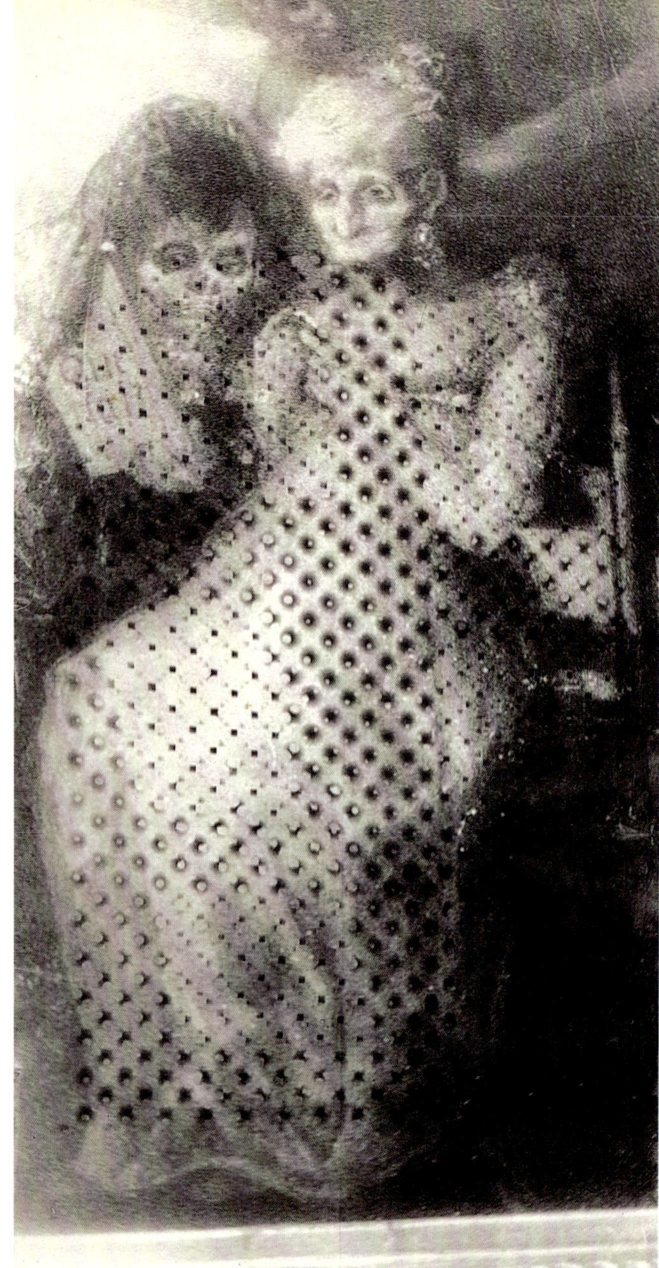

Above: Sigmar Polke, *Goya "Die Alten"* (The old women), 1984
Right: Sigmar Polke, *Fountain of Youth*, 1984

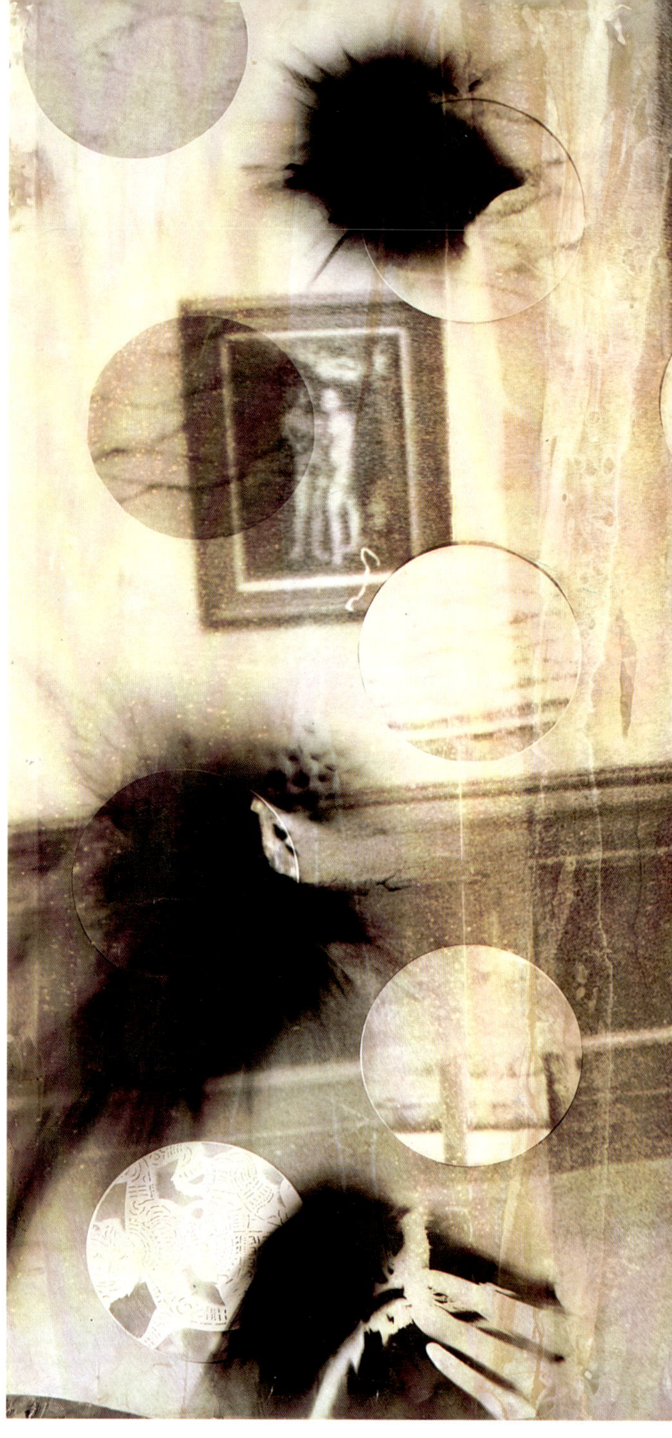

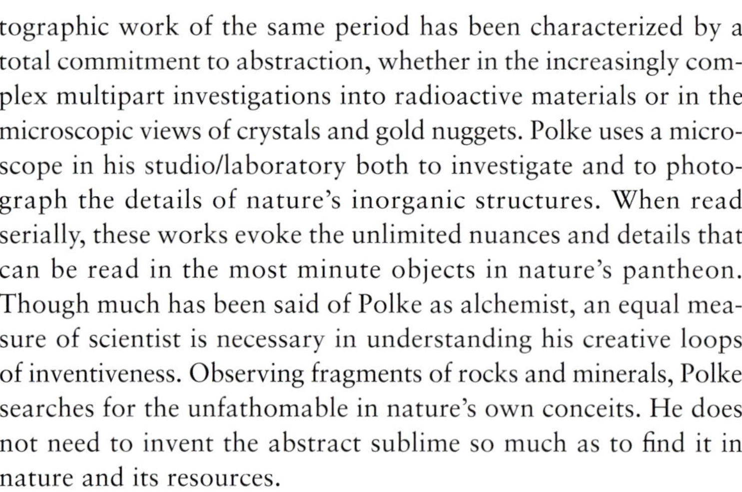

tographic work of the same period has been characterized by a total commitment to abstraction, whether in the increasingly complex multipart investigations into radioactive materials or in the microscopic views of crystals and gold nuggets. Polke uses a microscope in his studio/laboratory both to investigate and to photograph the details of nature's inorganic structures. When read serially, these works evoke the unlimited nuances and details that can be read in the most minute objects in nature's pantheon. Though much has been said of Polke as alchemist, an equal measure of scientist is necessary in understanding his creative loops of inventiveness. Observing fragments of rocks and minerals, Polke searches for the unfathomable in nature's own conceits. He does not need to invent the abstract sublime so much as to find it in nature and its resources.

An anarchist by nature, Polke has always implicitly understood the limitations of painting, even when he used it to undermine traditional notions of originality and creativity. He has sought to create an art that moves seamlessly between the activities of the studio and the activities of life. Photography gave him the opportunity to explore the complex layering of popular, intellectual, personal, social, and scientific elements. More than any other medium, photography begs the question of authorship. This thorny issue is in fact at the very foundation of Polke's photographic work. He uses photography to "borrow" from the real world; these "appropriations" are often complicated by the fact that Polke frequently collaborated with other artists in the first decade of his mature work, and has again in his recent project "Aachener Strasse," a collaboration with Augustina von Nagel. Up until the mid 1970s, Polke

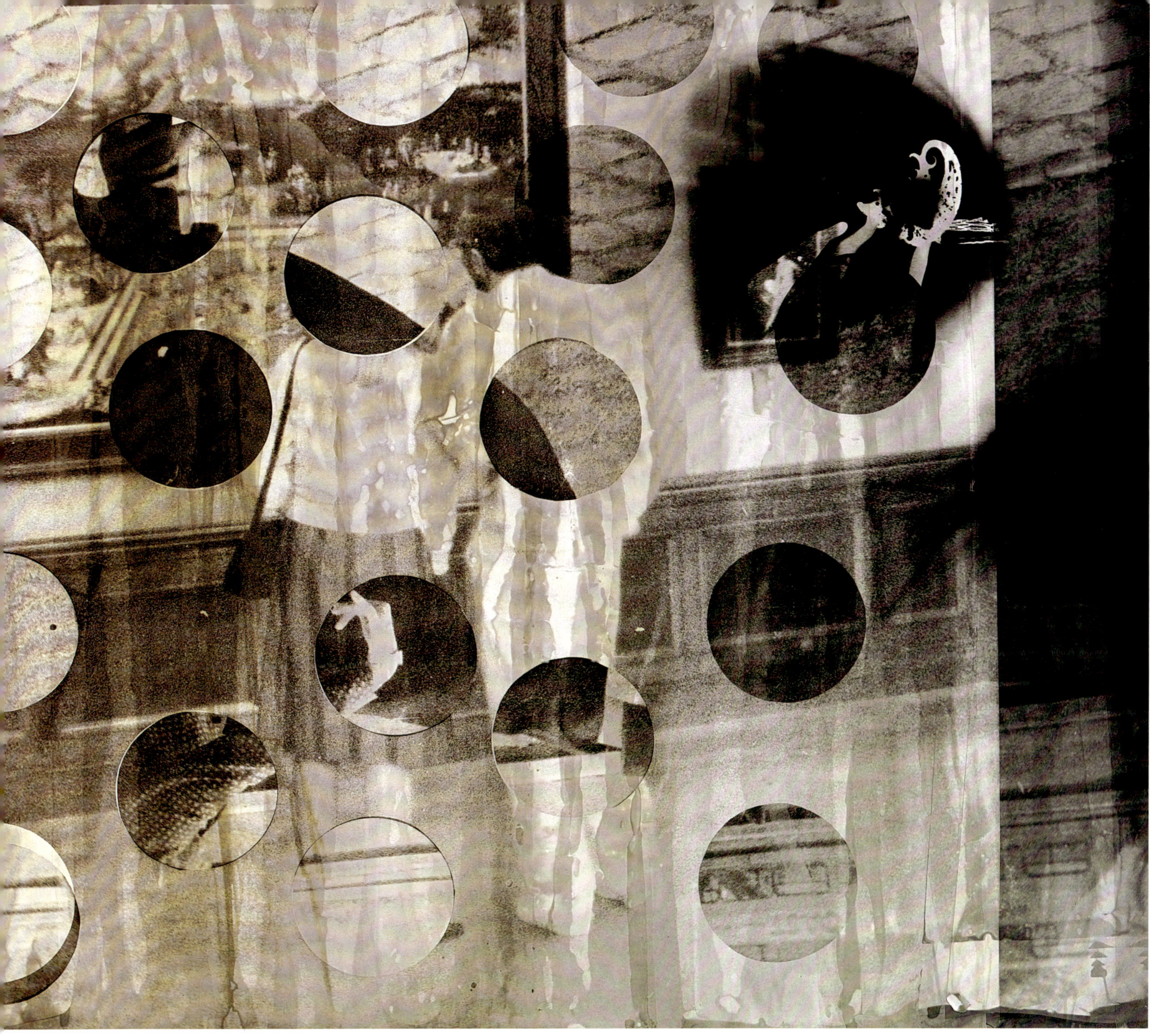

had collaborated separately with three living artists: Gerhard Richter, Christoph Kohlhofer, and Achim Duchow. These collaborations denied a certain consistency of authorship, which fits with Polke's belief that there should be no distinction between that which higher beings command you to do, that which you find in collaboration with colleagues, and that which you can take from nature.

This deeply revealing body of work represents the communal nature of his life at that time. Like the work itself, he was to go through a significant transformation in the early 1980s characterized by more experiments in the studio and darkroom and isolation from the community of artists that had figured in his earlier working milieu.

In Polke's search for altered states of reality, he first relied on chemicals found in nature to alter his perception of the world. More recently, he has found in nature itself representations that express an altered state of vision. Yet, in his exchange of drugs for crystals Polke has given up none of his fierce search for the immortal.

This text was excerpted from Schimmel's essay in *Sigmar Polke Photoworks: When Pictures Vanish*, the catalog to a major traveling exhibition organized by the Museum of Contemporary Art, Los Angeles. The exhibition is scheduled to appear at the Corcoran Gallery of Art, Washington, D.C., from September 21, 1996 to January 6, 1997.

1. Conversation with the artist, 1995.

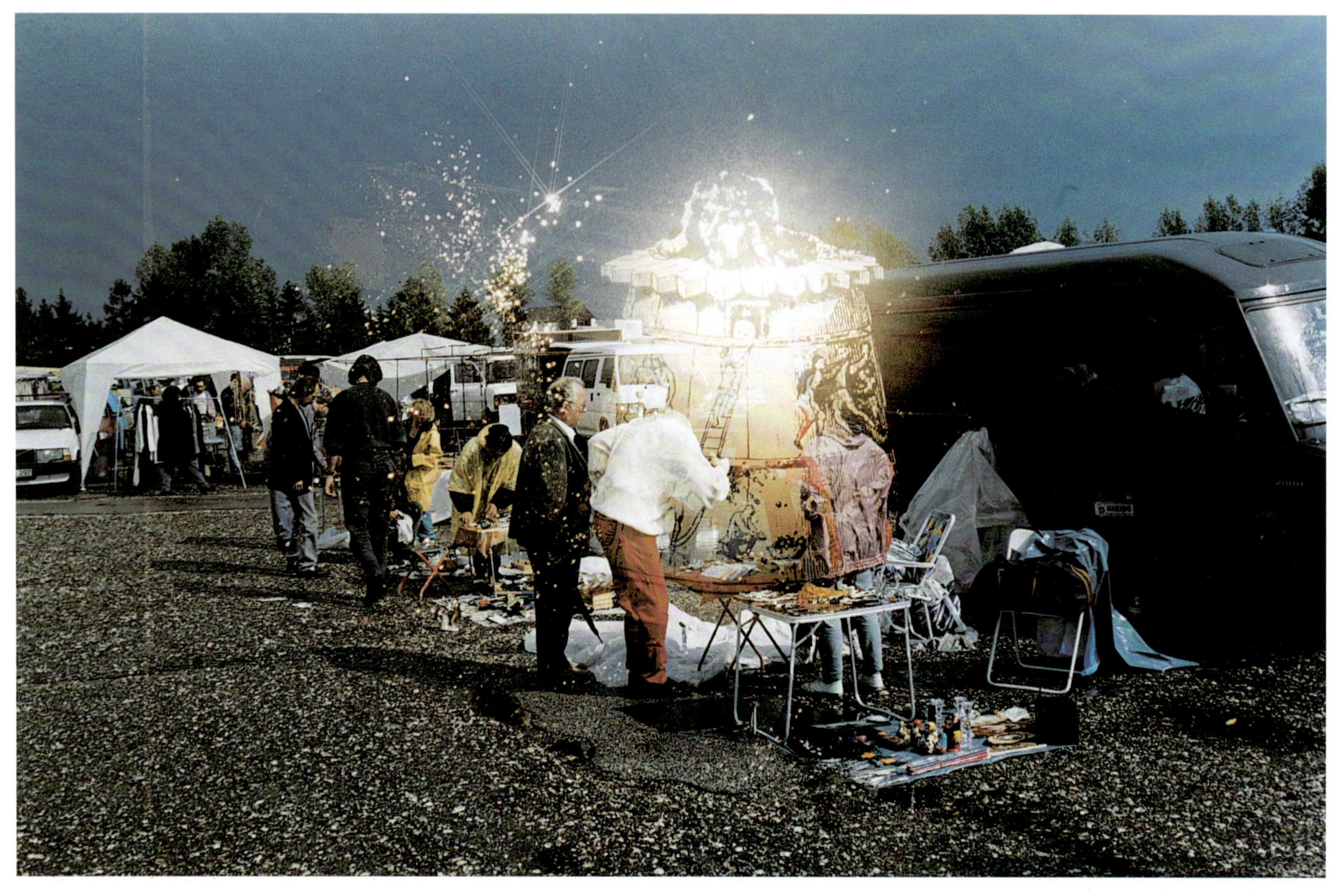

Above, below, and opposite: Sigmar Polke and Augustina von Nagel, from the series "Aachener Strasse," 1995

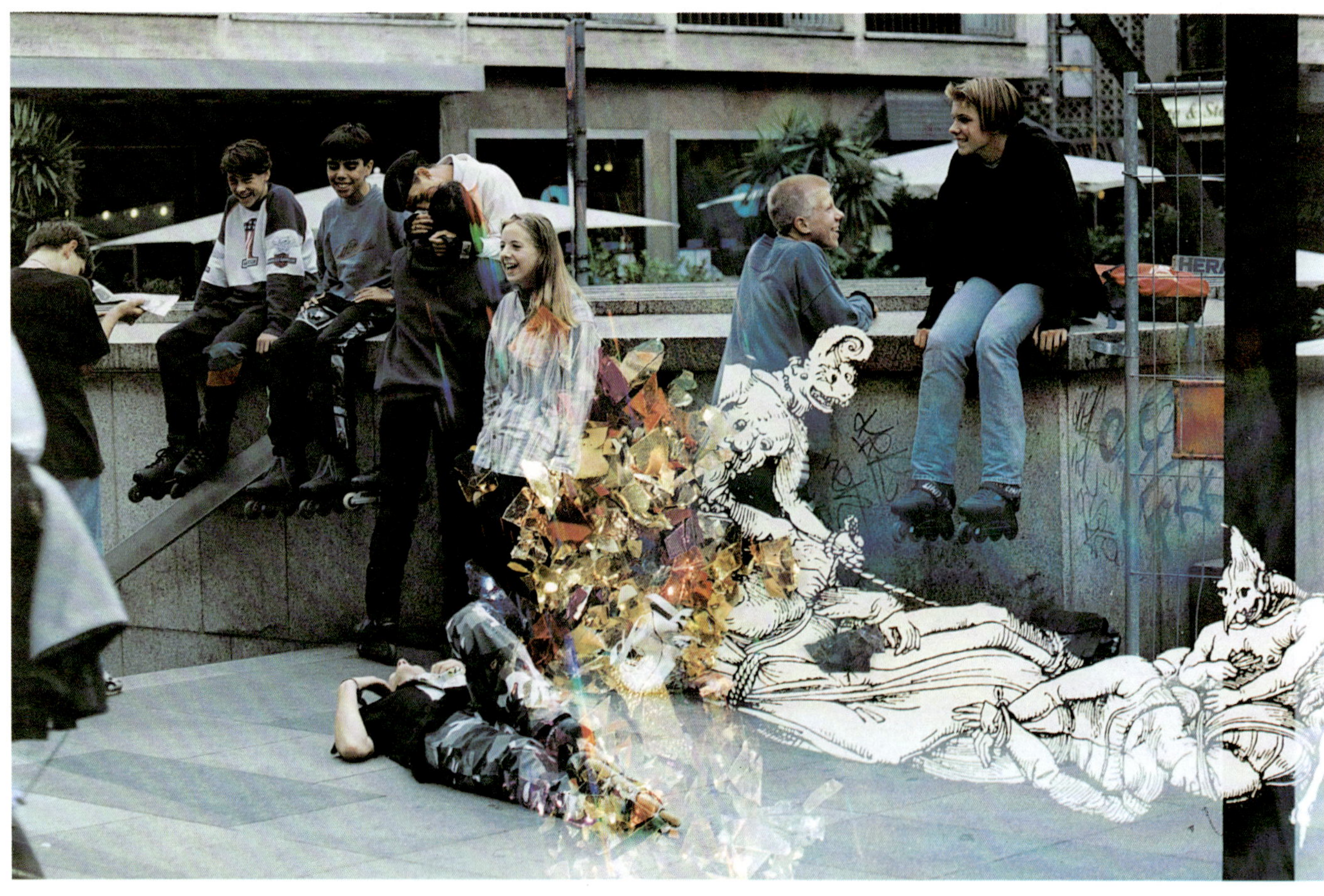

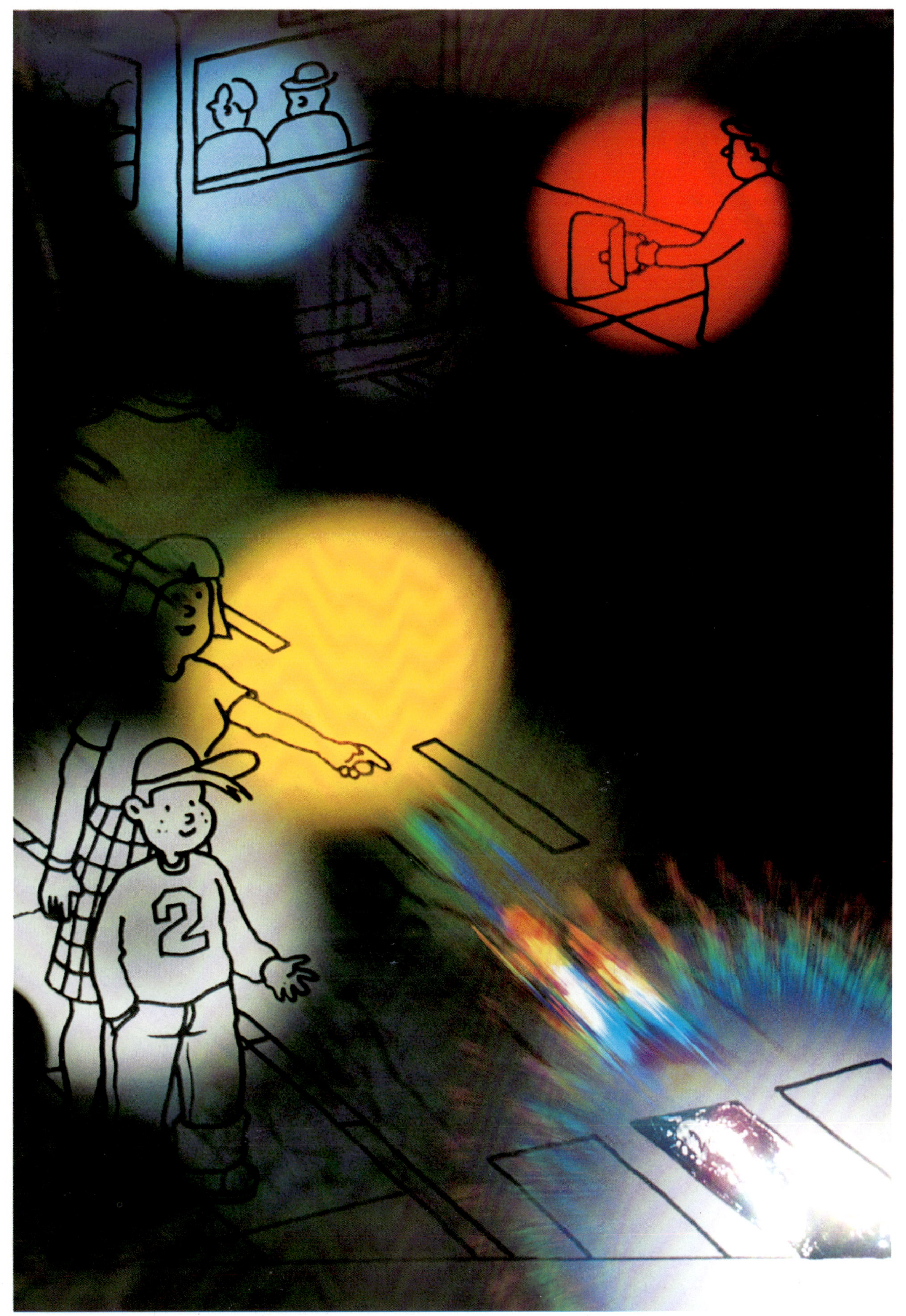
2

LOUISE LAWLER: SOUVENIR MEMORIES

Using photographs in unexpected ways, Louise Lawler addresses the role of art as commodity and as spectacle.

BY ROSALIND KRAUSS

1. We begin with the assumption of spectacle. It is there in the idea of an exhibition that will include slide projections to be seen at night through the storefront window of a gallery, the miragelike image hovering in the darkened space like an exhibitionistic ghost. It is there in the display of the paperweights, in their combined references to the jewelry store and the peep show. For if the jewelry store is signaled by the rows of chest-high pedestals with their Plexiglas tops, within which the little crystal half-globes are on show as so many identically precious objects, the peep show is triggered by the action of the objects' semispherical "lenses," which narrow down the viewer's gaze to an almost impossibly small point of entry into the work's visual field he or she must hunch over to see—Duchamp's *Etant donnés* rewritten as tiny, kitsch souvenirs.

Making works of art whose supports are consistently drawn from the lowest rungs of commodity culture, from matchbooks, from dime-store glassware, but also from the visual vocabularies of journalistic and commercial photography, Louise Lawler has a relation to these supports that is not ironic but meditative, almost loving. Onto the shiny red covers of a set of matchbooks she letters the subheadings from Roland Barthes's *Lover's Discourse*—"angoisse," "askesis," "corps"—hand-setting each letter meticulously and hot-stamping the type in foil. She photographs a Pollock hanging over a dining-room sideboard; the picture is pure *House & Garden* or *Vogue Interiors*, half soup-tureen, half violently dripped canvas; but she has so effaced herself before the spectacle language that it is hard to find the anger or the contempt or any of the other avant-garde modes of outrage in the image. She photographs a wall from the showroom at Sotheby's installed for a contemporary art auction; the picture is strangely cropped so that while we notice the glassy varnish on the surface of a Warhol whose contents we can therefore barely discern, our noses are also pressed against the stains and dirt of the carpet-lined walls and the crooked, tattered card that hawks this painting as so much merchandise. Siding momentarily with photojournalism, Lawler's image then relapses, however, into the strangely stunned but tender neutrality that one would have to identify as her "style."

2. That style takes the condition of spectacle as a fact of life. Writing in the 1930s, Walter Benjamin had imagined the revolutionary effect—whether for good or evil—of photographic reproduction on the work of art, the "destruction of its aura," both in terms of

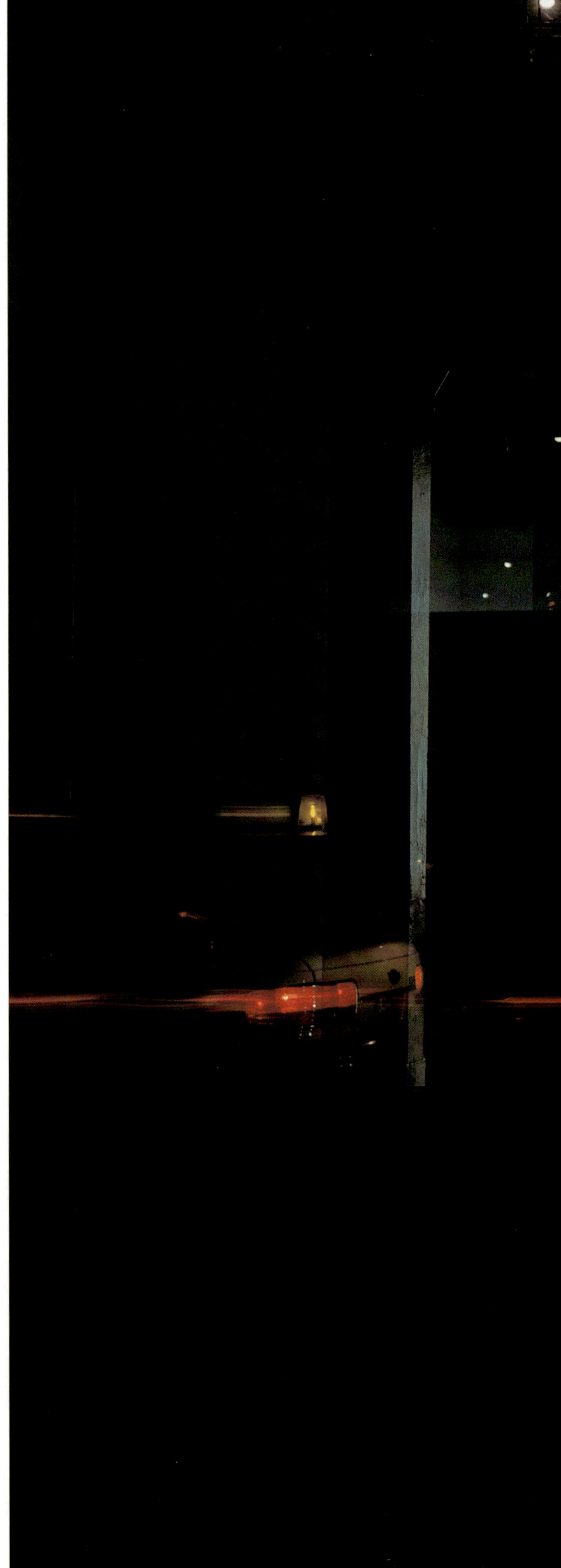

Louise Lawler, *External Simulation View at Night*, 1994

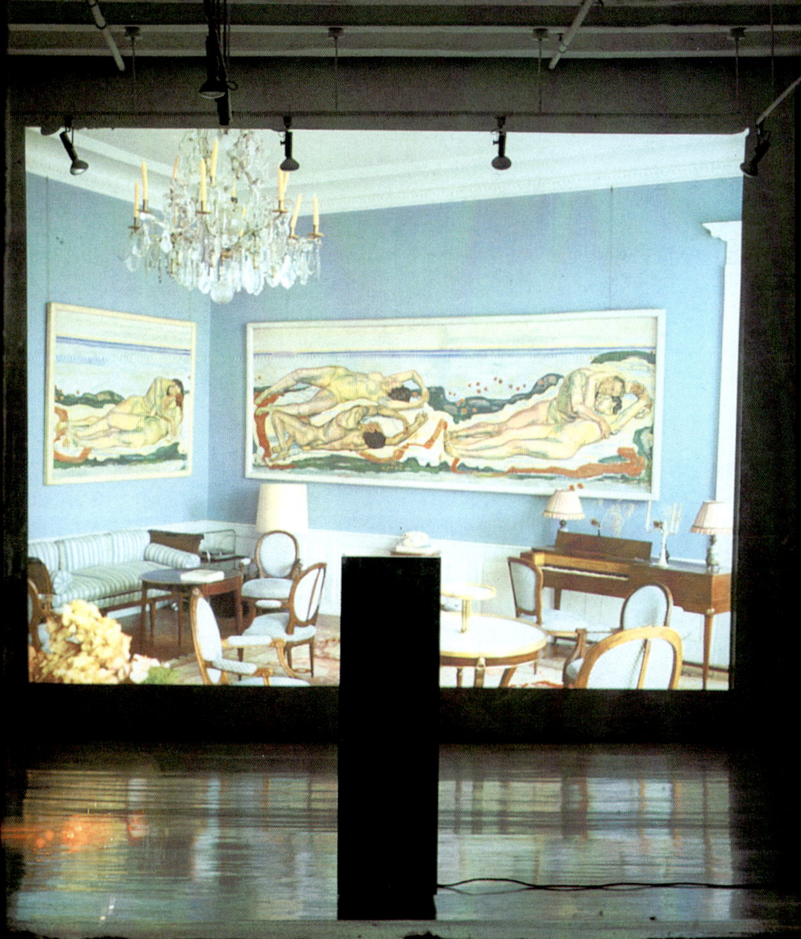

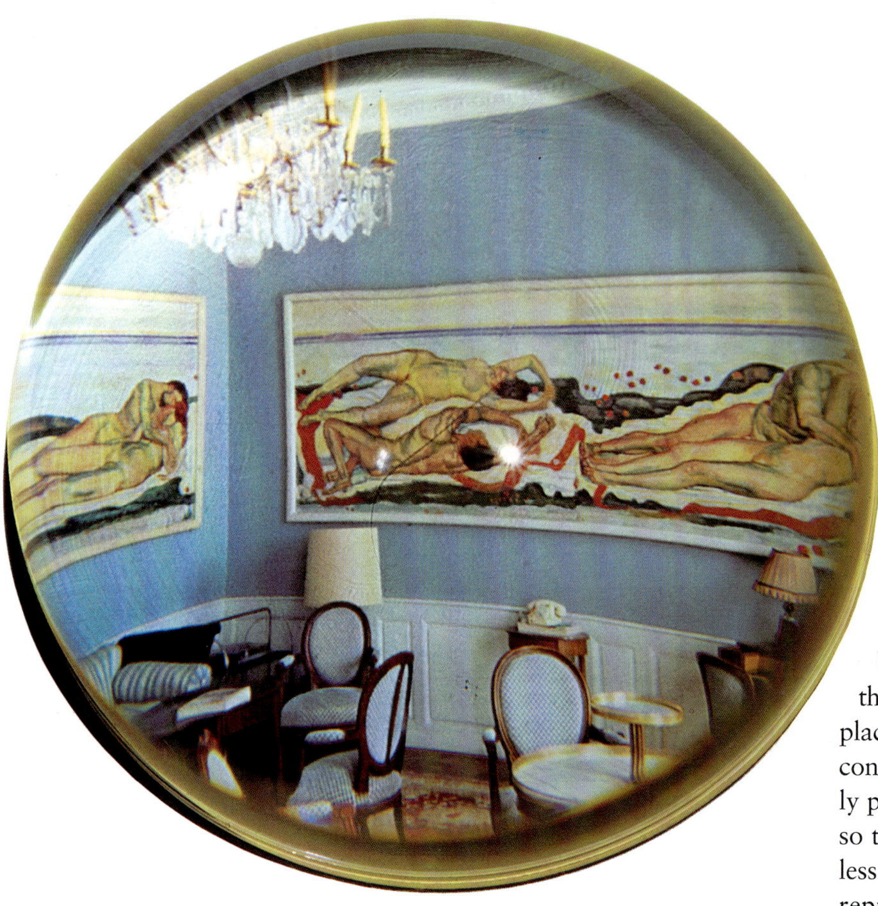

Louise Lawler, *Untitled (Salon Hodler)*, 1992
Write a story, do, about a young man, the son of a serf, a former grocery boy, a choirsinger, a high school pupil and university student, brought up to respect rank, to kiss the hands of priests, to truckle to the ideas of others—a young man who expressed thanks for every piece of bread, who was whipped many times, who went without galoshes to do his tutoring, who used his fists, tortured animals, was fond of dining with rich relatives, was a hypocrite in his dealing with God and men, needlessly, solely out of a realization of his own insignificance—write how this young man squeezes the slave out of himself, drop by drop, and how, on awakening one fine morning, he feels that the blood coursing through his veins is no longer that of a slave but that of a real human being.

Using as their vehicle the kitsch-level, mass-cultural object, these works enact their relation to photography not only in their obvious condition as multiples, but more interestingly in the way each crystal half-sphere presents itself as a lens, one through which one peers as though through a camera's viewfinder.

its condition as unique, and its embeddedness in a tradition of rich associations, by delivering the aesthetic image to the system of its own replication and dissemination: what would later come to be called "sign exchange." But however vivid his imagination, Benjamin could not know what it would be like for these effects to have become the totality of one's experience. He could not know the degree to which the oppositions that run through his own work, structuring its logic—oppositions such as those between the storyteller and the journalist, or the collector and the consumer—would collapse under the simulacral force of spectacle.

What Lawler takes for granted is the result of this force and its absolute pervasiveness. It is no longer the case that painting has a resistant opacity—due to its material presence, its objectifiable surface—while photography is nothing but the pure transparency of a slippery illusionism through which we are sucked into the half-truths of the world of media. Under the pressures of spectacle, the logic of this opposition has become warped into something that looks more like a pretzel or a Möbius strip than it does a straightforward binary. For, within the conditions of a culture of the spectacle, the values of opacity and transparency have, it would seem, changed places. As Andy Warhol had already made perfectly clear, media has constructed its own supposedly transparent world as a space entirely peopled by commodities (the Marilyns, the Jackies, the Elvises), so that the signs that circulate within it are as opaque and depthless as one could want. And on the other hand, the conditions of reproduction, as they seep across the boundary into high art, a boundary they have rendered altogether porous, have turned every gesture and every seemingly resistant surface of painting, into the glitteringly transparent sign of its own subordination to a spectacle world in which it no longer operates in relation to values like spontaneity or authenticity, but functions as a pure token of sign-exchange.

And there is another transformation that has become a corollary of this: if the opacity of the Modernist pictorial surface was an index of the materiality of the picture plane, it acted to force that plane onto a level continuous with other physical bodies thereby declaring the work of art a function of public space. The displacement of that index into the world of reproductions—where the gesture is always already an image of itself—is a function of the solipcism of media, of a condition of spectacle that means that its public is impossibly dispersed and privatized, each viewer isolated in front of a television set, each positioned at the aperture of the peep show. This too is the work of what we could call the photographic as it operates on all the arts.

To assume this condition of spectacle as the very texture of one's own world, the fabric of one's very sensibility, is to observe that world through the eyes of spectacle. It is to see everything mutate into at least two versions of itself: the "original" object and the sign for that object, although within the logic of spectacle's mirror reflections it is never clear which is which. The gleams and reflections that interest Lawler, as she photographs works of Modernist art within their present condition of commodification—a Frank Stella "protractor" painting, for example, photographed as nothing but its own rainbowlike reflection in the polished floor of its display space—are avatars of this pervasive condition of the sign.

But it is not only recent art that is so infected. As Lawler photographs the salon of a Swiss collector, its decorous little tables and chairs seem to have migrated from the world of rarefied antiques and to have entered the space of the reproduction, the elegant room now resembling nothing so much as a upper-class hotel lobby. But even more disconcertingly the two paintings by Ferdinand Hodler that dominate the salon undergo the same internal mutation. For Hodler has pictured three pairs of lovers, two in one painting, one in the other, their bodies locked together in turn-of-the-century symbolist erotic intensity. Each of the pairings is slightly different, an index of the measure to which lovers are unique in each other's eyes, revered with feelings that are never to be duplicated, nor repeated. Looking at this display through Lawler's gaze—so attentive and yet so dispassionate—what we see is not the uniqueness of these pairs but their repetition, each becoming the redoubled sign of the other, as though despite whatever he had intended, Hodler had flattened and debased and emptied out his own world.

3. It is the photograph of the "Hodler salon" that stands sentinel over Lawler's subsequent displays of the paperweights (one of which contains the "Hodler salon" in miniature) as a series. Using as their vehicle the kitsch level, mass cultural object, these works enact their relation to photography not only in their obvious condition as multiples, but more interestingly in the way each crystal half-sphere presents itself as a lens, one through which one peers as though through a camera's viewfinder. And by means of that line of sight, that unifocal vector, one is summoned to perform on *this* side of the lens the very closing out of public space that has emerged as the result of the mediated world of photography. Substituting for the shared space within which culture formerly operated, a position that can only be occupied by one viewer at a time, the lens enforces a situation in which the only public thing that can occur in the space in which these works are displayed, is a form of voyeurism in which one either watches someone else looking or takes one's own visual pleasure with the concomitant sensation of being watched.

And on the *other* side of the lens, the one that gathers a world of objects into its view, what we encounter is a kind of brilliant summary of the lessons Walter Benjamin read to us in his various essays on photography—lessons about photography's bringing far-away things close to us, miniaturizing them for us so as to give us a sense of possessing them. Lessons as well about how photography would utterly transform art, forcing it to renounce its earlier cult-value and even its subsequent exhibition-value for a new, modern, postphotographical value, which he linked to documentary. Benjamin had high hopes, of course, for the revolutionary potential of this documentary, hopes that Lawler does not allow herself, here, to share. But the documentation she nonetheless brings us is about the fate of art in the private spaces of its commodification as it is also about the fate of the museum. For the little half-orb of the paperweight produces its own counter-discourse about the museum's stated ambitions to assemble disparate objects into a single space and to bestow on them the intellectual, aesthetic, and categorical coherence of a collection, conserving these objects for posterity, one symbol for which is the obsessive placing of them under glass.

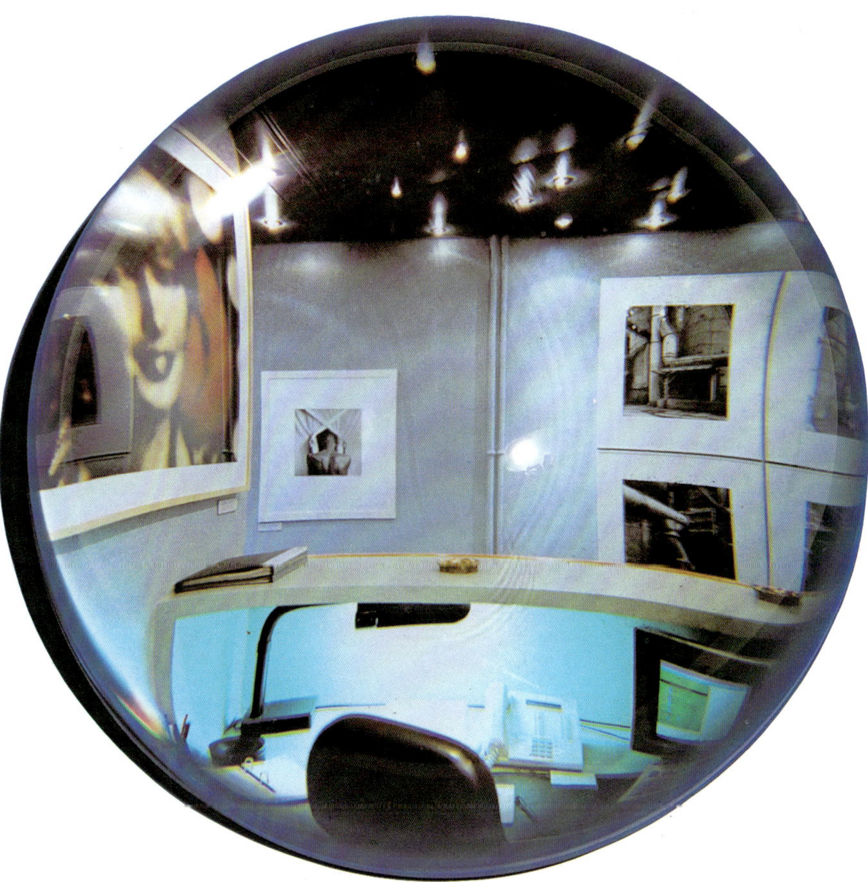

Louise Lawler, *Untitled (Computer)*, 1993

Yet even while it announces the shrivelling and diminution of these aspirations within the trivialization of the spectacle world, this symbol also reminds us of the utopian aspects of the museum's early project, insofar as the museum presented an original that in its material presence seemed to oppose itself, all the way down the line, to the simulacral drive of photography. And, indeed, what one could call the utopian dimension of Lawler's paperweight objects is that they are never completely or satisfactorily open to their own photographic reproduction: the lens producing, here, its own form of opacity and thus of resistance. It is somewhere in the thickness of the works' orbs of crystal—part photographic lens, part vitrine, part protective glazing—that these two fates—art's and photography's—have met and become intertwined. And strangely, photography seems now to have taken up the cause of art's presumed uniqueness, its supposed resistance to commodification both at the level of the object and at the level of its conditions of viewing. Which is to say that this paradoxical form of the photograph—itself never completely reproducible—seems to have taken up the cause of uniqueness and at the same time to be showing it to us from an extraordinary distance, bodying forth what might be seen as the sensuous equivalent of what we could call the past.

An extended version of this essay will appear in the catalog to "A Spot on the Wall," an exhibition organized by the Kunstverein, Munich; Neue Galerie, Graz; and De Appel, Amsterdam.

GERHARD RICHTER

The ongoing dialogue between painting and photography over the course of Gerhard Richter's career sheds light on the boundaries of both media.

PHOTOGRAPHS AND NOTES

Painter, teacher, iconoclast, Gerhard Richter has exerted a far-reaching and complex influence on contemporary art and artists. Richter has also explored every imaginable intersection of painting and photography: from photo-realistic paintings, to painting on photographs, from 1:1-scale photographs of paintings, to paintings that evoke the blurred transit of motion captured by a camera. A more compelling argument for the breakdown of distinctions between modes of expression would be hard to find.

In *Atlas*, a collection of roughly five thousand photographs on six hundred panels, Richter has assembled perhaps the ultimate picture archive, which contains everything from snapshots to installation sketches, from pornography to the still-life, landscape, and portrait photographs that he has since realized as quasi-photographic paintings.

Richter's many interviews and writings—recently compiled in *Gerhard Richter: The Daily Practice of Painting*—overlap and contradict one another at every turn, and yet, taken together, they provide unexpected inroads into a deeper understanding of the dialectic between representational and abstract art. He is intensely demanding of himself, and no less so of those who attempt to read meaning into his works. "Many amateur photographs are more beautiful than a Cézanne," he once said, simultaneously thumbing his nose at the art historical canon and elevating the ephemeral or casual image to High Art. A selection of Richter's images, and of his thoughts on painting and photography, follows.

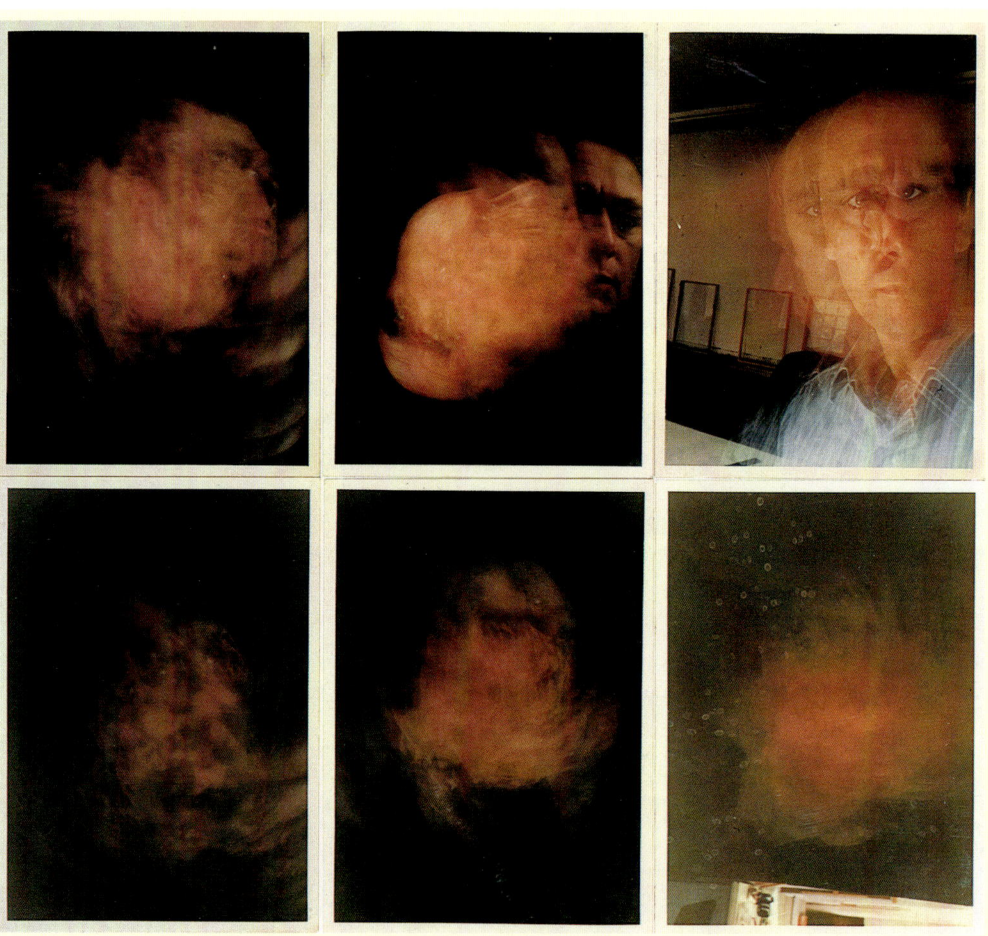

Gerhard Richter, *Doppelbelichtungen (*Double exposures*)*, 1970

Belief is something with many sides to it. Believing in pictures is like believing in God—or believing in pictures in a practical sense, at a time when painting is rather out of favour. . . . We're always creating pictures; take fashion, for example. We put something on because we believe in it, and we thereby offer a picture of ourselves that tells other people who we are and what we're like. The same happens in other ways—we're always creating pictures for other people to understand if they can. —G.R., 1992

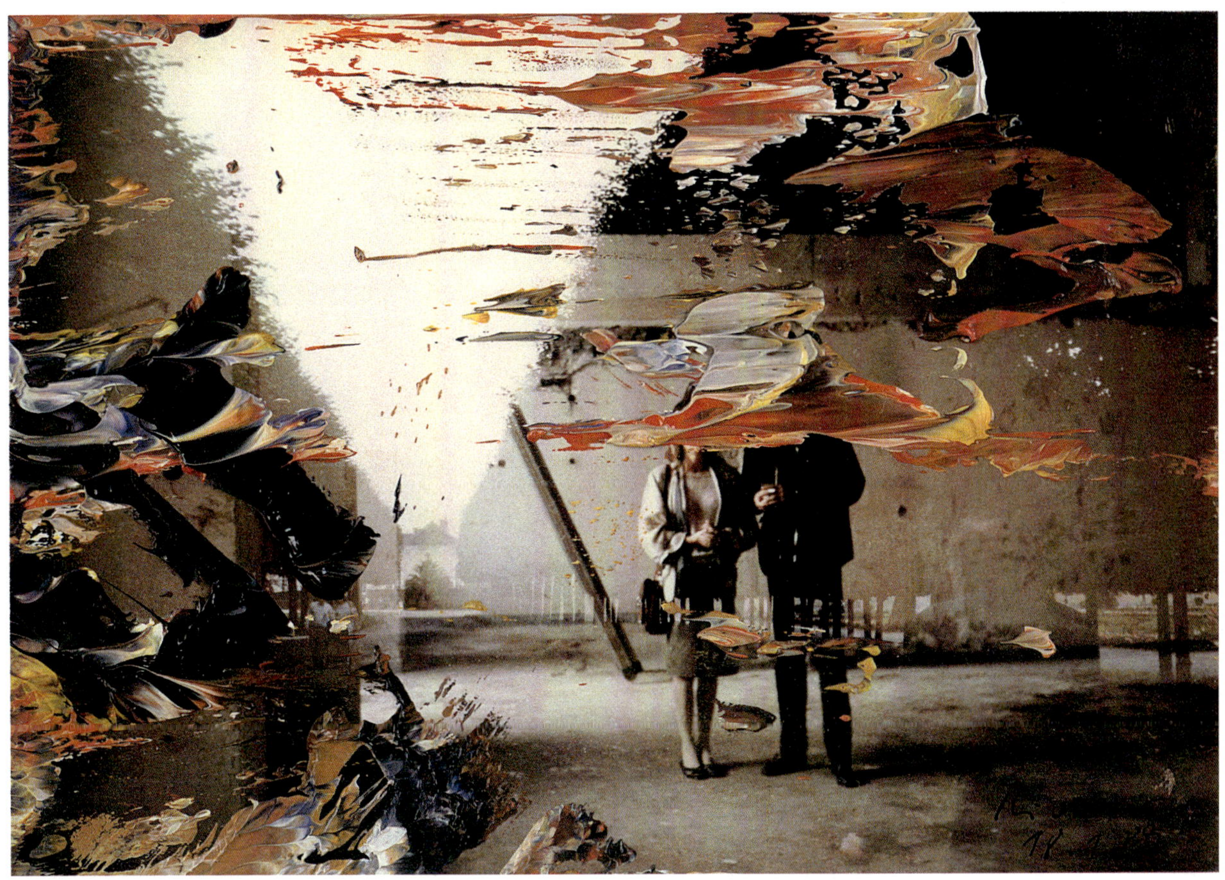

Above: Gerhard Richter, *18.1.89*, 1989

Below: Gerhard Richter, *1.Juli 94*, 1994

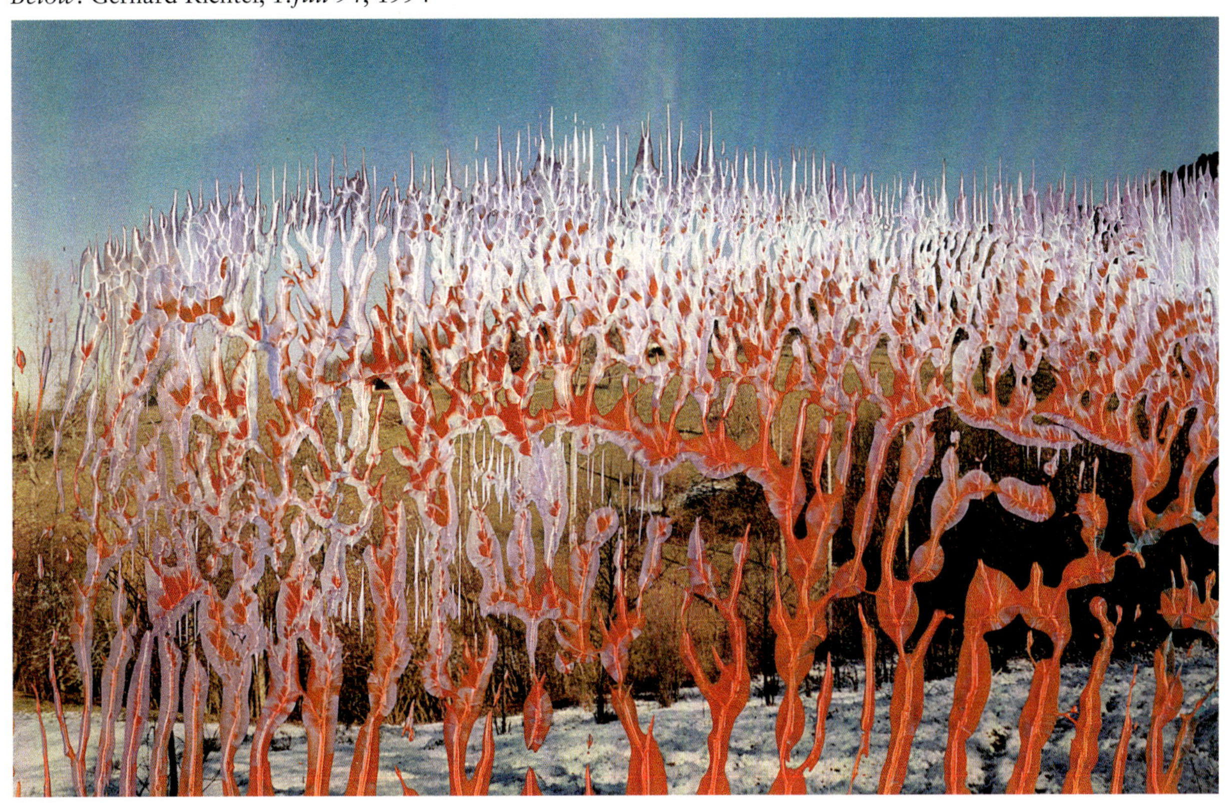

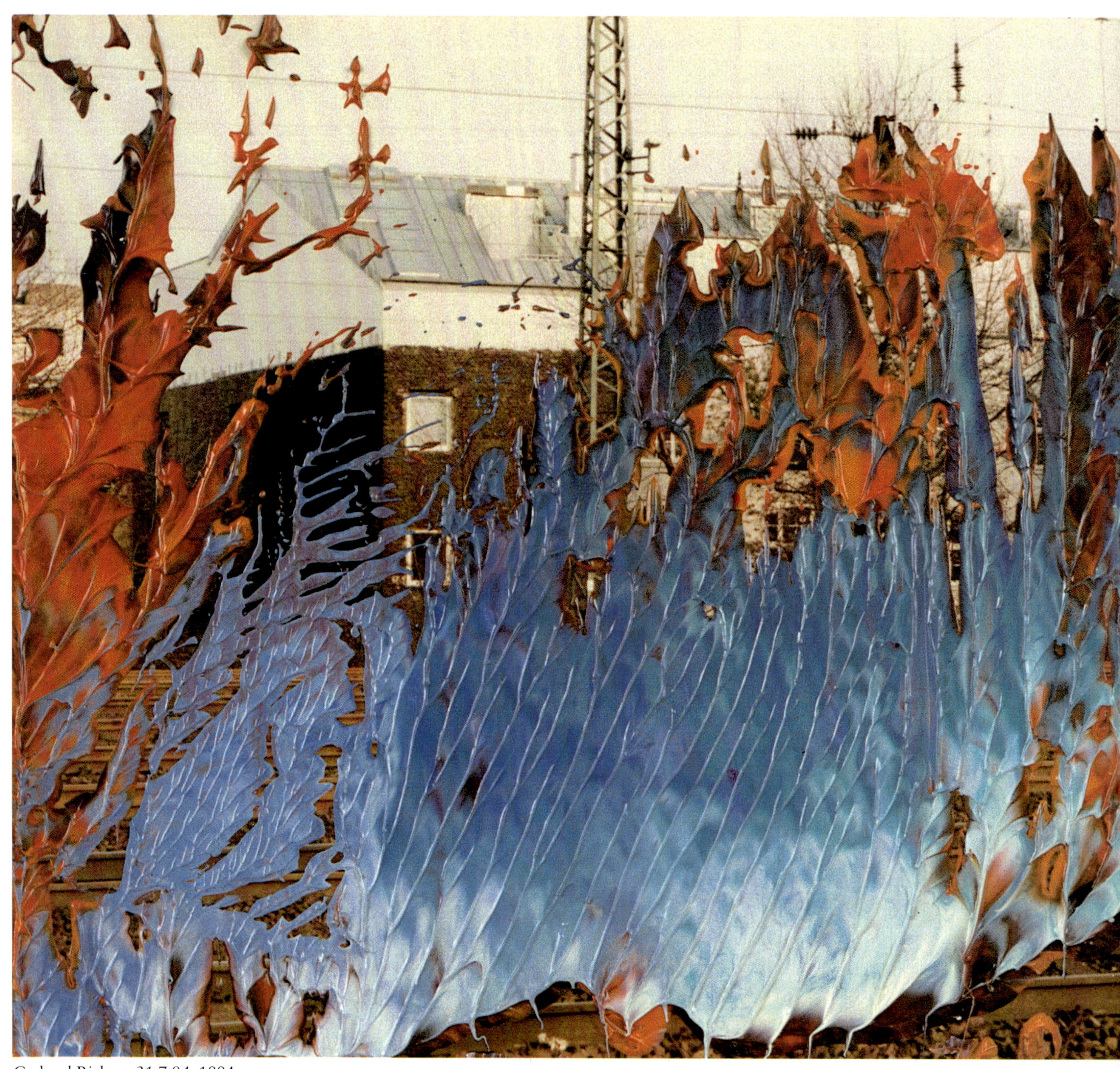
Gerhard Richter, *31.7.94*, 1994

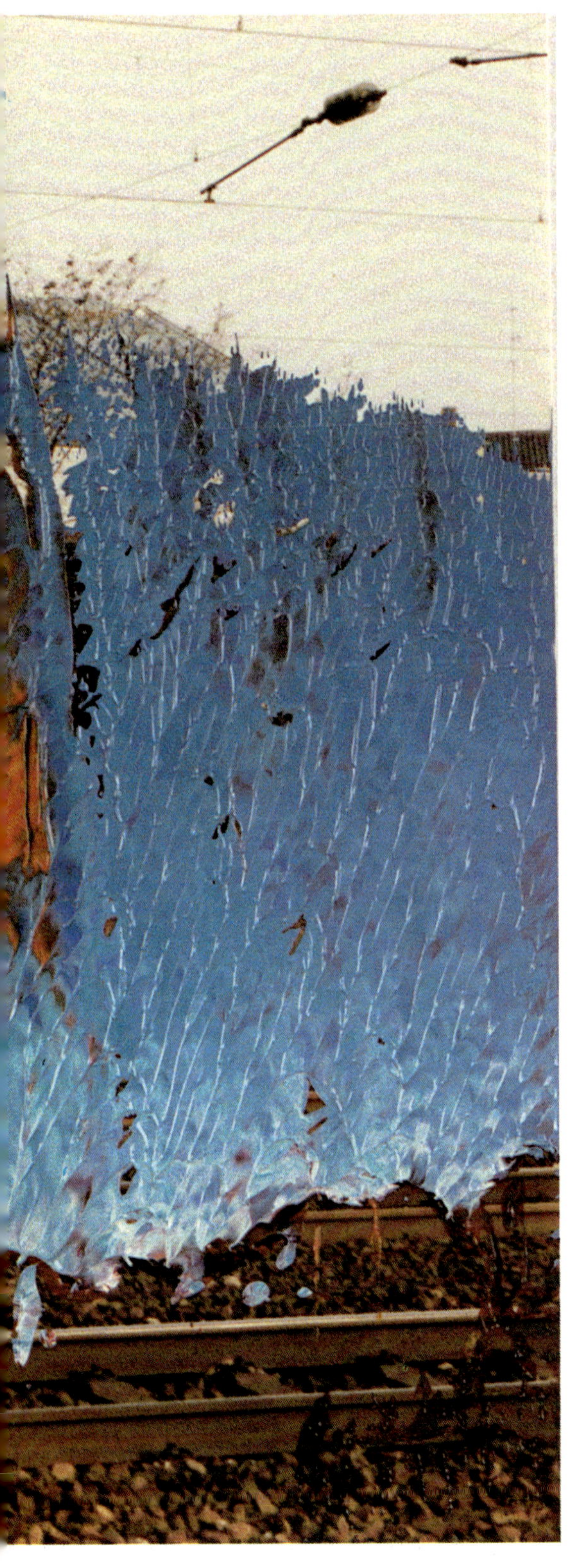

*The legitimate pictures are the photographs—
the devotional pictures that people hang or set up in
their homes. We then sometimes use them for art,
and that may well be illegitimate.* —G.R., 1993

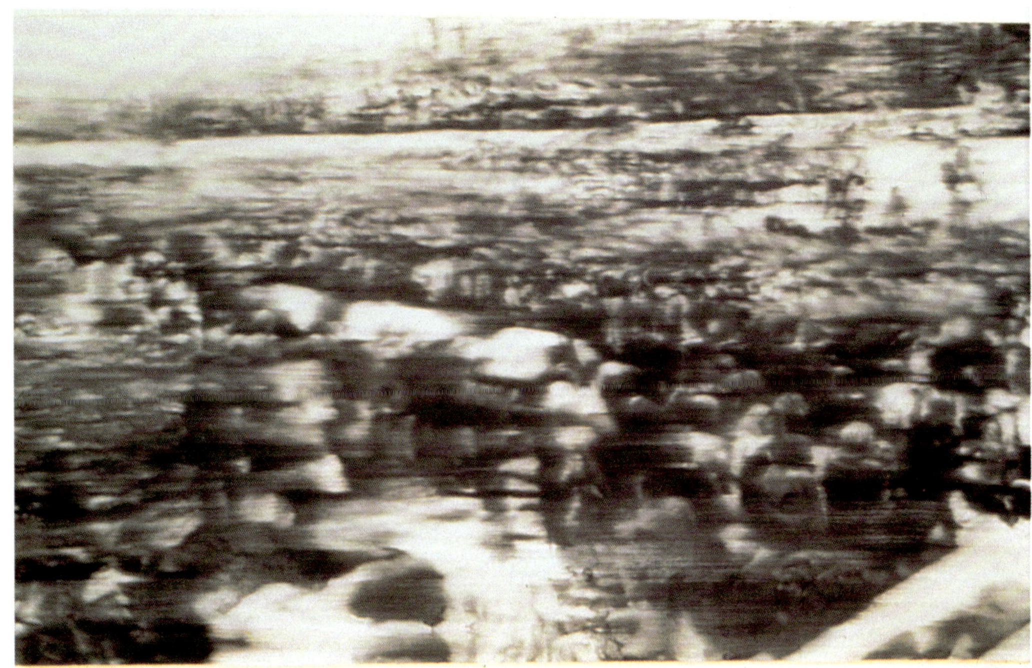

Gerhard Richter, *Beerdigung* (Funeral), 1988

The Photo Realists . . . painted photographs in a finicky, detailed way. I haven't the patience for that; and then there are the distracting perceptual factors that find their way in. One is the outsize format, and the other is the admiration of the labour involved: the fact that it takes a whole year, the response of marveling at the way it looks "just like a photo." I wanted to avoid all that by cheapening the production values. You can see that a photograph is meant, but it hasn't been laboriously copied and duplicated. This worked, and the pictures had the basic resemblance to photography without looking like copies of photographs. —G.R., 1993

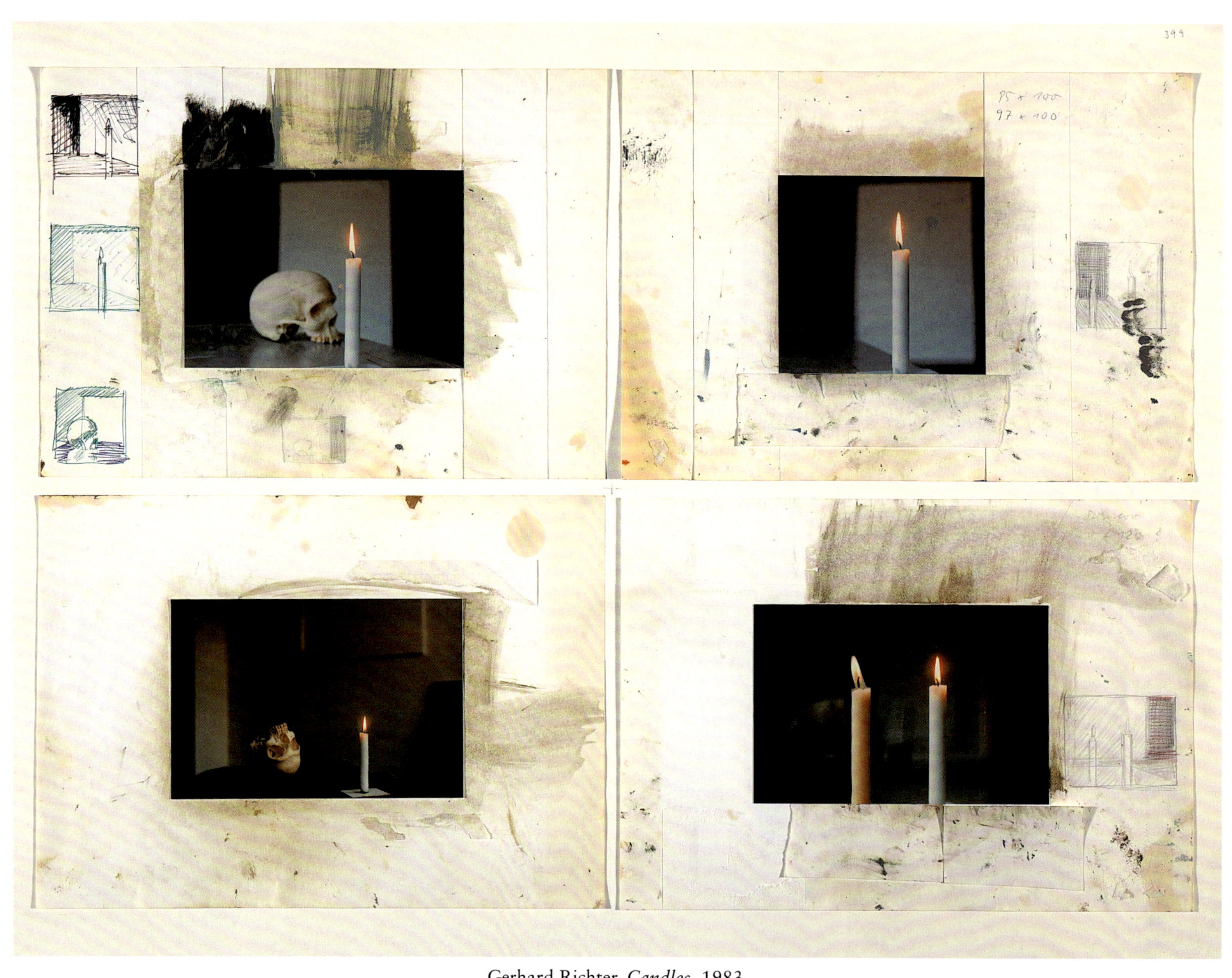

Gerhard Richter, *Candles*, 1983

. . . I needed the greater objectivity of the photograph in order to correct my own way of seeing: for instance, if I draw an object from nature, I start to stylize and change it in accordance with my personal vision and my training. But if I paint from a photograph, I can forget all the criteria that I get from these sources. I can paint against my will, as it were. And that, to me, felt like an enrichment. —G.R., 1972

Gerhard Richter, *Two Candles*, 1983

AN EDGE OF BLACK

*From monumental wax sculptures to whirling photographic moments—
Petah Coyne's dizzying forays into photography.*

PHOTOGRAPHS AND TEXT BY PETAH COYNE

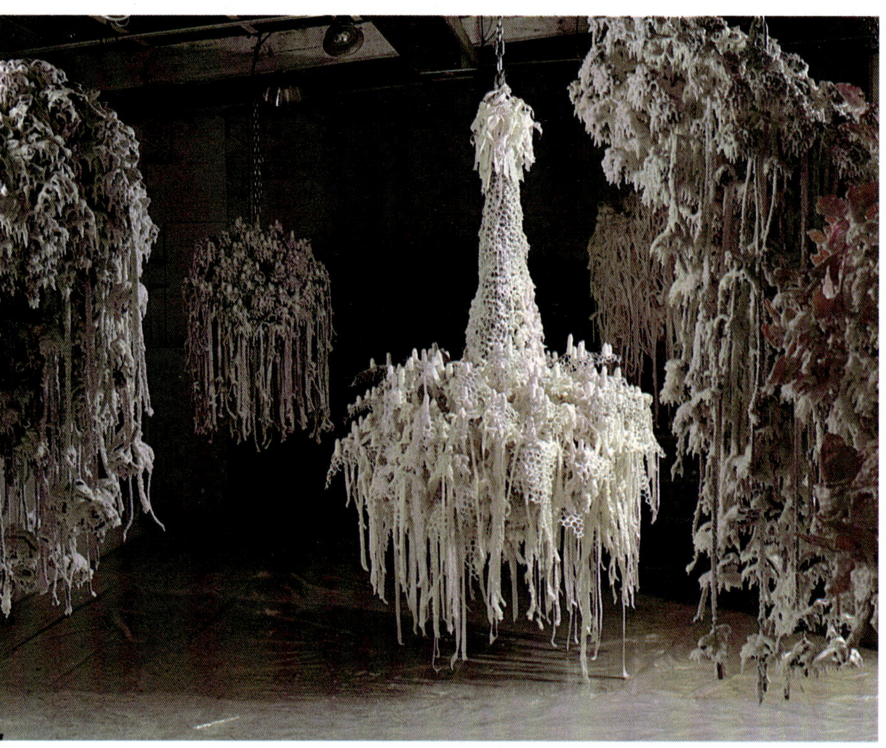

Petah Coyne, *Untitled*, 1992–94

As these images move in space, sometimes gathering gale-force speed, I watch in amazement and sometimes in horror. I want desperately to move with them, to fly like the piñatas and run as free as the monks.

I have always seen the world moving at an incredibly fast pace, as if I've been hurled from a slingshot, and I seem never to land. I try desperately to keep up with it all—running, always moving. I believe no generation before ours has ever had to navigate, with such agility, through so many different kinds of space and thought so quickly. Amazingly, the pace only increases with the added years.

My sculpture is all about this continual change and pace. It is a perpetual process, adding layer upon layer of texture and shape. This constant tending and never reaching completion is like the care of invalids. My photography is also about continual movement and change, but the elimination of it, the removal of excess. My search is to see what lies underneath.

I try to breathe deeply while hurricanes of spinning objects fly past my vision, seeing it all as I would a movie at close range. New images come into focus, my mind is not able to make sense of the "true" meaning, it wanders uncontrollably into other territories. Finding great pleasure in my newfound vision, I even hate to close my eyes at night, afraid I will miss some luscious visual sensation.

Through this blur of motion I look out and focus in on details. My eyes and mind pause on them, tracing an edge of black or a transparent surface. I seem never to focus on the whole; it is far too much to grasp. Instead, my vision is filled with small details or patches, from which I try to make sense of the whole.

My body feels pulled forward and my face often stops just short of the vision. I feel so close I can smell the environment that surrounds it. But even these tumbling details cannot be seen completely in focus, as you would if you were sitting still. Only parts come into focus, the rest is an abstract blue. These patches appear like an accident taking place in slow motion, repeated again and again through my mind. With each replay I focus on a new feature, allowing my mind to play with the images. As these images move in space, sometimes gathering gale-force speed, I watch in amazement and sometimes in horror. I want desperately to move with them, to fly like the piñatas and run as free as the monks. I want to belong.

But I find myself out of step, once again at a high-school dance and the only person with no concept of rhythm. I shudder with dread, but eventually go along with it, moving within my own awkward rhythm. My jerky movements against the activity of my subjects make not just a blurry photograph but one person's subtle shifting against another's. Here everything stops. These are the moments of simple silence so enmeshed in emotion and poignant clarity that all else falls away.

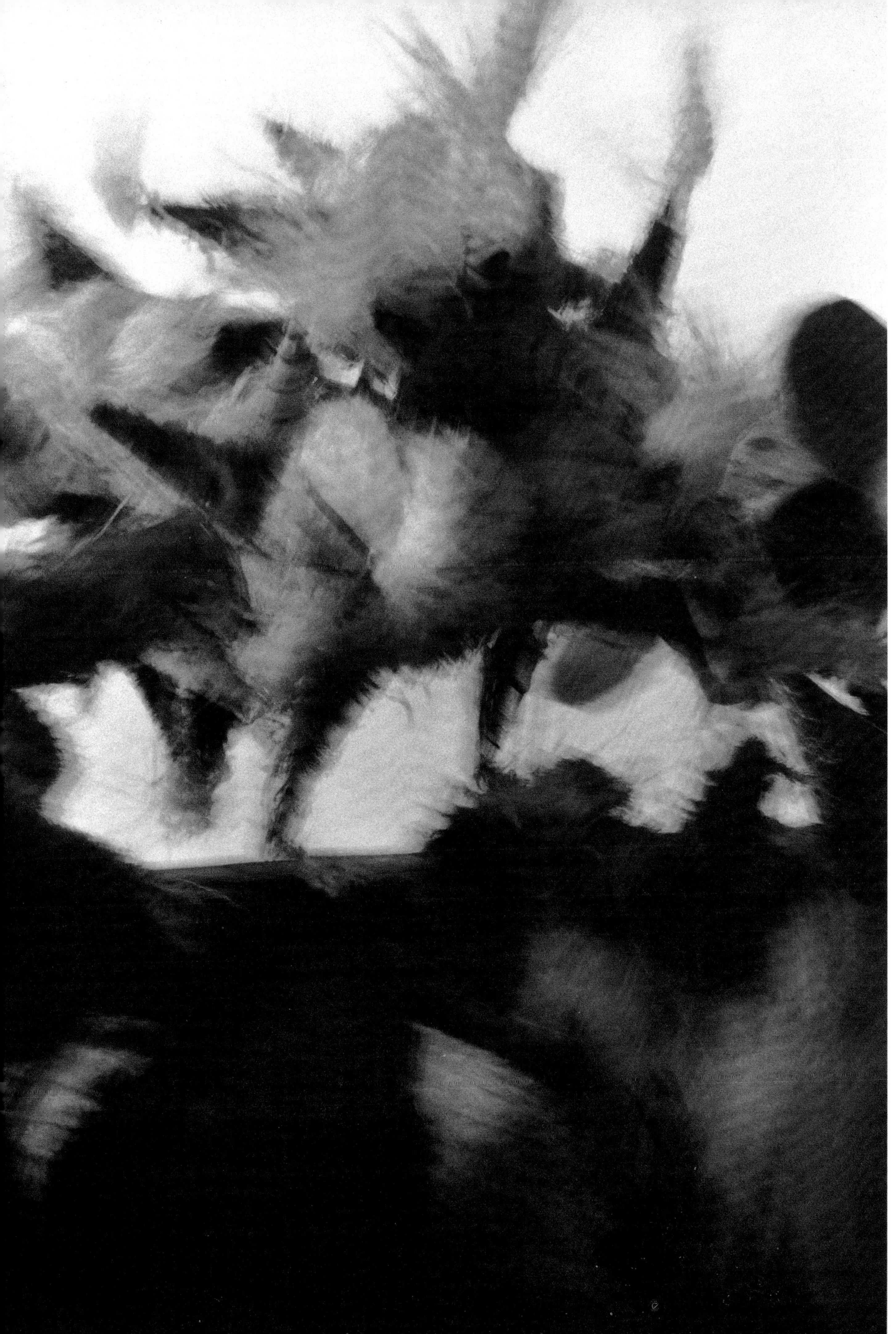

Petah Coyne,
Untitled, 1994

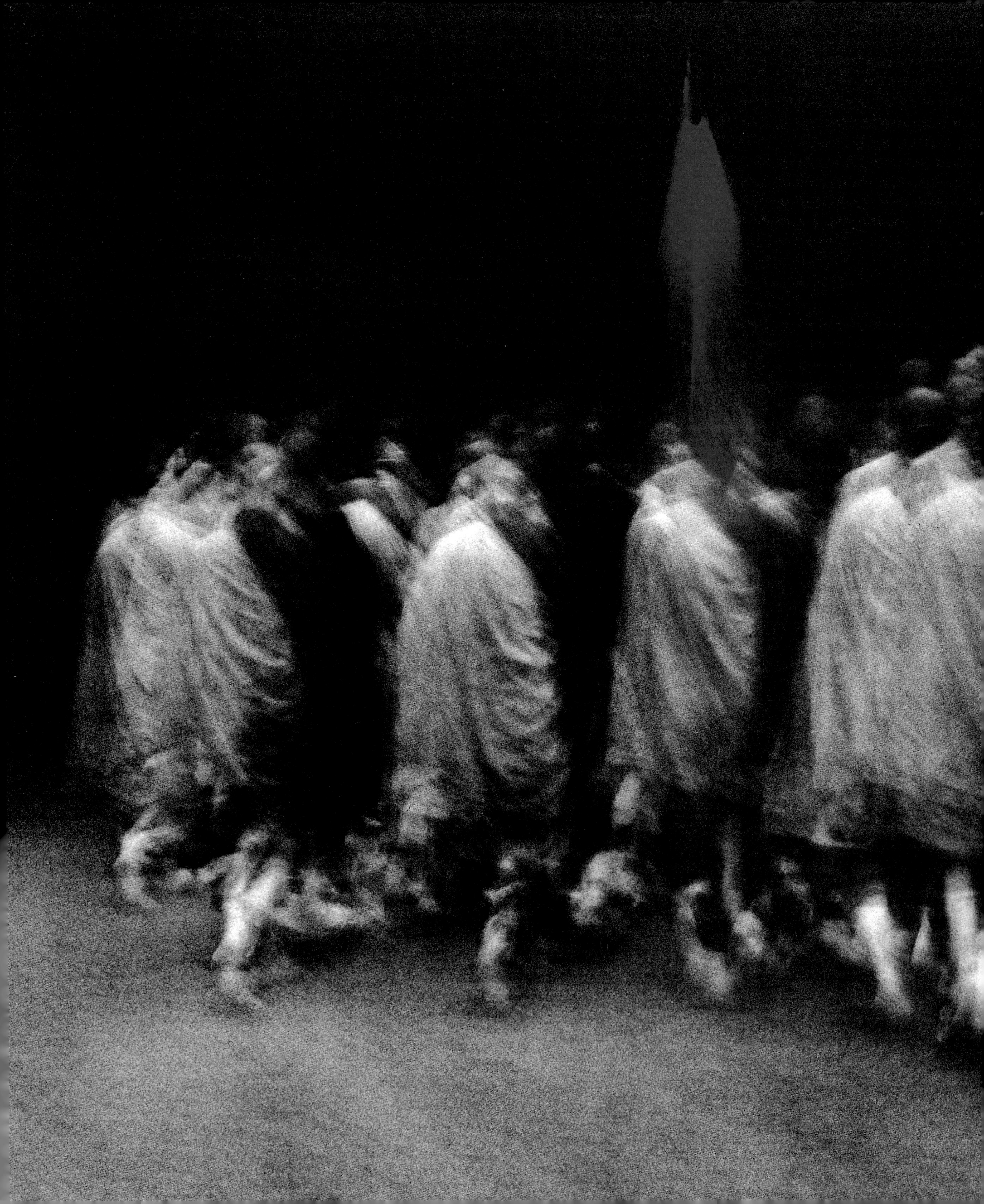

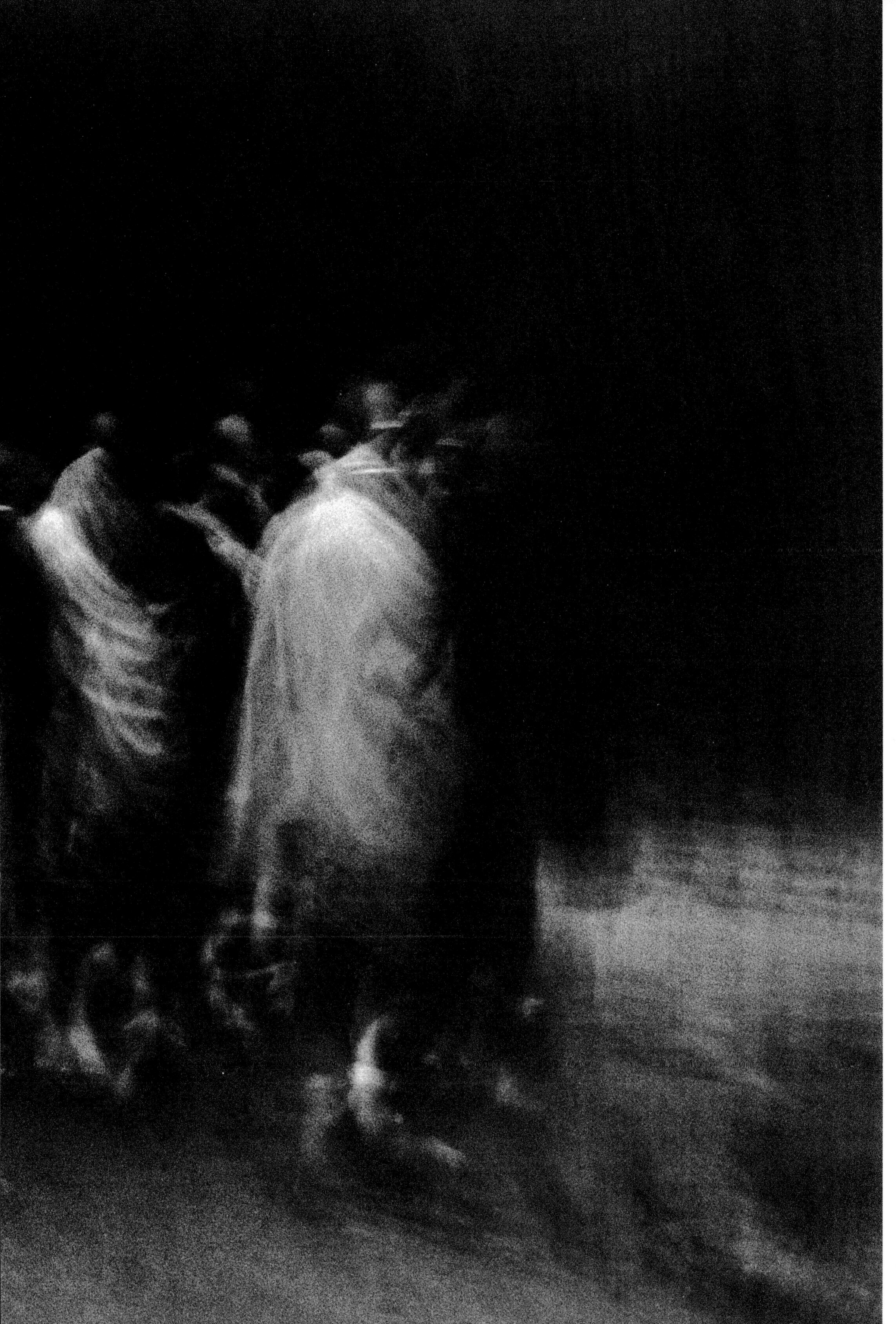

Petah Coyne,
Untitled, 1994

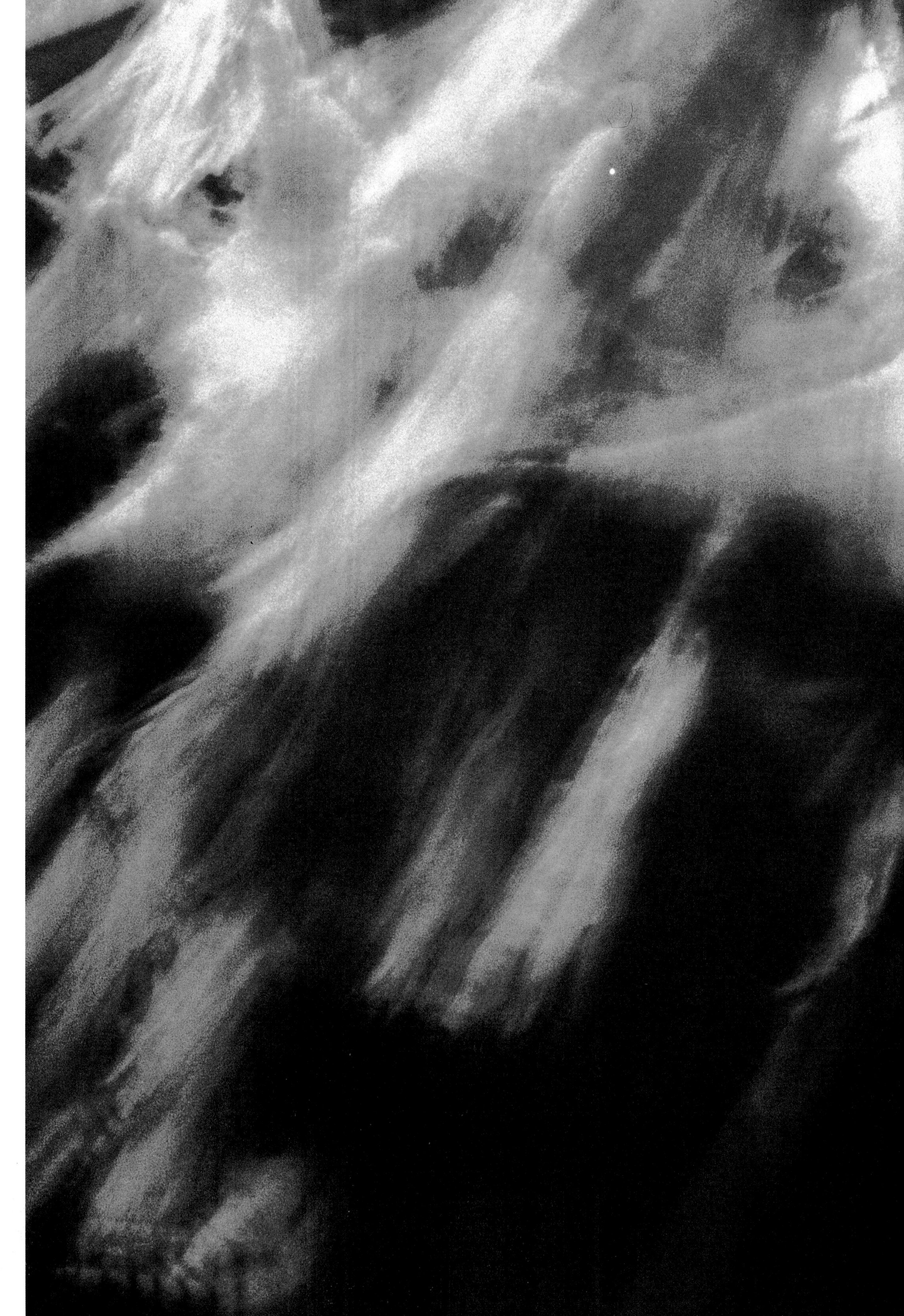

Petah Coyne, *Untitled*, 1994

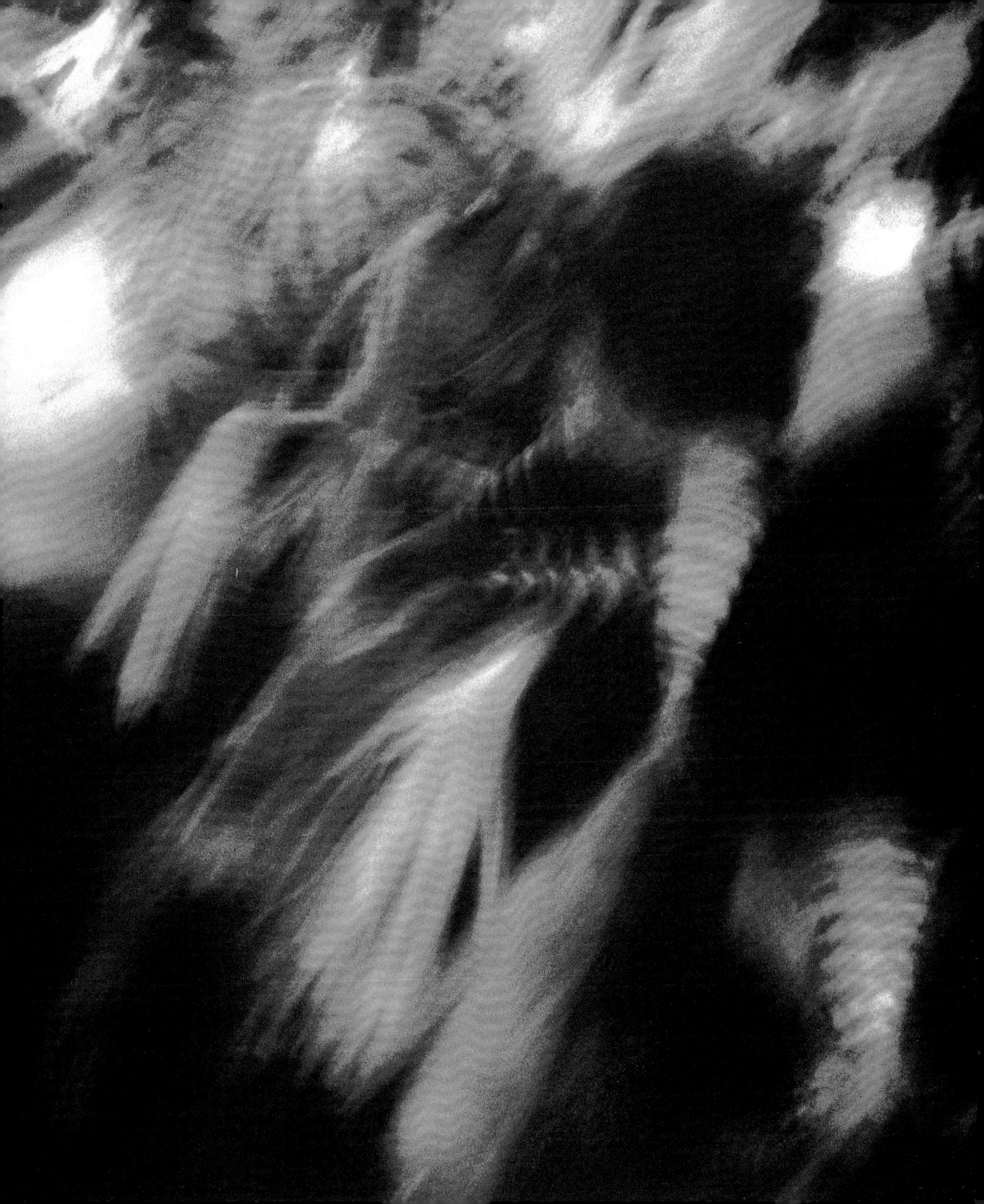

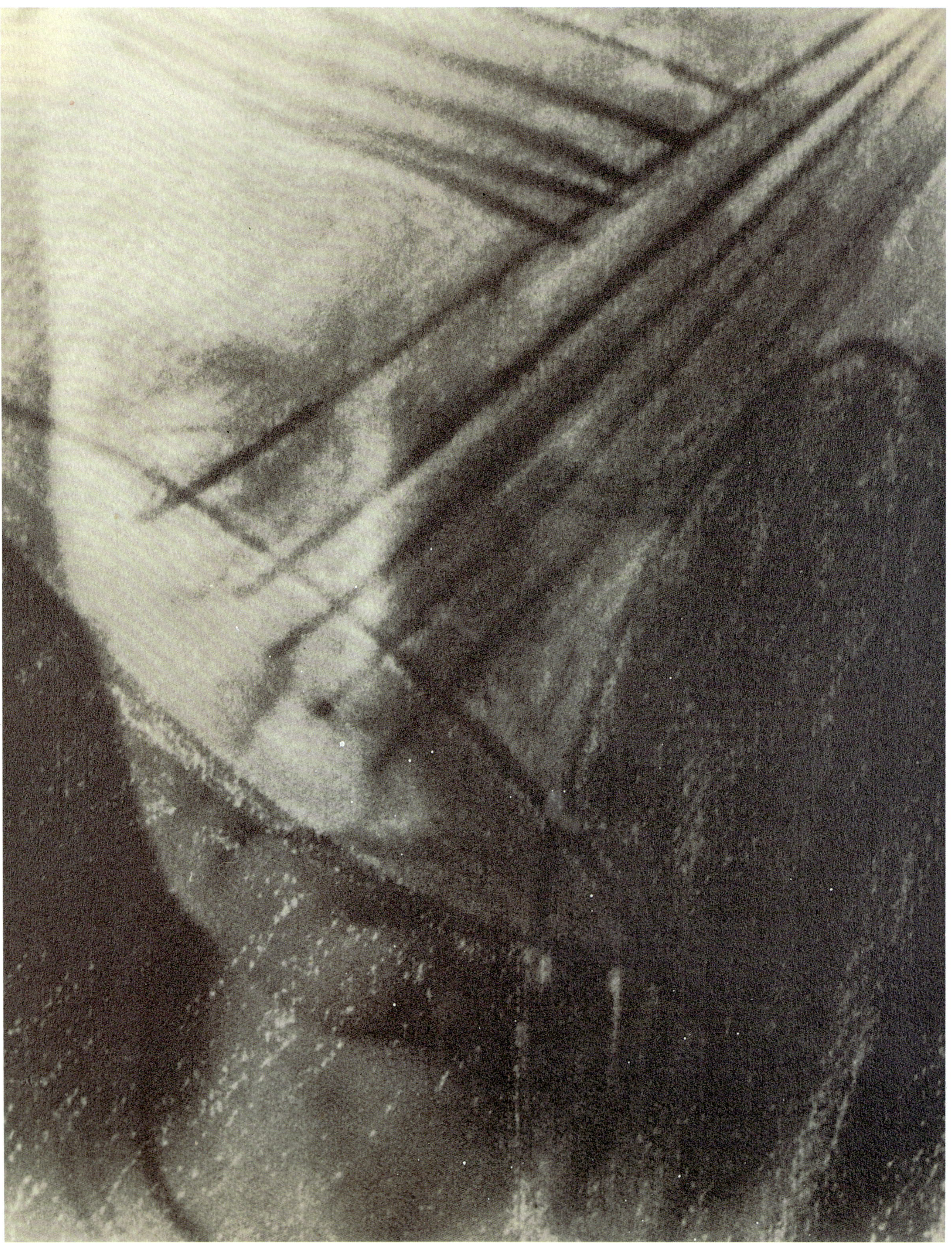

RICHARD POUSETTE-DART

Well-known as an Abstract Expressionist painter, Richard Pousette-Dart also possessed an insightful eye for photographic portraiture.

PHOTOGRAPHS AND JOURNAL ENTRIES

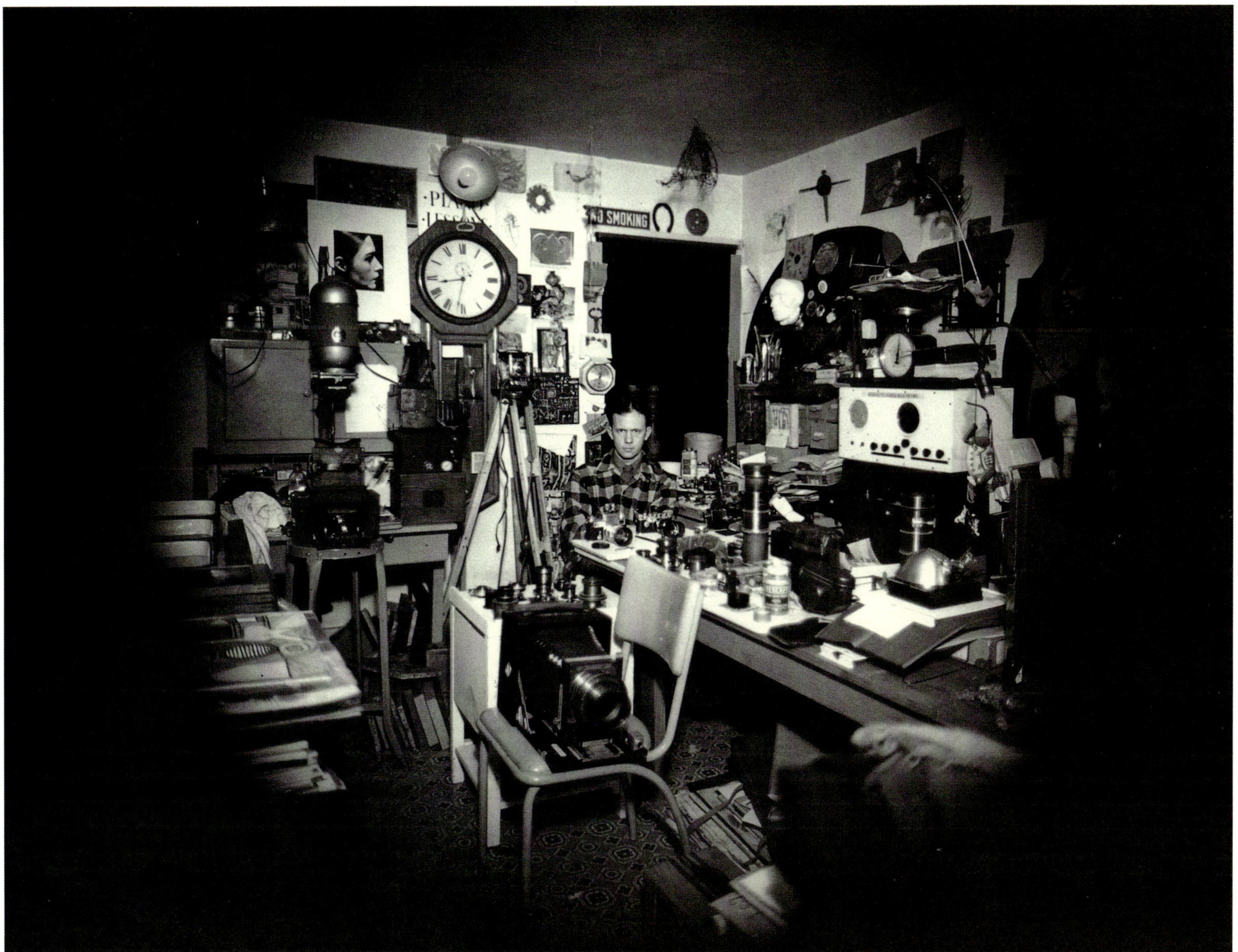

Opposite: Richard Pousette-Dart, *Betty Parsons*, ca. 1948

Above: Richard Pousette-Dart, *Self-Portrait in Darkroom/Workshop*, 1951

Although he was best known as an abstract painter of the New York School in the 1940s and '50s, Richard Pousette-Dart was an active and inventive photographer throughout his career. His portrait and landscape photographs, in particular, reveal a continual process of experimentation and exploration. Remarkably, Pousette-Dart's photographic work was largely overlooked until a posthumous exhibition was presented earlier this year at Zabriskie Gallery in New York City. His notebooks and artist's journals—caked in the red, yellow, and white paint that brought his canvases to life, and thick with pithy and often poetic meditations on art—also reveal a mind that thought deeply about the relationship between his passionate, even spiritual engagement with painting, and his similarly intense involvement with photography. Excerpts from those journals appear here, along with Pousette-Dart's portraits of Betty Parsons, whose gallery he joined in 1946, and of some of the friends and artists in his circle.

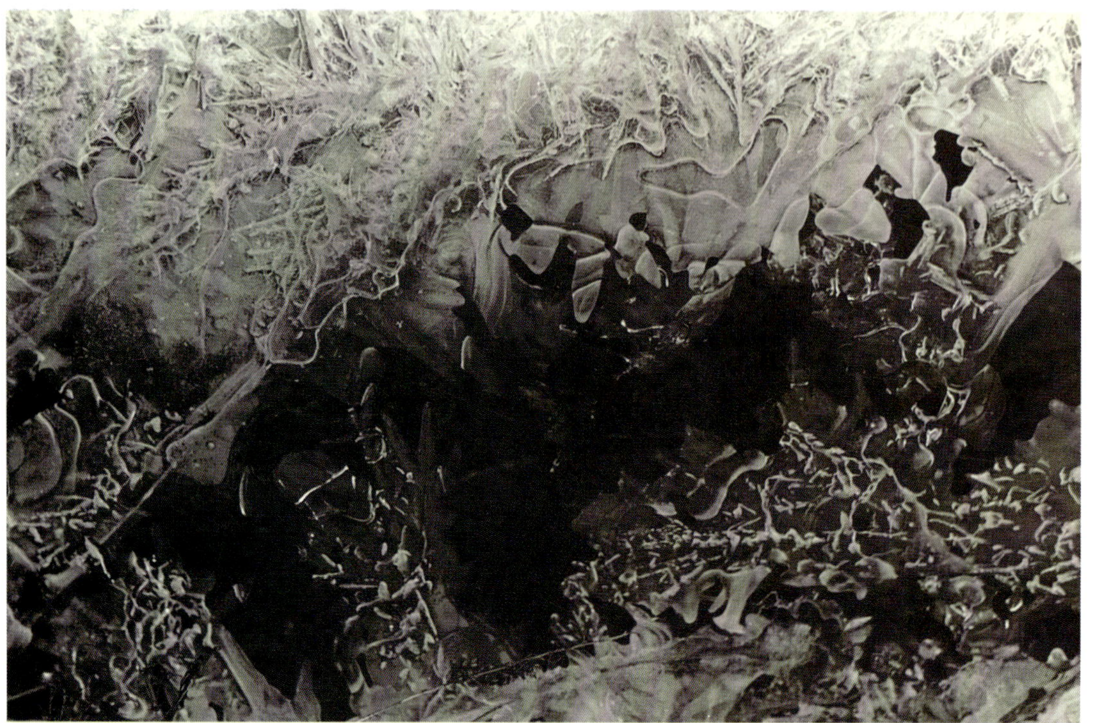

Richard Pousette-Dart, *Ice Study*, ca. 1950

white and black and
every color in between
spells joy and life and
nothingness
paint until you get
beyond painting
beyond art, beyond
yourself

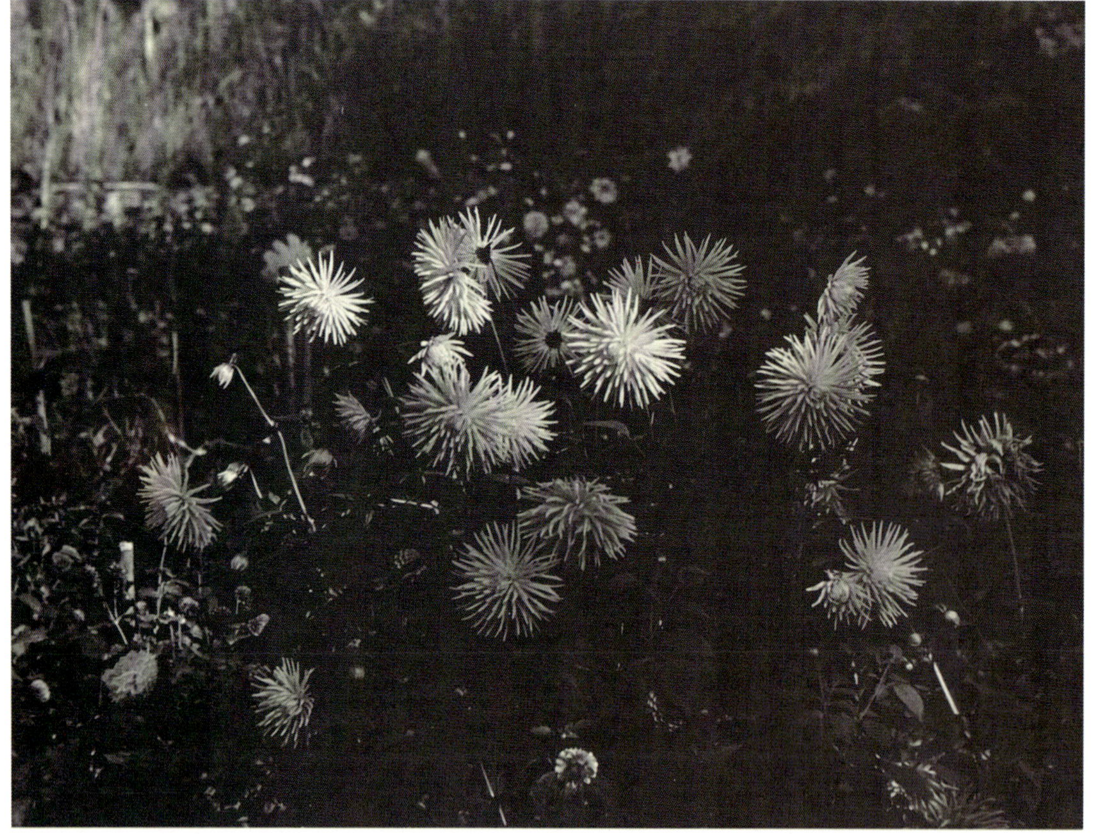

Richard Pousette-Dart, *Straw Flowers*, ca. 1950

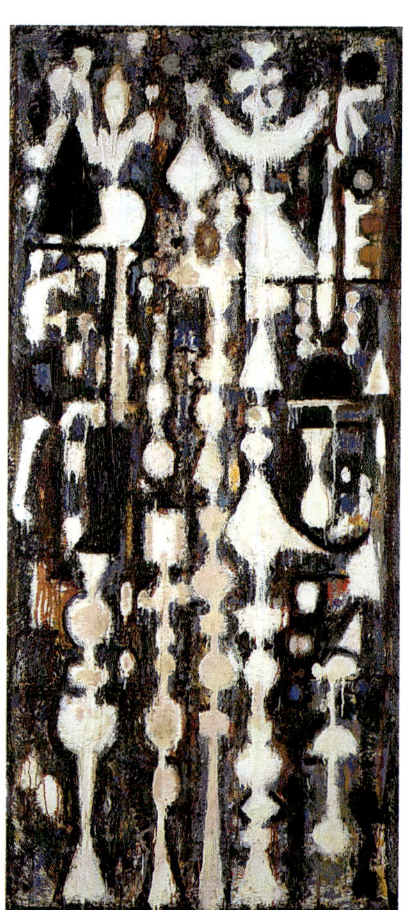

Above: Richard Pousette-Dart, *Pillars of Odysseus*, 1949–50
Opposite: Richard Pousette-Dart, *Betty Parsons*, ca. 1950

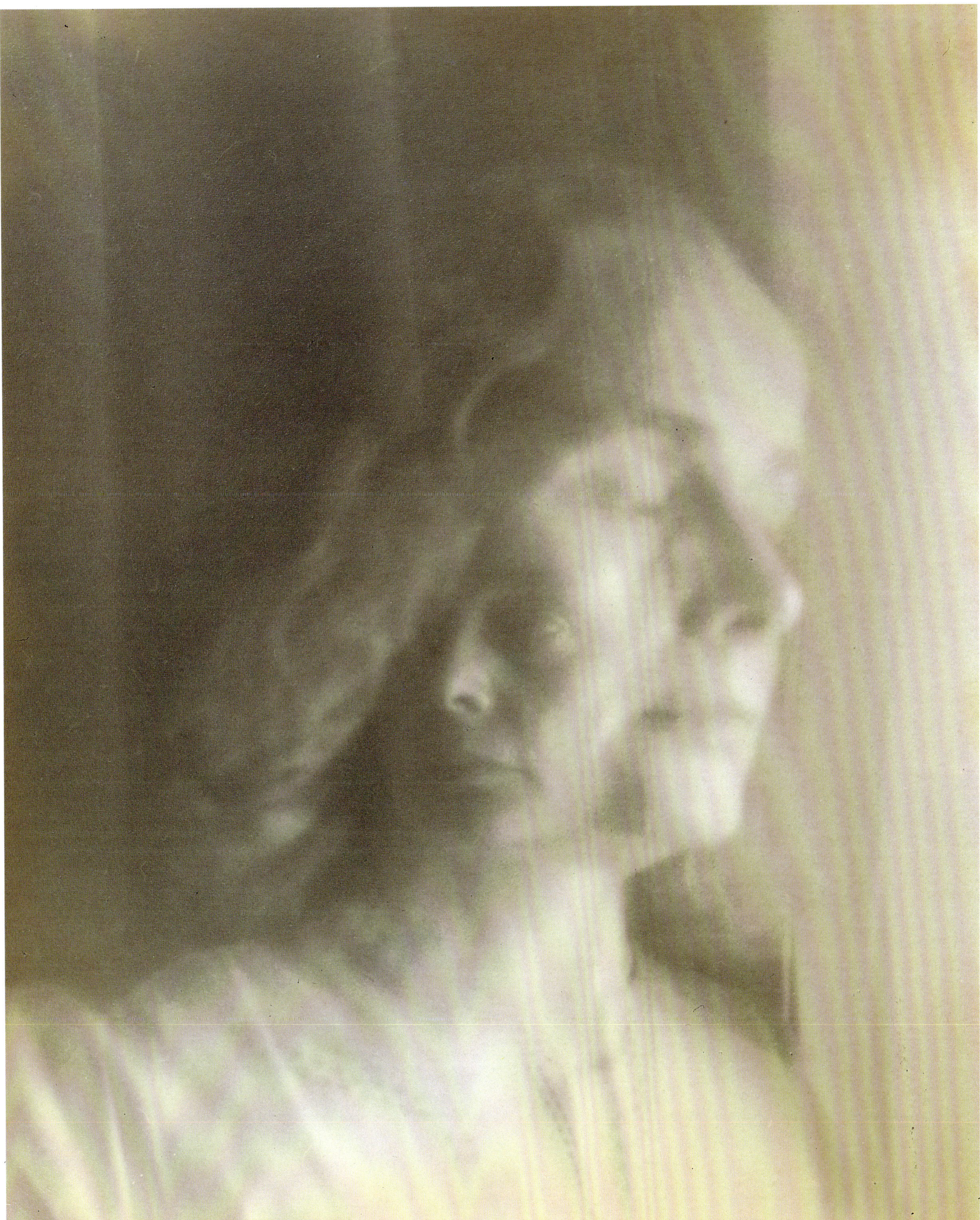

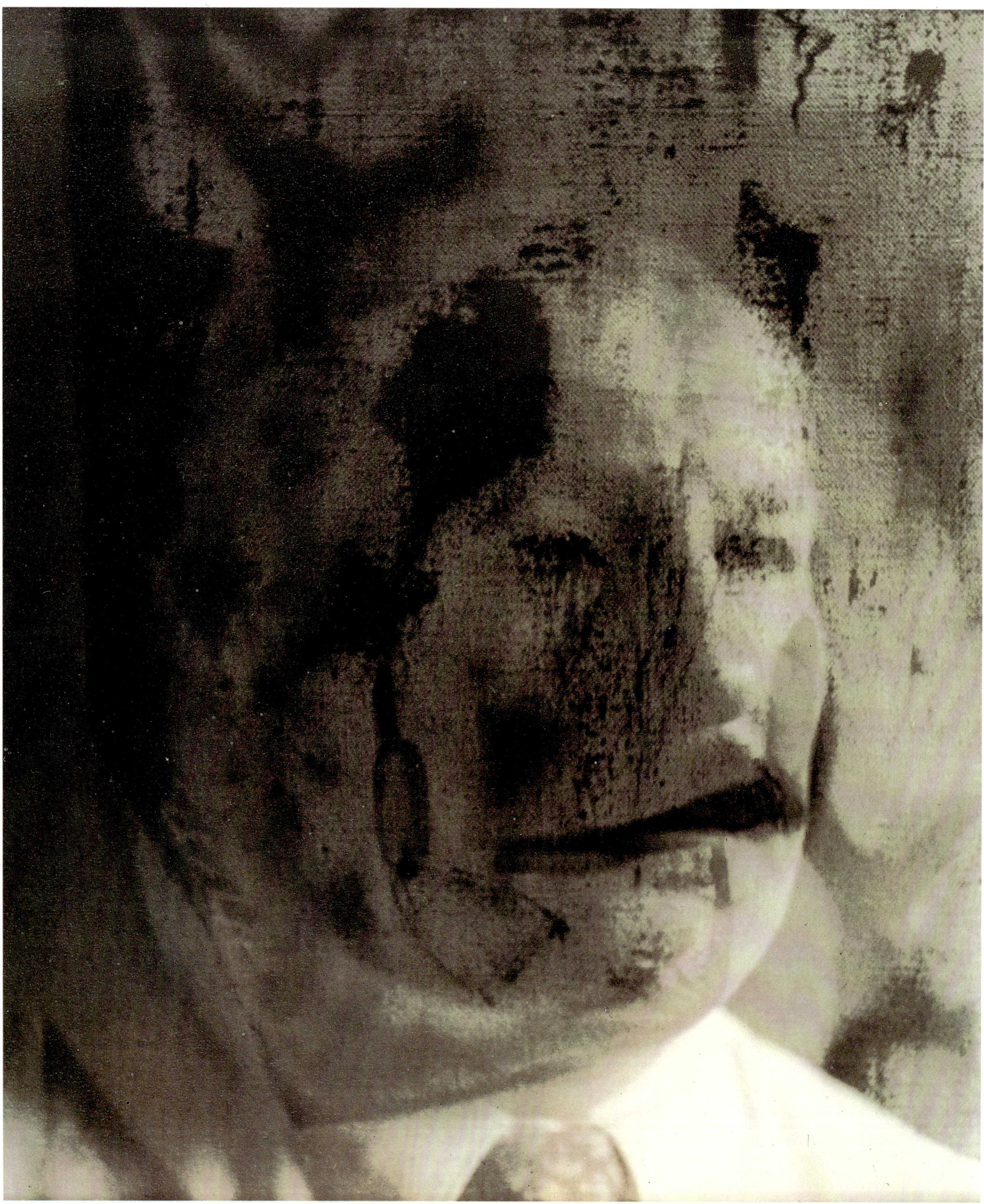

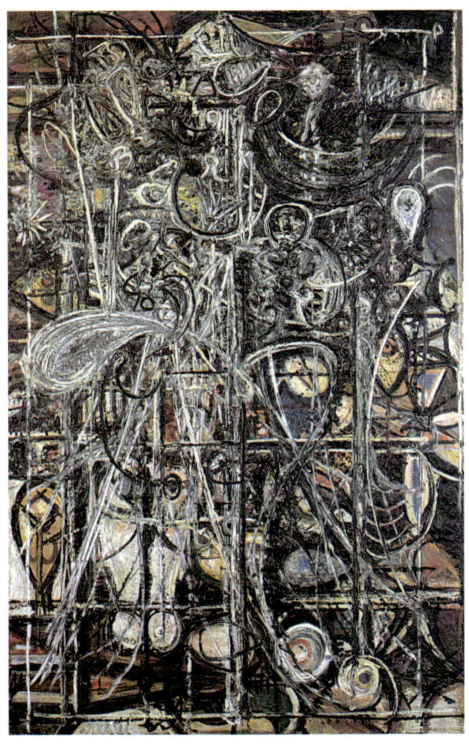

Above: Richard Pousette-Dart, *Figure*, 1944–45
Opposite: Richard Pousette-Dart, *Barnett Newman*, ca. 1944

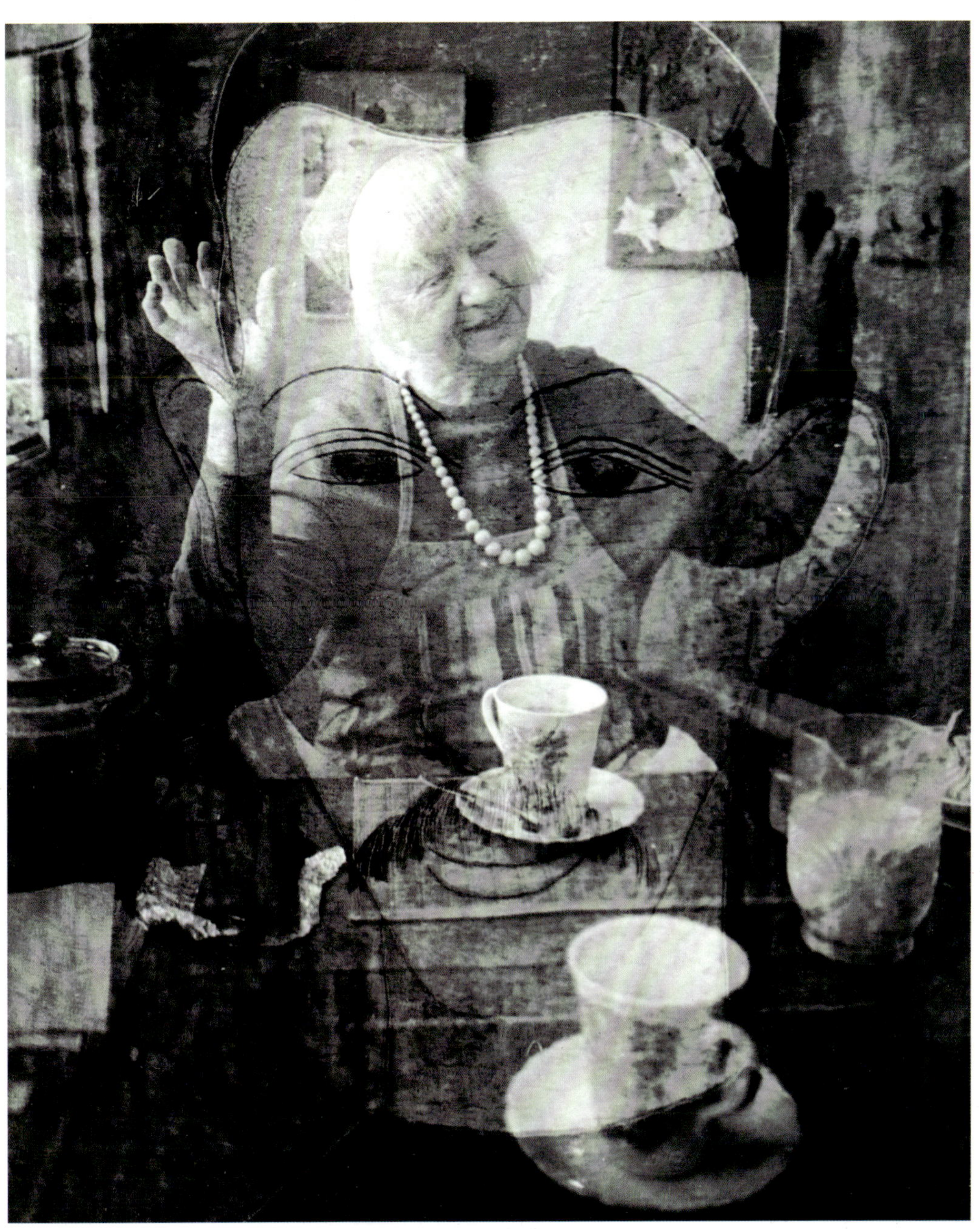

Richard Pousette-Dart, *Martha Ryther*, ca. 1967

. . . to be my own light meter, calculator, computer, miracle of the mind, those human measurements, sized by intuition, soul, feeling, the mind and spirit of creative imagination, give me the perfection and the imperfection of the human hand and heart, give me the sublimity the realization and the fulfillment of what is right in front of my eyes.

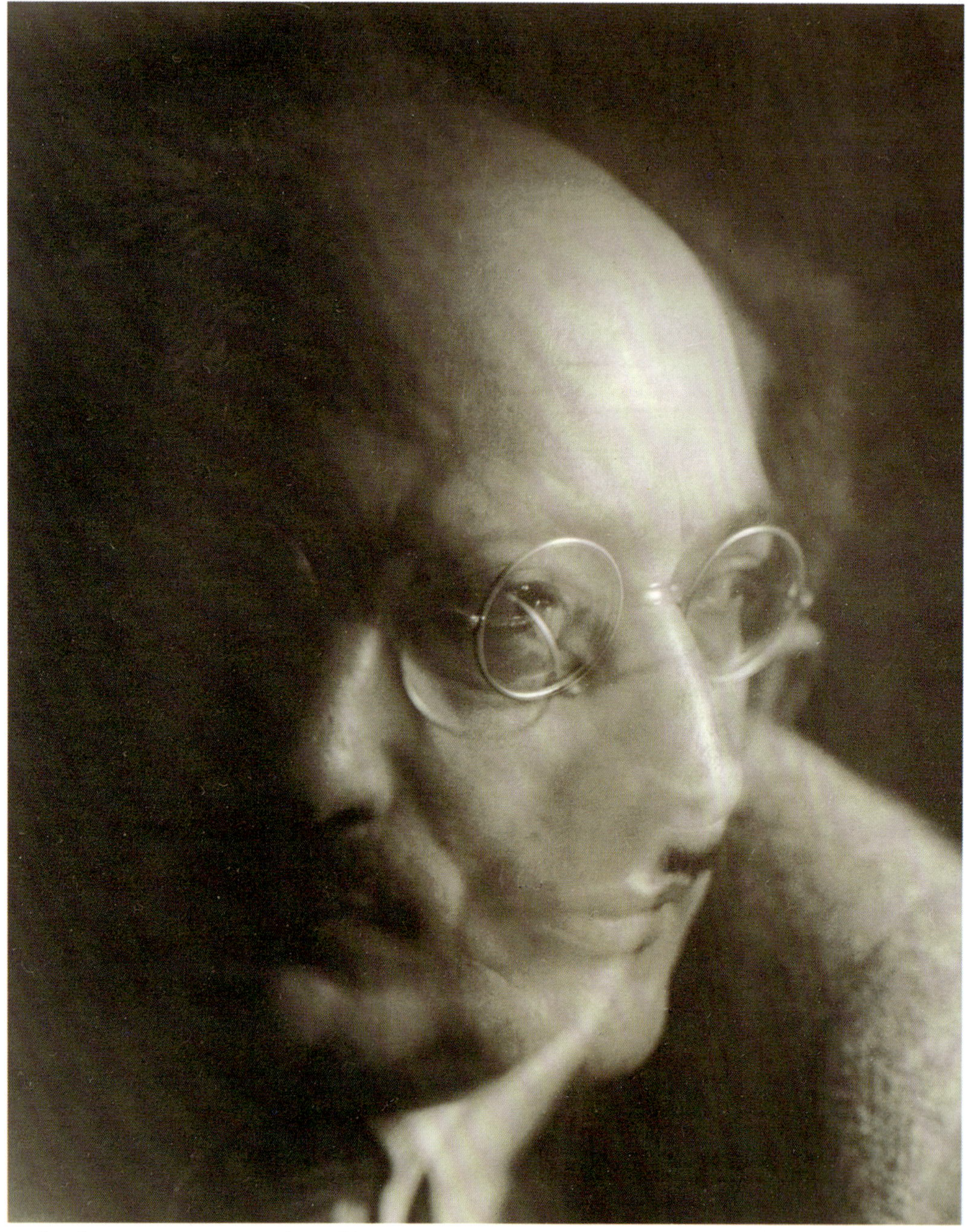

Richard Pousette-Dart, *Mark Rothko*, ca. 1949

everything is a lens
through which we may see

through and through far
enough
to travel through and see
beyond

not to see the polish
not to see reflections
not to see the scratches
not to see imperfections

through and through to find
the source of our own eyes
for what is there is always
more

a presence here + now
a miracle beyond

The camera is blind. It is you who must see your own picture and persevere until you capture whomever, within their own light, and with all that you cannot capture the reality of anyone. We all remain free and unrecordable.

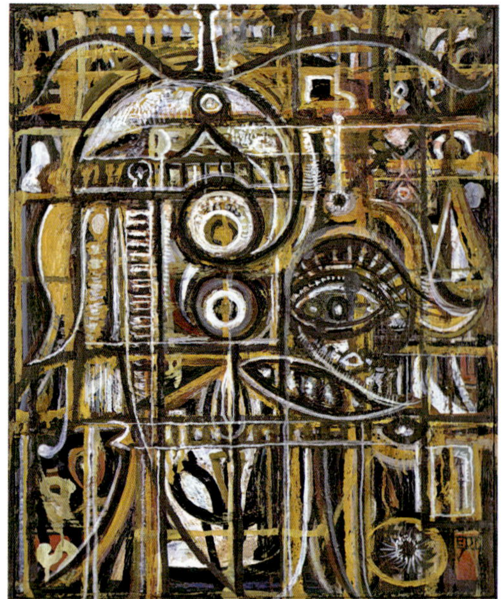

Above: Richard Pousette-Dart, *Abstract Eye*, 1941–43
Opposite: Richard Pousette-Dart, *Betty Parsons*, ca. 1945

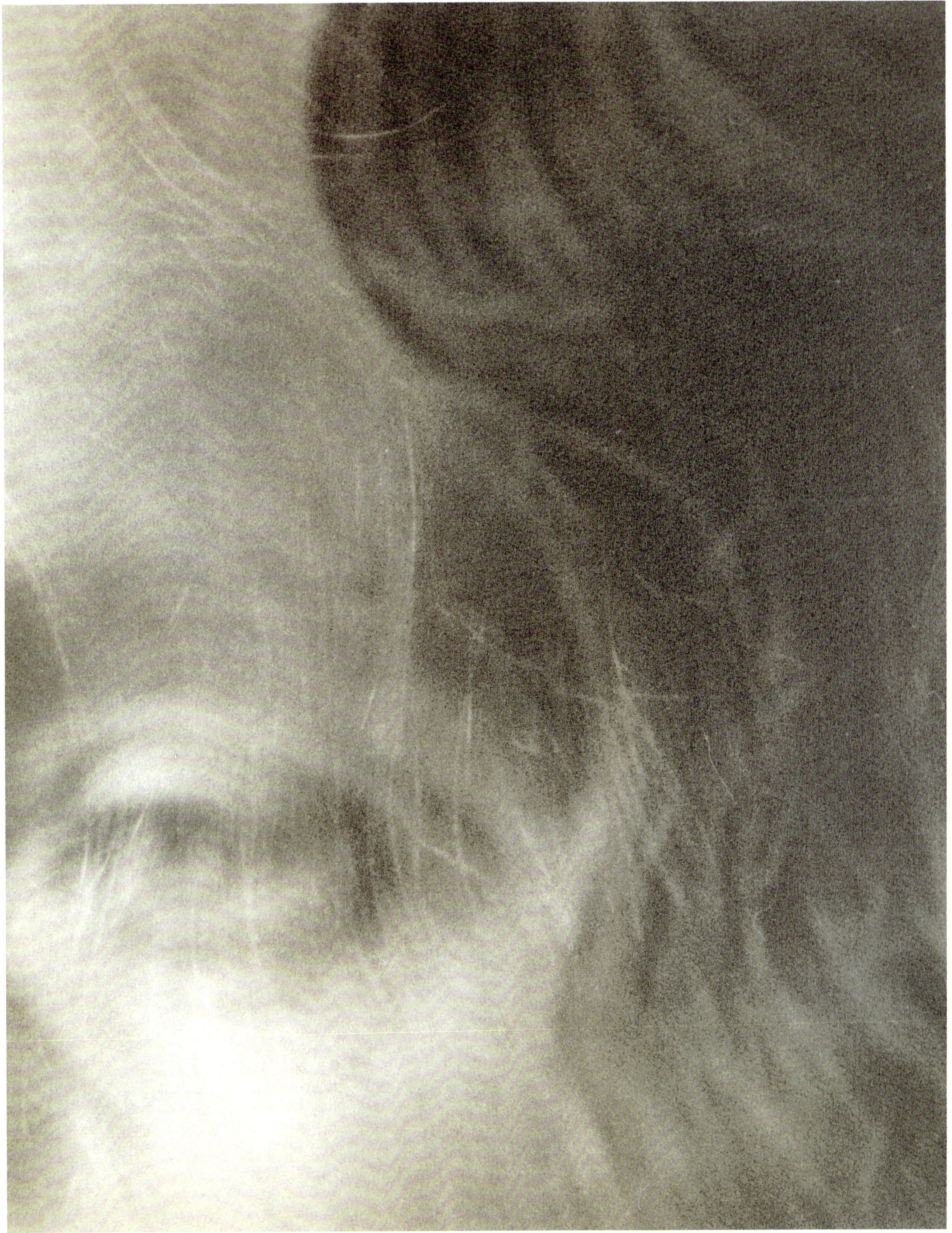

CHRIS MARKER'S REALITY BYTES

BY JAN-CHRISTOPHER HORAK

Filmmaker Chris Marker's inventive narratives, including the cult classics Sans Soleil *and* La Jetée, *explore the ways that still photographs and moving images act on human memory.*

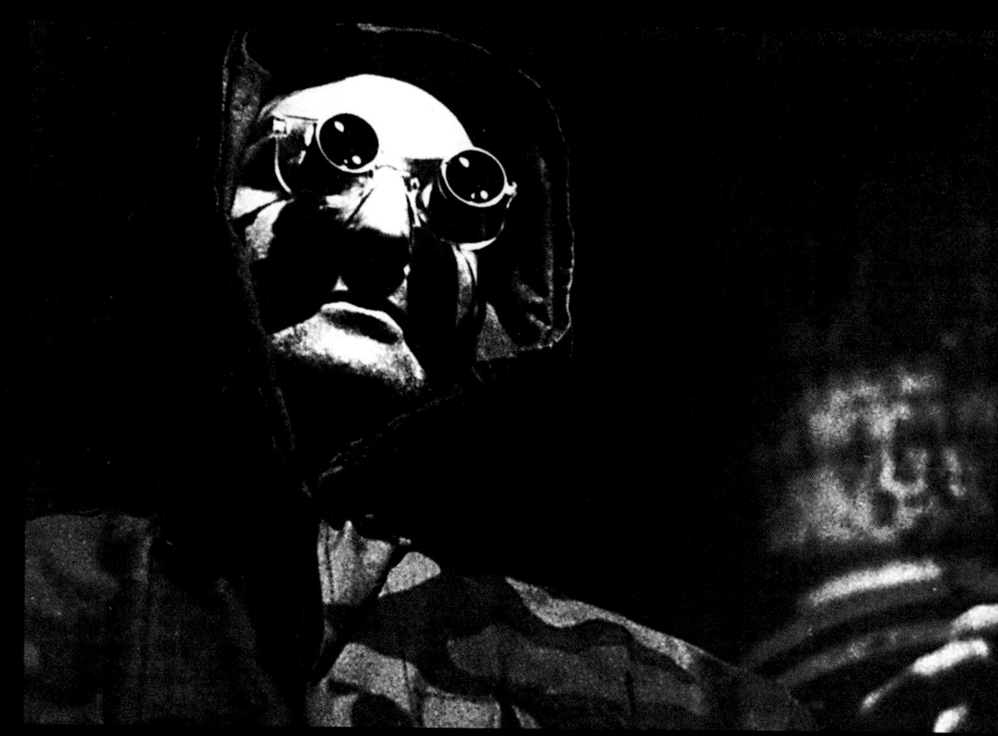

Above, below, right: Chris Marker, *La Jetée*, 1963.

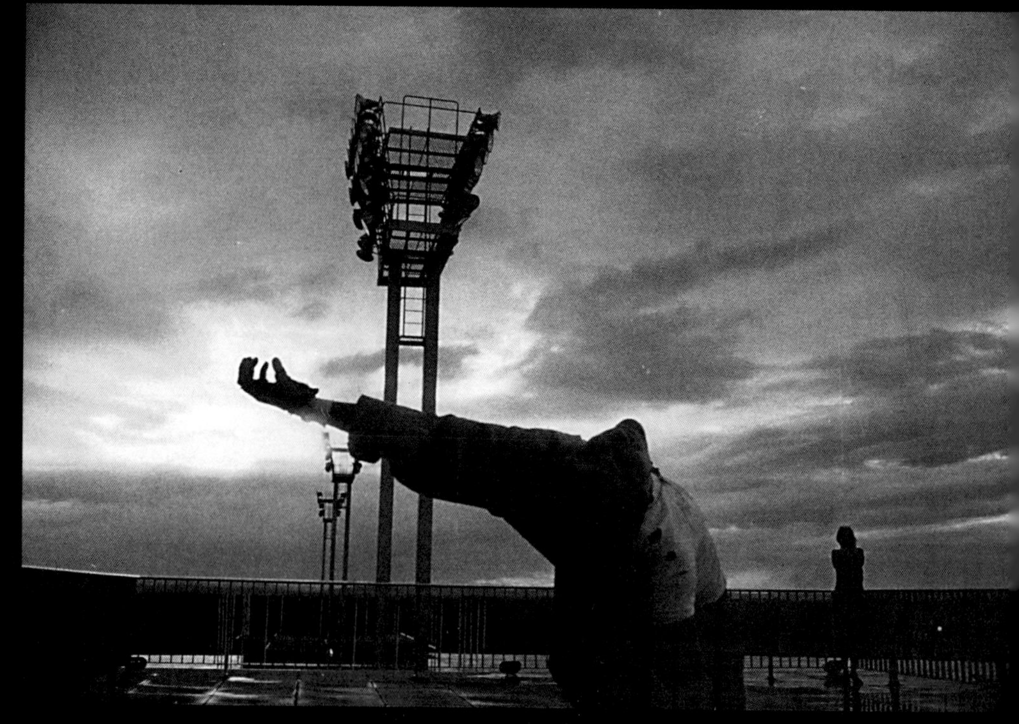

Formerly a journalist, novelist, essayist, and assistant director to Alain Resnais, Chris Marker has had a brilliant career as a documentary filmmaker, but less well known is his work as a photographer. Marker's five photo-books, like his films, are a mixture of documentary, diary, essay, memoir, and fiction.[1] His works are constructed as multiple, even contradictory texts, consisting of juxtapositions of word and image, music and language, pictures and music, the whole coming together as a stream of consciousness that no longer differentiates between objectivity and subjectivity, reality and dreams, fact and desire, the past, the present, and the future.

In Marker's films and photography real geographical places are captured in images and transformed through the act of reception into subjective visions. The camera is utilized as a tool for the objective documentation of reality bytes, but the result is a consciously constructed aesthetic subjectivity. This subjectivity is the result of the juxtaposition of word and image, the editing process, and the production of a sound track.

One of Chris Marker's earliest films, *Sunday in Peking*,[2] begins with the statement: "For thirty years I have dreamt of Beijing without knowing it. In my memory I had an image out of a children's book, without knowing exactly where it had come from, an image of the city gate of Beijing: the path to the Ming Dynasty memorial. Suddenly one day I was there. It was a special feeling to wander through an image from my childhood."[3] The film's point of view, that of a subjective observer from France, is emphasized through the

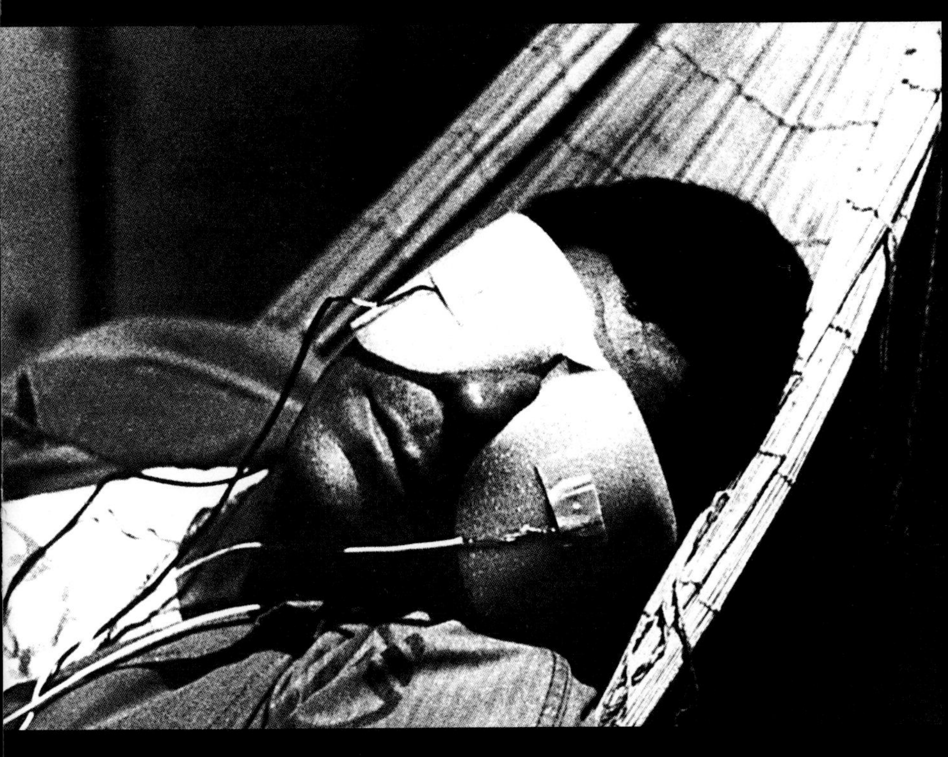

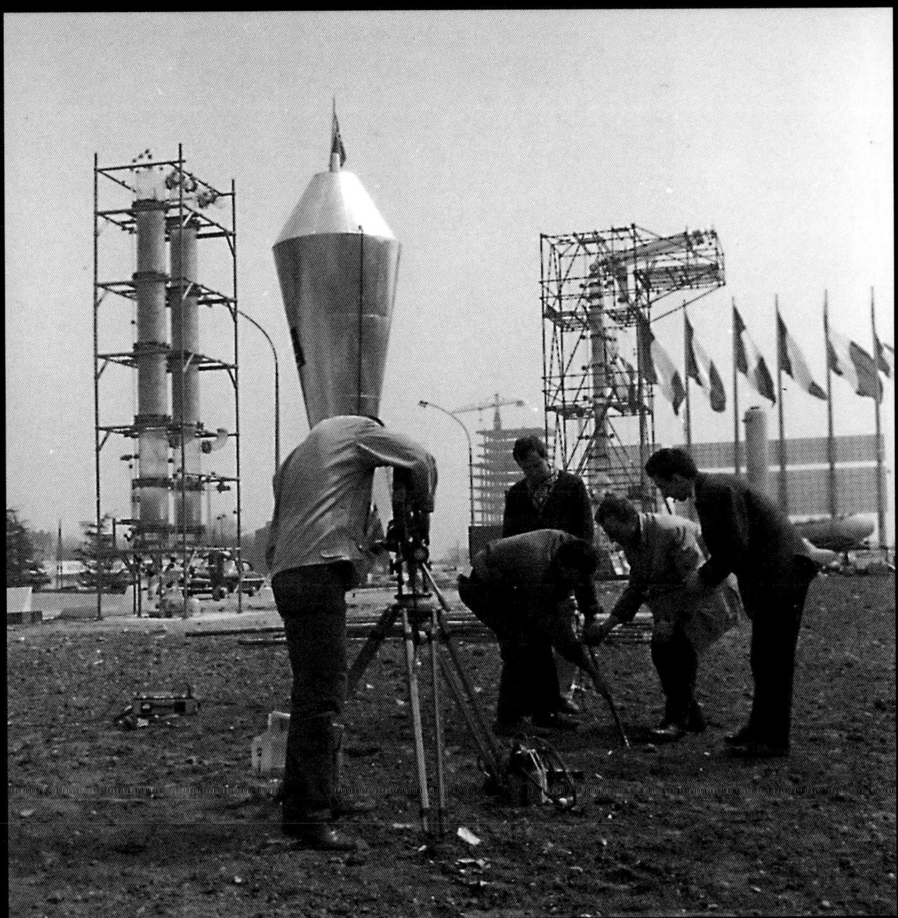

Chris Marker, *Le Joli Mai*, 1963

"To create is to remember. Memory is the basis of everything."

visuals: in the first shot Marker pans over childhood toys, then up to the Eiffel Tower, then down again to an open book with a large photograph of the Beijing street scene, before fading out and into Marker's own reconstruction of the scene on film in 1955.

An image from childhood also defines Chris Marker's science-fiction short *La Jetée* (1964), which consists exclusively of photographs. As in Marker's first film, the whole story originates from the opening image. The human ability to remember, to recall a visual, nonverbal imprint in the brain as experience and knowledge, is a never-ending preoccupation for Marker. The narrator in *La Jetée* says from off-screen: "Moments in one's memory are like other moments. They remain conscious only because of the scars they leave behind." In another film, *Sans Soleil*, he writes: "He liked the fragility of those moments suspended in time. His memories, their only function to leave behind nothing but memories."[4] His four-hour, monumental documentary history of the New Left, *Le fonde l'air est rouge* (1977), released in Great Britain in the early 1980s in a three-hour version as *A Grin Without a Cat*, also begins with a childhood memory, but one that is already mediated: it is the memory of an image of maggot-infested meat, followed by the aborted execution of *Russian Sailors from Potemkin* (1925). Likewise, Marker's latest project, the video installation *Silent Movie* (1995), has its genesis in memories from his childhood movie experience: film scenes with Clara Bow and Simone Genevoix reworked as still photographs on video, actresses whom Marker calls his "amours enfantines."

According to Marker, all these images exist in his head in a precognitive state, at the level of pure perception, i.e., they are images between the subconscious and consciousness, between actual experience and the imaginary. Marker transforms these rediscovered images into a discourse on photographic images, into a discourse about human imagination and the images in people's heads. In *A.K.* (1985), Marker's meditation on Akira Kurasawa, the filmmaker connects the very act of aesthetic creation with memory. Holding a close-up on a hand-held tape recorder while a Japanese TV screen is seen flickering in the background, Marker notes at the beginning of his film: "To create is to remember. Memory is the basis of everything."

A photograph takes a moment of time, 1/100 or 1/60 of a second, and transports it into timelessness. As a sign, the photographic image remains independent of time. Even a syntactical ordering of individual photographs, for example in a photoreportage or photo-*roman*, does not alter this fact. While photographs may be chronologically or thematically organized, explanatory captions and the reader's cognitive capabilities must still create the temporal connections between these photographic moments frozen in time.

This principle is clearly demonstrated in *Commentaires 1 et 2*, the two volumes of Chris Marker's collected screenplays (1953–1966). Since Marker's films are not just dependent on his narratives, but rather consist of juxtapositions between words and images, he has attempted to visualize his film scripts through film stills. The photographs are integrated into the text in various sizes, sometimes taking up a whole page, sometimes only half a page, sometimes only as a small image at the edge of the text. The reader assumes that Marker has included all the most important shots in the film, yet the photographs remain strangely abstract. In two-dimensional form they can only function as indices of film scenes, giving the reader a visual taste while he or she reads the verbal narration to the film. Any attempt to read the "illustrations" in *Commentaires* as a syntactical construction, however, is bound to fail, because the spaces between images are too great. The selection of film stills (why these and not other images?) remains mysterious. It is a mixture of long shots and close-ups, panoramas of cityscapes and landscapes, as well as portraits of human beings, interspersed with the products of visual culture: comics, advertising, propaganda billboards, television, paintings, and statues. These film stills hardly outline, even in general terms, the contours of

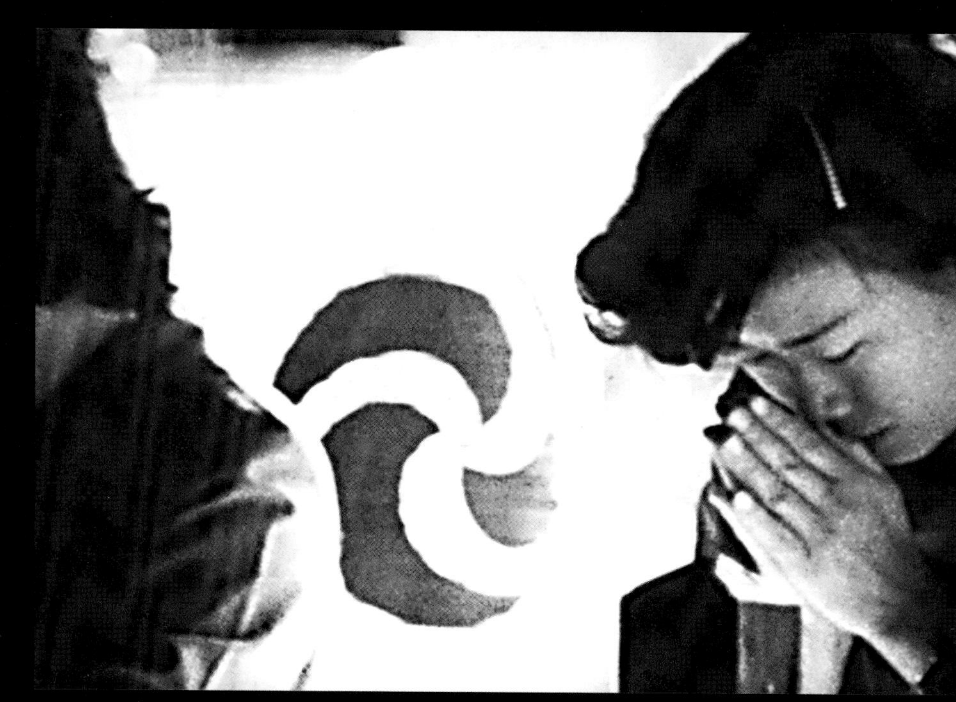

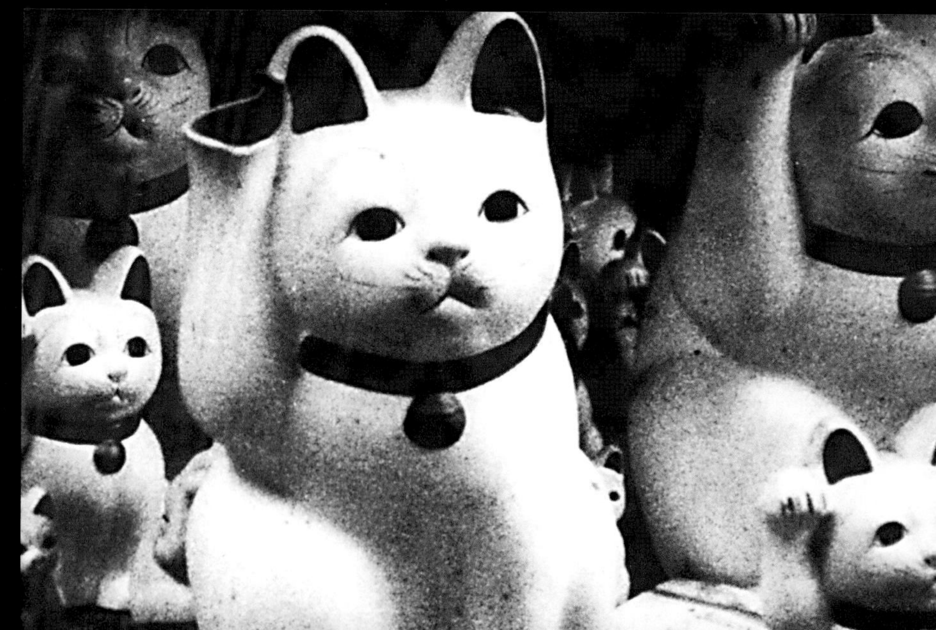

Top and bottom: Chris Marker, *Sans Soleil*, 1981

"He liked the fragility of those moments suspended in time. His memories, their only function to leave behind nothing but memories."

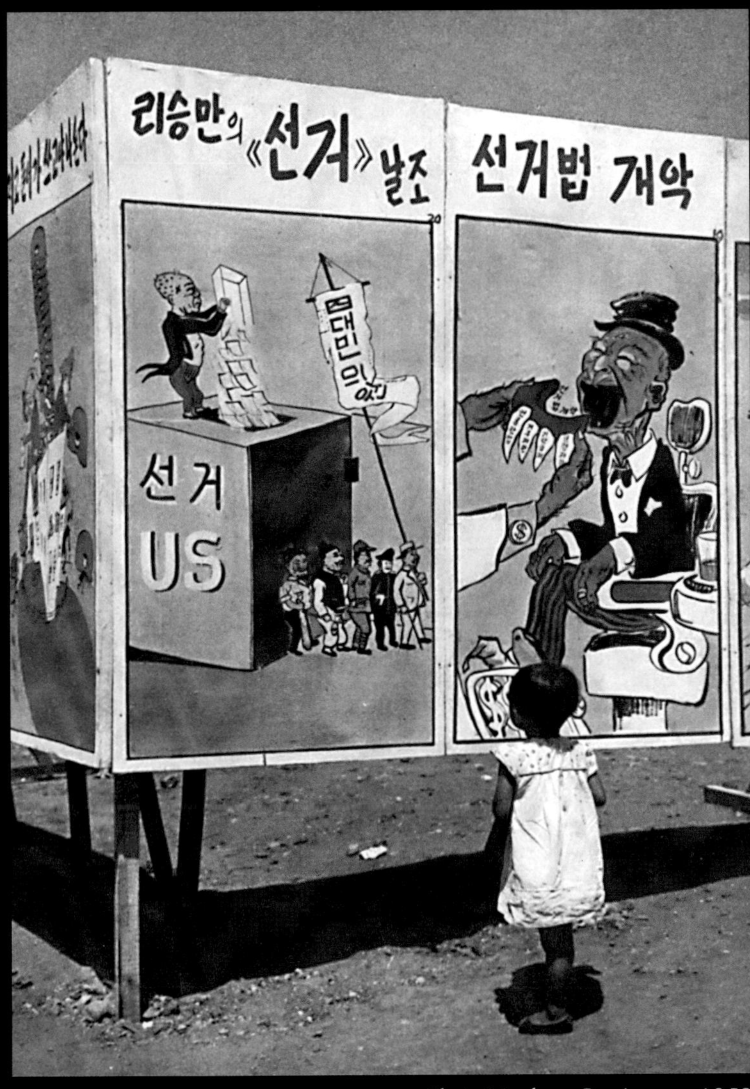

Chris Marker, *Coréennes*, 1959

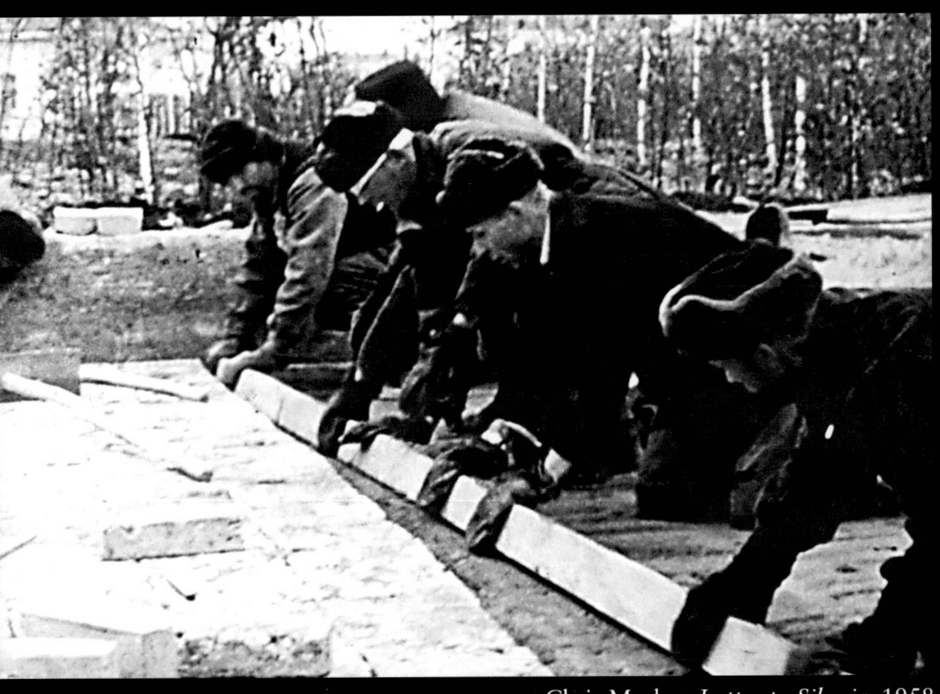

Chris Marker, *Letter to Siberia*, 1958

the actual film; rather they are Marker's representation of the film as text.

The difficulty in making semantic sense of the illustrations is heightened when the reader realizes that individual photographs, i.e., film stills appearing in *Commentaires*, don't actually appear in the film. For example, Marker publishes no less than thirty-five photographs in his film script for *Si j'avais quatre Dromadaires* which are not to be found in the actual film, while others are framed completely differently. In the script for *Sunday in Peking* Marker likewise reframes many of the stills. One can therefore assume that Marker sees the film scripts in *Commentaires* as completely independent works, which have the privilege of being "incomplete." Not surprisingly, the book includes at least two film scripts for films which were never made and which Marker designates as *films imaginaires*: they are called *L'Amérique Rêve* and *Soy Mexico*.

In contrast to other photographers who publish books, it is noteworthy that Marker uses photographs relatively sparingly in his *Commentaires*. The published narration (German translation) of *Sans Soleil* eschews photographs and stills altogether. Even Marker's photography books *Coréennes* (which documents his impressions of a trip to North Korea) and *Le Dépays* (which concerns Japan) consist of very long texts, in which photographs are inserted. They are neither independent image sequences with full-page photographs, as can be found in most photography books, nor merely illustrations to the text. Each level of communication, visual and verbal, remains to a certain extent independent. Marker writes at the beginning of *Le Dépays*: "The text provides very little commentary to the images, just as the images hardly illustrate the text. In fact, they are two series of ideas, and at times they cross or point to each other, but to confront them would be useless and tiresome."[5] One need not take Marker's statement at face value. Clearly, though, language and a literary aesthetic dominate the text, possibly because Marker's language creates its own images, and because the photographs need words to escape from their ambiguity. Word and image are related, just as they are related in Marker's films, which show a predilection toward a continuous flow of narration from off-screen. His films use language and words the way other films use sound—as a perpetual stimulus.

Photography signifies not only time, but also space differently from the cinema. Marker's utilization of photographic images in *La Jetée* and *Si j'avais quatre Dromadaires* allows him to reflect on the relationship between the two media—film and photography—in terms of their space and time coordinates. The conventions of central perspective allow for the projection of a real three-dimensional space on a two-dimensional surface. Through the cognitive capabilities of the viewer, the illusion of the third dimension is abstracted. In *Si j'avais quatre Dromadaires* Marker presents a whole catalog of possibilities for the signification of space through photography, concentrated into a single sequence. Some photos demonstrate depth of focus (Great Wall of China) or the depth of field through a wide-angle lens (Göta Canal in Sweden); others lack any depth at all, thereby emphasizing an abstract pattern (the square in front of the Cathedral of Notre Dame, taken from above), or flatten space (the Negev Desert).

The preponderance of portraits in the film indicates that Marker sees this genre as particularly suited to photography. But Marker's portraits, both in his films as well as in his photography books, never exclude their subjects' environment. The close-up portraits by other photographers, where the focus is on the landscape of the face, would be anathema to Marker. He needs to include the physical space of the subject in his composition, since it is through the cultural definition of that space that he can engage his own subjectivity. The same impulse feeds Marker's portraits of women's faces in his video installation *Silent Movie*, only in this case, it is the fetishistic quality of Hollywood dreams that provides the context for his subjective vision.

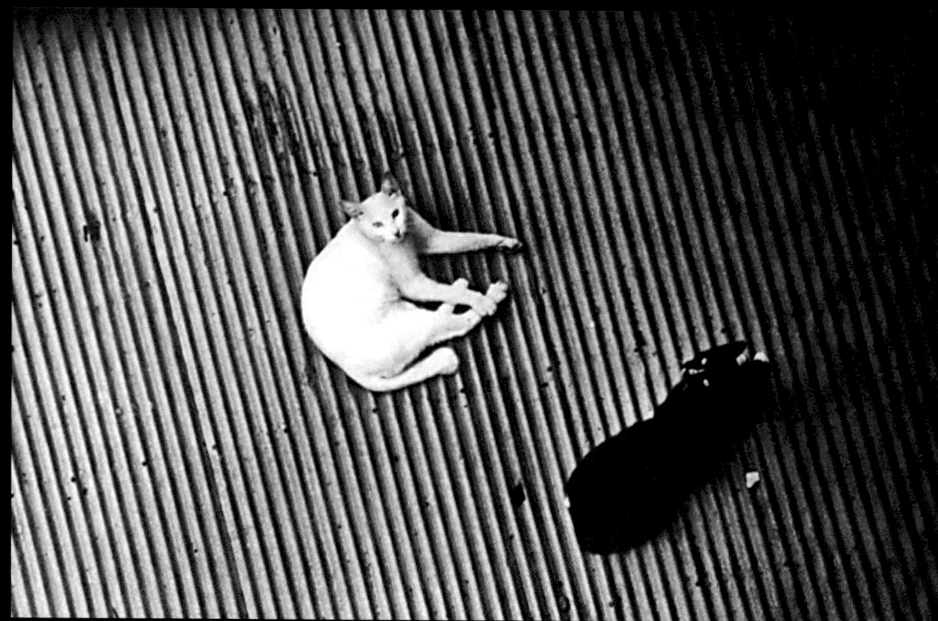

Above and below: Chris Marker, *Le Dépays*, 1982

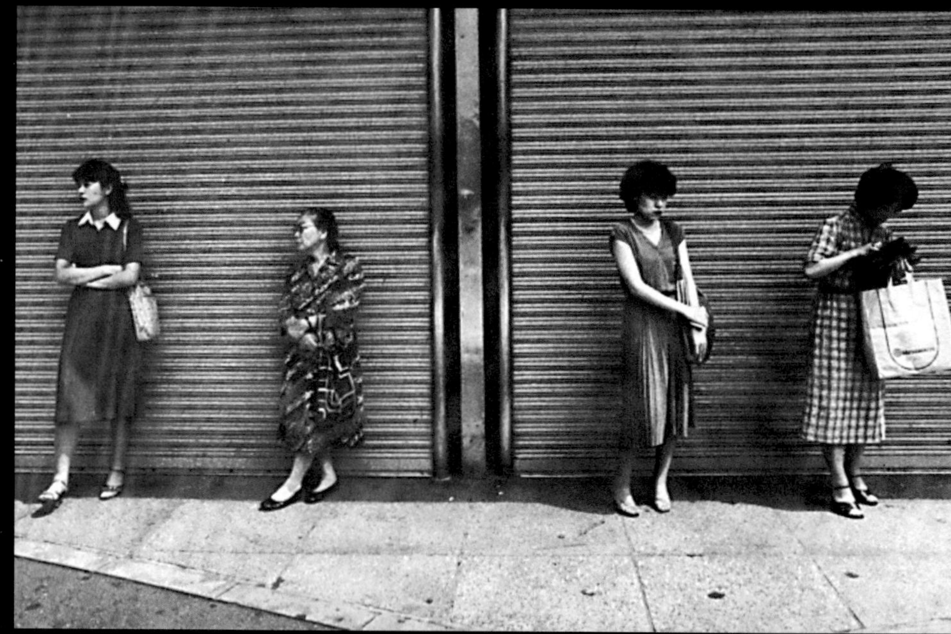

The close-up portraits by other photographers, where the focus is on the landscape of the face, would be an anathema to Marker. He needs to include the physical space of the subject in his composition, since it is through the cultural definition of that space that he can engage his own subjectivity.

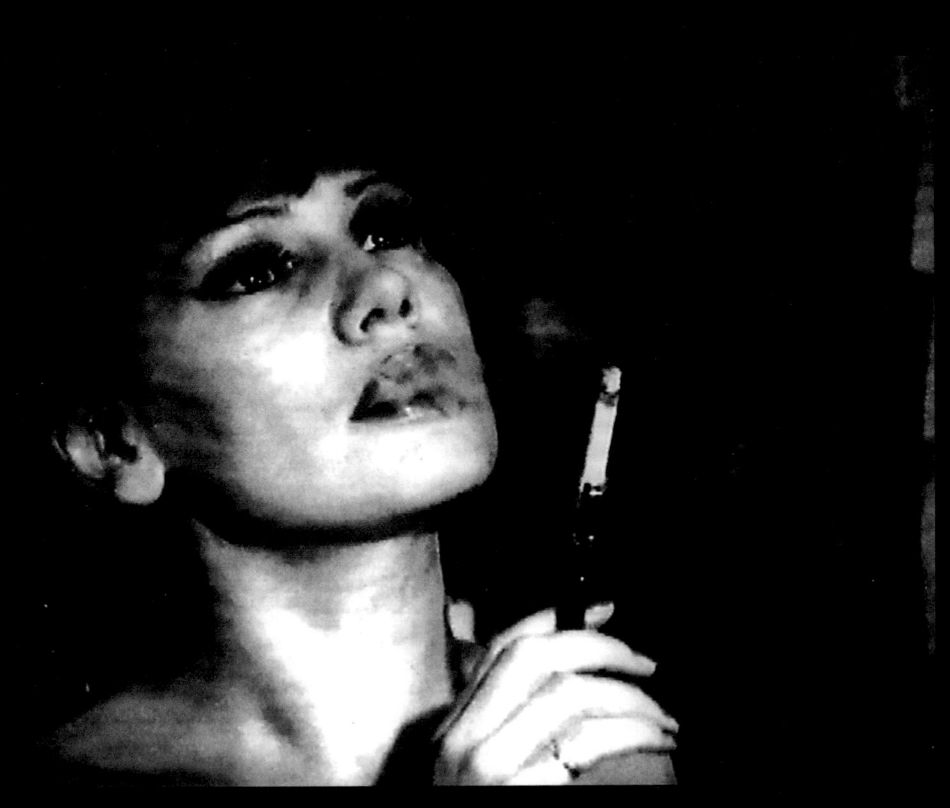

Above and below: Chris Marker, *Silent Movie*, 1994

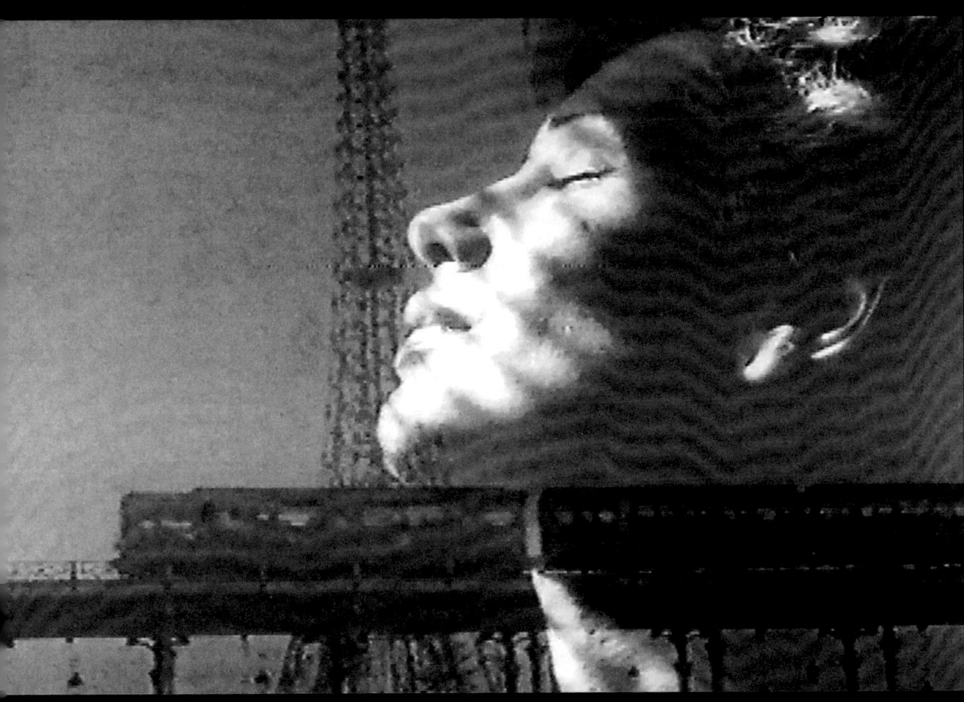

"The text provides very little commentary to the images, just as the images hardly illustrate the text. In fact, they are two series of ideas, and at times they cross or point to each other, but to confront them would be useless and tiresome."

In contrast to Marker's film images, which are seemingly representations of a real space, his photographs, especially those in his films, are visual documents of photographic representations of real space. Photographs in Marker's films are themselves merely objects signifying perception, the signs of cognition, never an actual experience of the world.

Like the hero of *La Jetée* whose transgalactic travels through space and time are only possible due to the strength of his imagination, Marker's focus is inward rather than outward into the real world. Not surprisingly, then, it seems that Marker ultimately refuses to differentiate between film and photography, since in the subconscious—in memory—both media function similarly. As a result, Marker has no qualms about inserting photographs into a film or freezing silent film images as stills on a video monitor. The photographic journeys of Chris Marker lead us not into the great wide world, rather they present us with an inner vision.

1. Photo-books by Marker are *Coréennes* (Paris: Éditions du Seuil, 1959), *La Chine: Porte ouverte* (Paris: Éditions du Seuil, 1956); *La réenfermée: La Corse* (Paris: Éditions du Seuil, 1981), with a text by Marie Susini; *Le Dépays* (Paris: Éditions Herscher, 1982), translated into German by Roland Platte and Andreas Eisenhart as *Das Fremdland* (Berlin: Galrev Verlag, 1985). See also Marker and Jean-Claude Carrière (text): "Effets et gestes," in *Vogue* (Paris), no. 752 (December 1994–January 1995), pp. 208–211, 263.

2. Marker's photo-book on China (1965) could not be found, although it would have certainly been germane to this study.

3. Quoted in Ian Cameron: "I am writing to you from a far country . . ." in: *Movie, No. 3* (October 1962), p. 14.

4. Text taken from 35mm print, distributed by New Yorker. The complete narration has been published in English as "Sunless" in *Semiotexte*, vol. IV, no. 3 ("Oasis" 1984), pp. 33–40. German translation: *Sans Soleil—Unsichtbare Sonne*, translated by Elmar Tophoven (Hamburg: 1983). There are discrepancies between the German and English texts.

5. Marker, 1985, n.p. Author's translation from the German.

ONCE

PHOTOGRAPHS AND STORIES BY WIM WENDERS

The internationally acclaimed filmmaker reflects on the power of the still image to provide a wealth of narrative detail.

Every photo,
every ONE SINGLE TIME
is also the beginning of a story
that starts "Once upon a time. . . ."
Every photo is also the first shot of a film.
Often the next moment,
the next tripping of the release a few steps farther,
is already tracking
the progression
of this story
in its intrinsic space
and its intrinsic time.
For me, in the course of time,
taking pictures has become more and more
a "tracking of stories."
That's why this book includes
more series of images
than individual shots.
"Editing" begins in every other picture,
the story announced in the first image
moves in its own direction,
marks out its sense of space
and gives an inkling of its sense of time.
Sometimes new performers emerge,
sometimes the alleged lead turns out
to be merely a minor role.

I firmly believe
in the story-telling power
of landscapes.
There are landscapes,
whether towns, deserts,
mountain ranges, or coastal stretches,
that simply cry for stories.
They evoke "THEIR STORIES,"
indeed CREATE them.
Landscapes themselves can be lead actors,
and the people in them merely extras.
And then I believe just as firmly
in the story-telling power of stage props.
Just think what the open newspaper
lying unheeded on a sofa in the corner
can report!
Or the billboard in the background!
Or the rusty car,
parked on the edge of the picture!
A chair!
It stands there, in such a way
that someone must have just gotten up from it!
An open book on a table,
of which you can read half the title!
The empty cigarette pack on the sidewalk!
The coffee cup with the spoon still in it!
In photos THINGS can be cheerful or sad,
why, even comical or tragic.

ONCE *I traveled to Australia*
via Thailand and Indonesia,
through the back door, so to speak,
to the city of Darwin
in the northernmost part of the country.

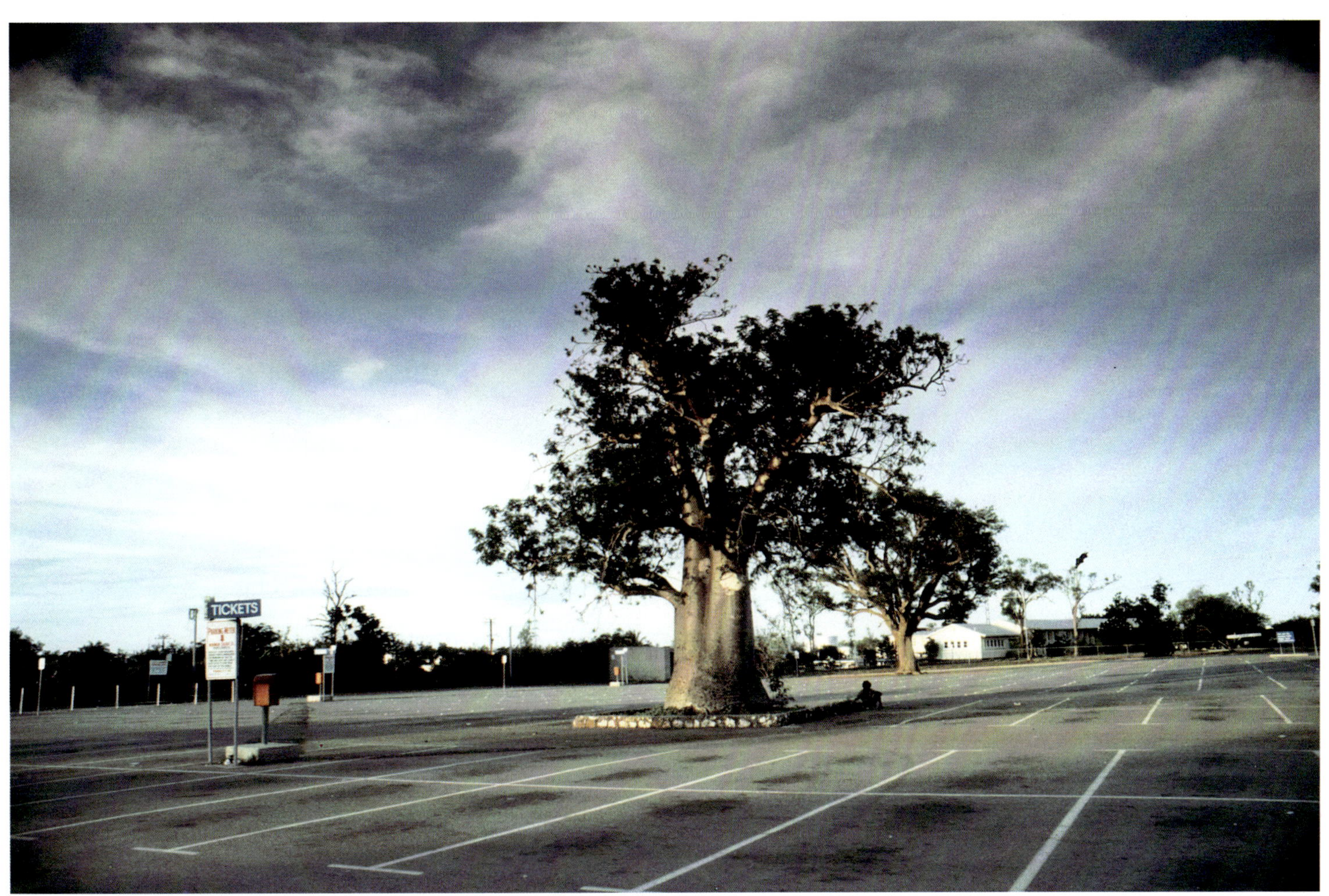

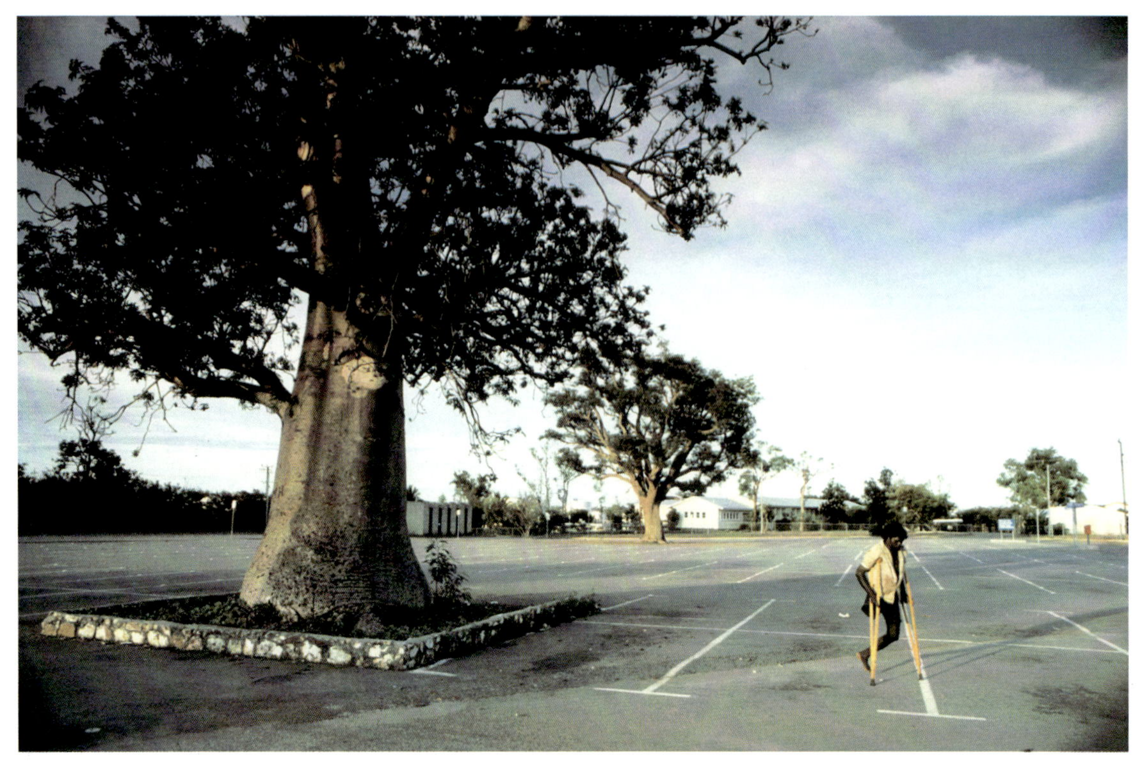

and thus I could experience an entire continent / through the eyes of a newcomer. / The evening of that first day / I saw a baobab tree for the first time / and the misery of the aborigines / for the first time.

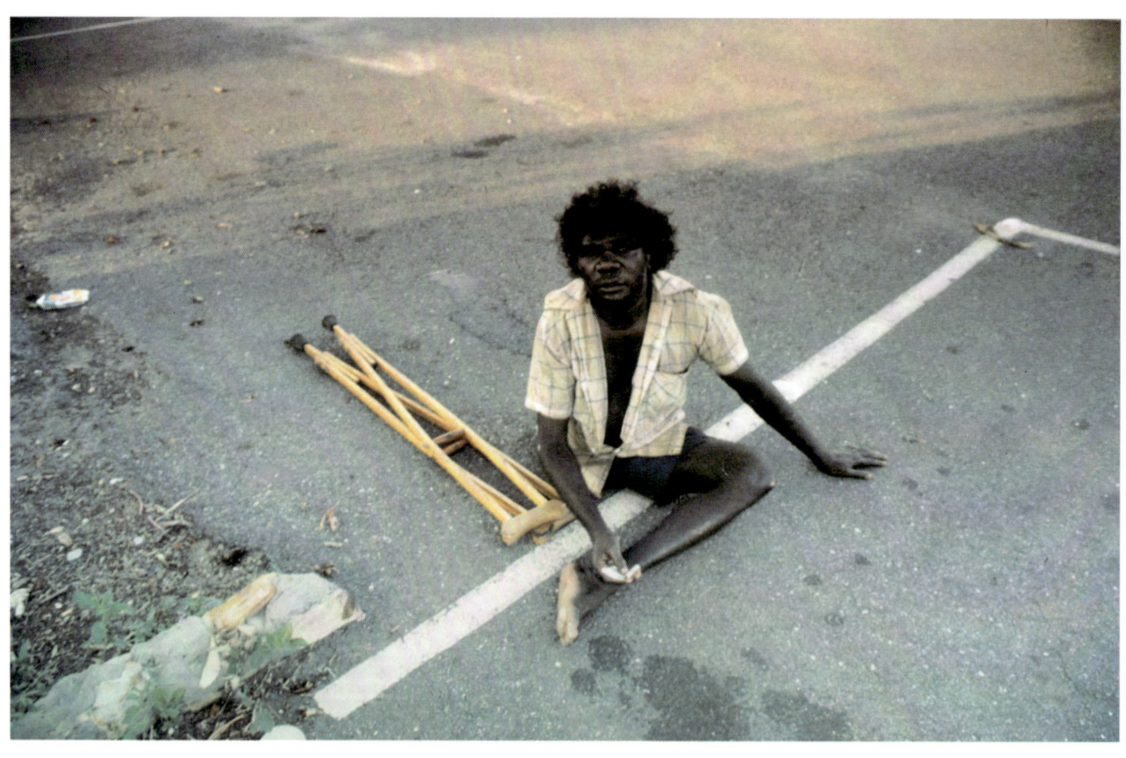

ONCE *I spent weeks*
crisscrossing through Texas.

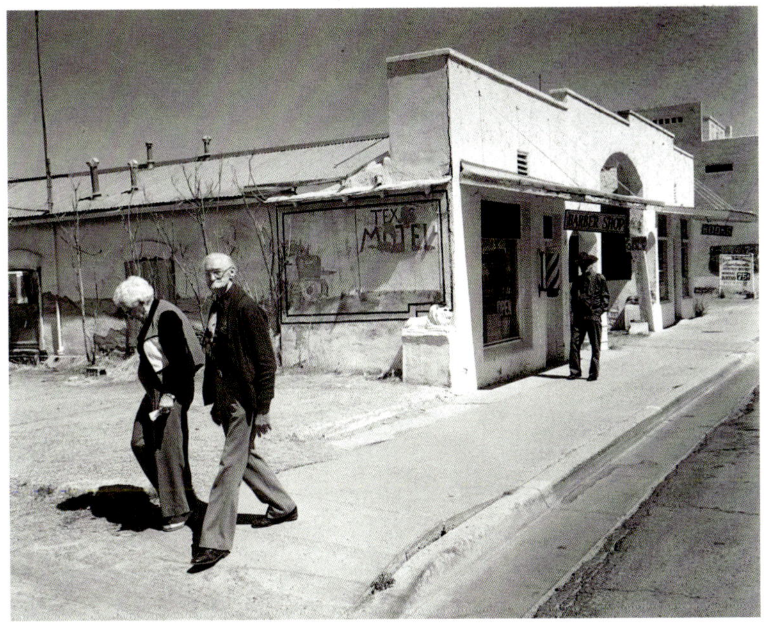

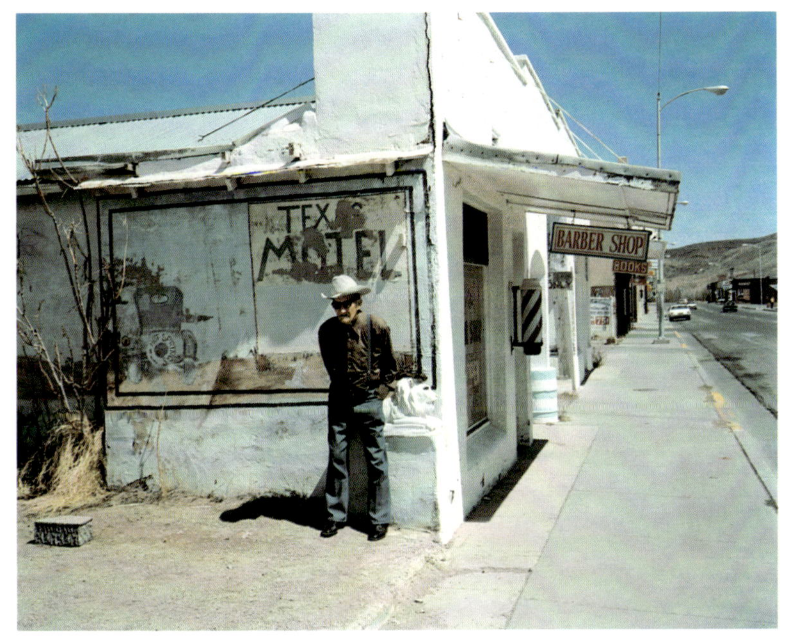

If I had to define Texas in a single image.
I would say:
An old man in a cowboy hat.

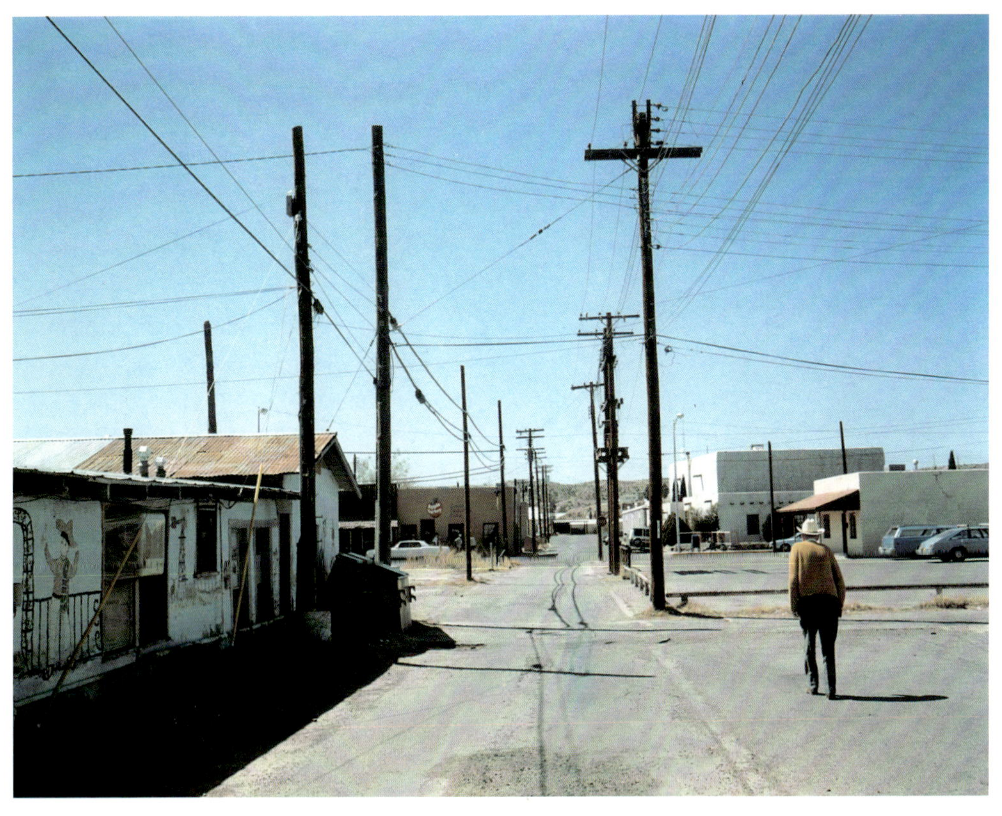

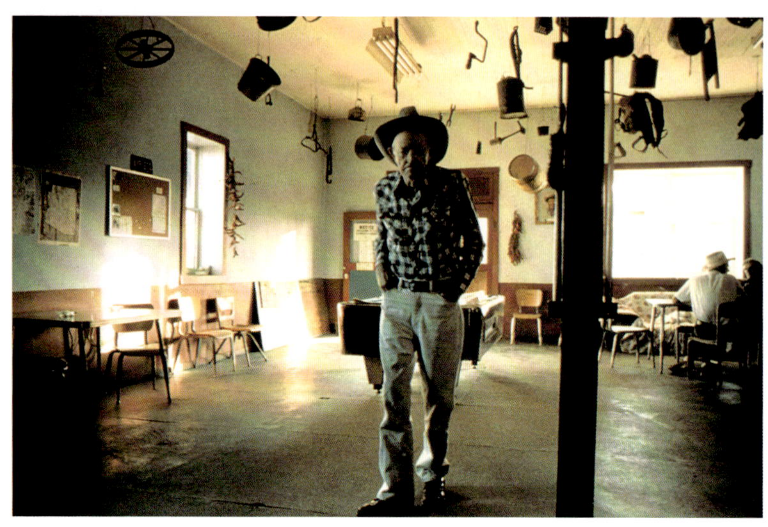

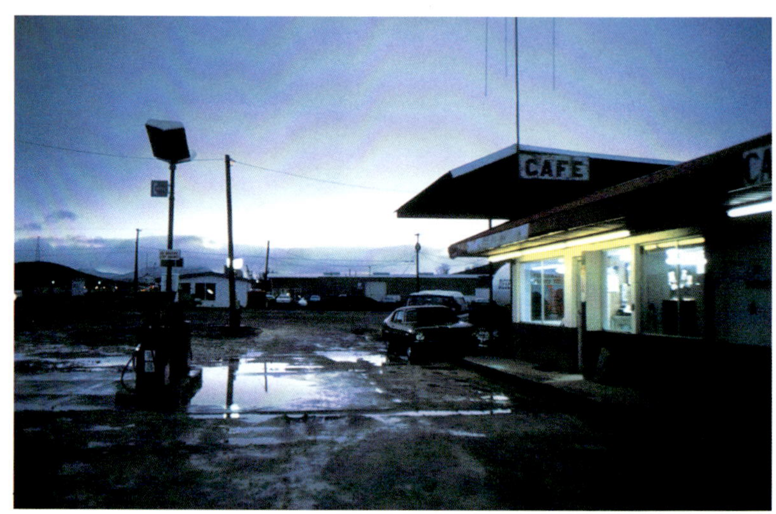

Old cowboys are the saddest and most touching figures.

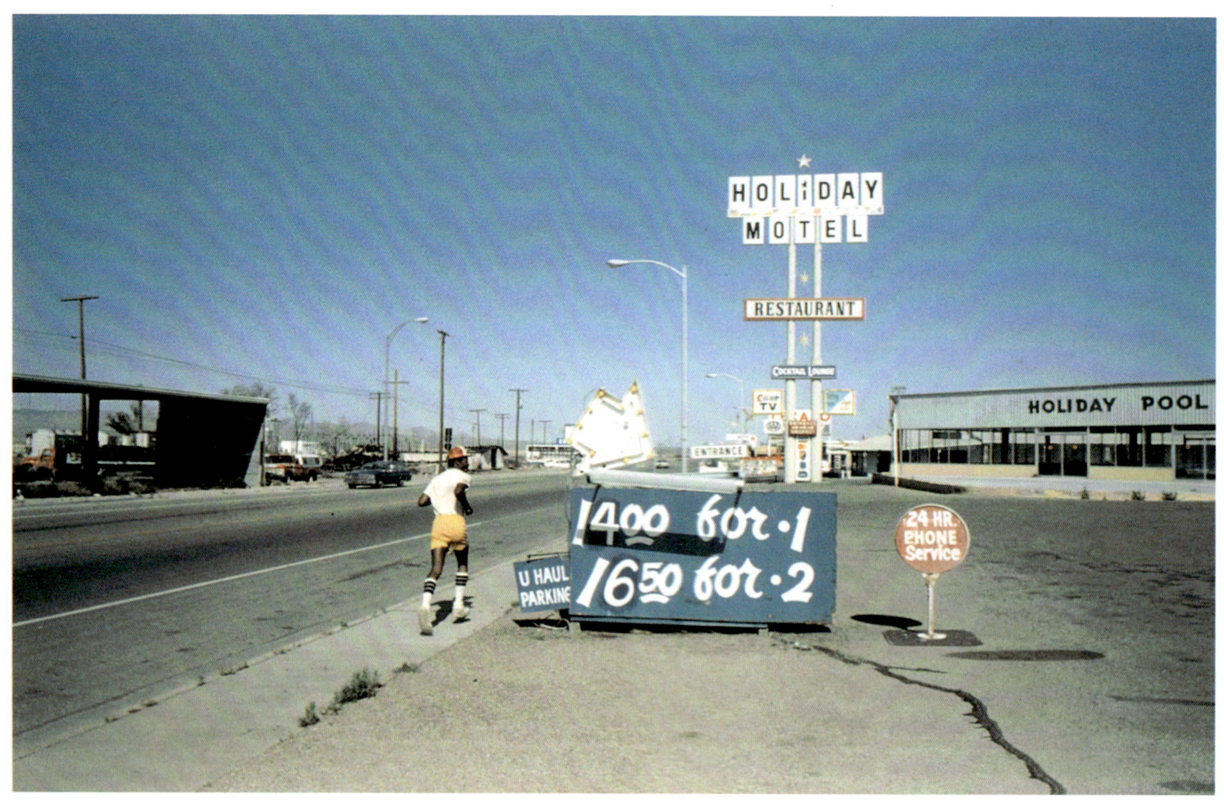

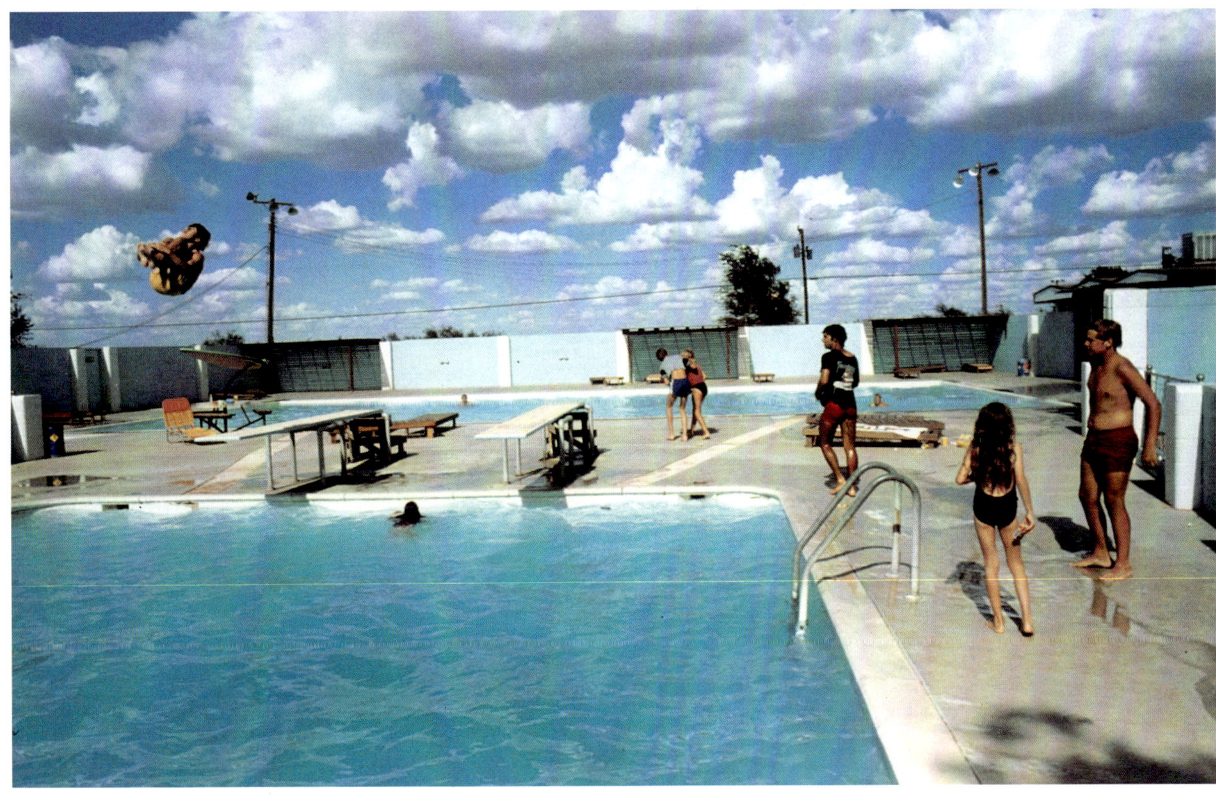

Everything appears only once in front of the camera,
and then every photo turns that ONCE into an ALWAYS.
It is only THROUGH
the captured image that time becomes visible,
and in the time BETWEEN
the first photo and the second
appears the story
that without these two images
would have passed into oblivion
for a different ALWAYS.

Just as in the moment of photographing
we wanted to vanish
into the world
and into things,
the world with its things now jumps out of the photo
and at every viewer
asking for attention, demanding duration.
"THERE" is where stories come into being,
there,
in the eye
of the viewer.

ONCE

"Once is not enough,"
goes an old saying.
As a child I always thought that
made a lot of sense.
But at least when you photograph
it's not true.
Then, ONCE is the ONLY TIME.

Translated from German by Joachim Neugroschel.

PEOPLE & IDEAS

INFLUENCE AND INSPIRATION: FRANCIS BACON, JOHN DEAKIN, AND PHOTOGRAPHY

by Peter Hay Halpert

"John Deakin—Photographs" at the National Portrait Gallery, London; and "Velázquez and Bacon: Paintings of Popes" at the National Gallery, London.

They were a particularly ambivalent yet strangely fitting pair of friends. Francis Bacon was one of the preeminent post-modernist painters of our times, while John Deakin, despite a prolific career as a photographer for British *Vogue*, remains a relative unknown. Now, a series of exhibitions in London and a new book are providing an opportunity to reassess Deakin's work, in the process shedding significant light on the influence and inspiration photography had on Bacon's painting. "John Deakin—Photographs," at the National Portrait Gallery, and curator Robin Muir's accompanying catalog (Schirmer/Mosel), represent the most significant contribution toward this reappraisal, while another Deakin show at the Zelda Cheatle Gallery fleshes out the picture of his career. "Velázquez and Bacon: Paintings of Popes," at London's National Gallery, also contains important clues to understanding the substantial role photography played in Bacon's work.

A self-taught painter, Bacon made conflicting claims about his use of photographs. In a conversation with Michel Archimbaud that took place in 1991, he said that "Photographs are only of interest to me as records. I know people think I've often used it [photography], but that isn't true. But when I say that to me photographs are merely records, I mean that I don't use them at all as a model. A photograph, basically, is a means of illustrating something and illustration doesn't interest me."[1] However, in the same discussion, Bacon explained that "Since the invention of photography, painting really has changed completely. We no longer have the same reasons for painting as before. The problem is that each generation has to find its own way of working. You see here in my studio, there are these photographs scattered about the floor, all damaged. I've used them to paint portraits of friends, and then kept them. It's easier for me to work from these records than from the people themselves, that way I can work alone and feel much freer. When I work, I don't want to see anyone, not even models. These photographs were my aide-mémoire, they helped me to convey certain features, certain details."

Bacon's disingenuousness at this stage in his life (he died a year later, in 1992), seems designed to contradict earlier statements made in a noteworthy series of interviews with his friend the art historian David Sylvester. In those discussions, which began in 1962 and continued through 1974, Bacon spoke much more specifically about his use of photography. "The thing of doing series may possibly have come from looking at those books of Muybridge with the stages of movement shown in separate photographs. I've also always had a book of photographs that's influenced me very much called *Positioning in Radiography*, with a lot of photographs showing the positioning of the body for the X-ray photographs to be taken, and also of the X-rays themselves."[2] Later, referring to photographs by Marius Maxwell which he admired in the 1924 publication *Stalking Big Game with a Camera in Equatorial Africa*, Bacon acknowledges that "one image can be deeply suggestive in relation to another. I had the idea that . . . textures should be very much thicker, and therefore the texture of, for instance, a rhinoceros skin would help me to think about the texture

John Deakin, *Muriel Belcher*, n.d.

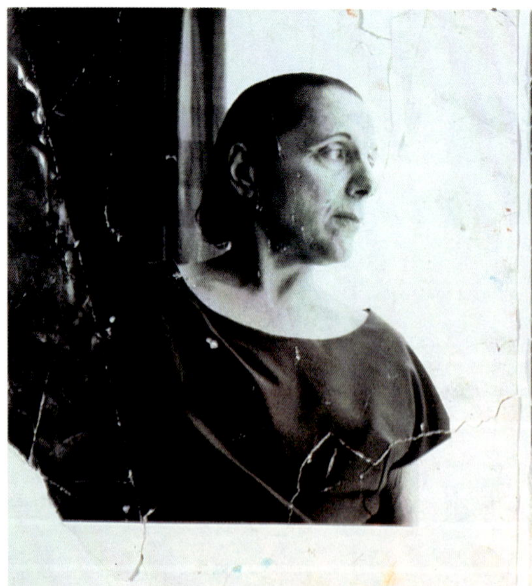

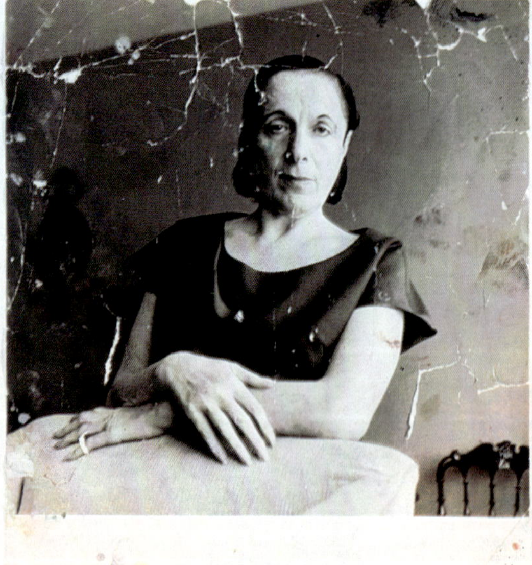

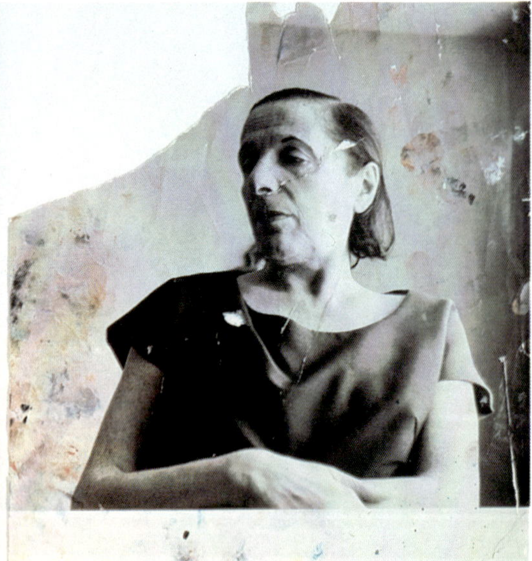

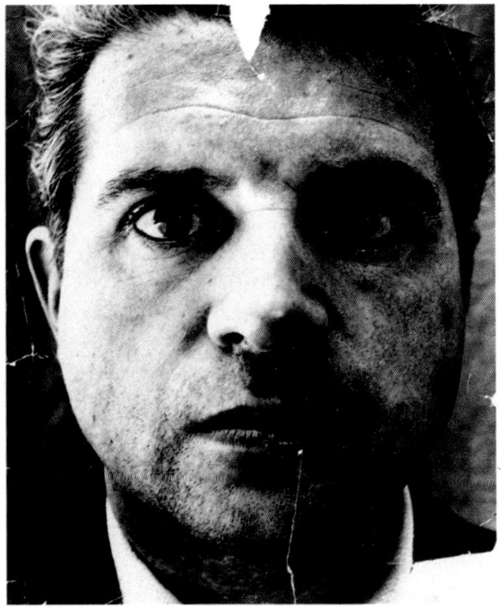

John Deakin, *Francis Bacon (head shot)*, 1952

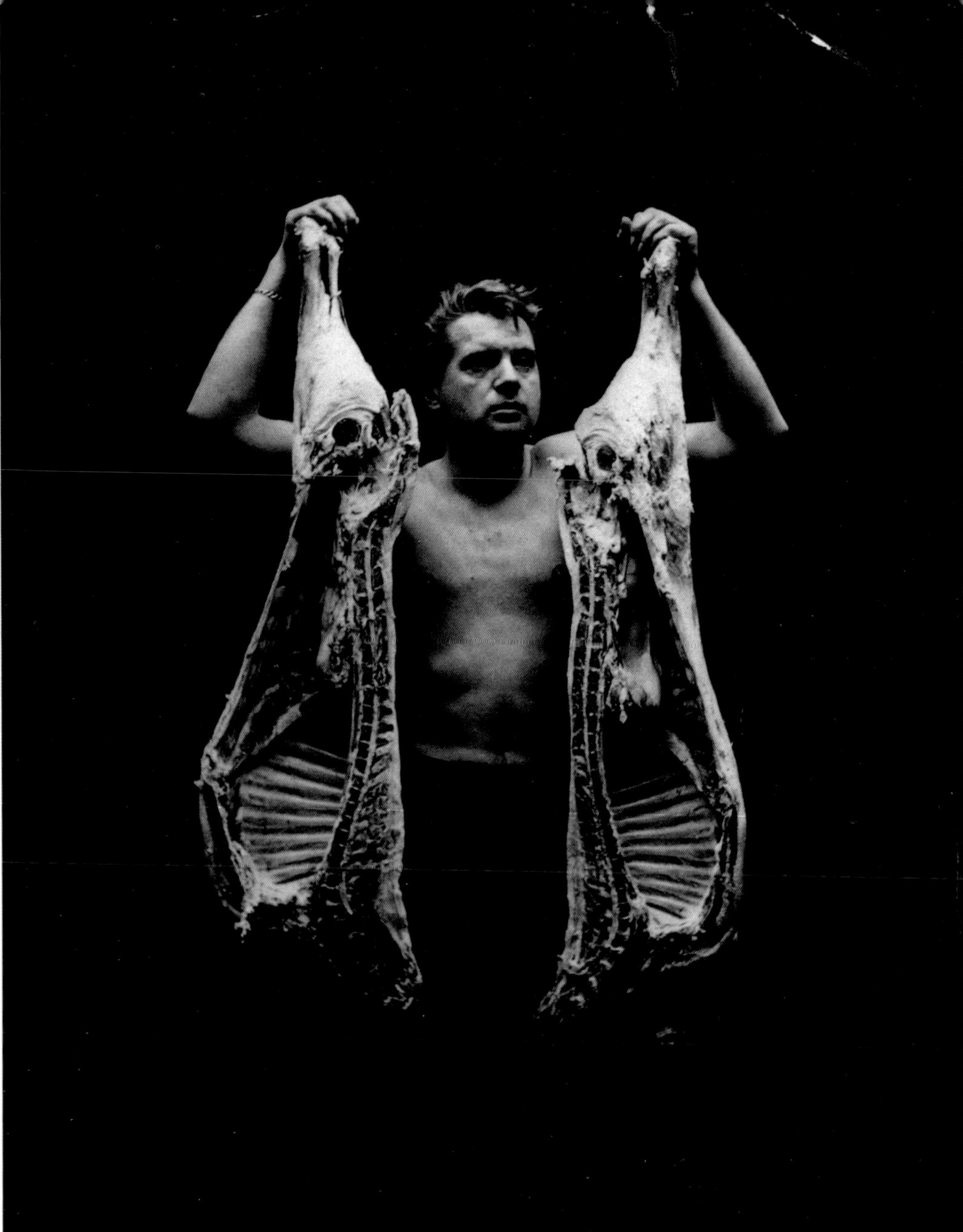

John Deakin, *Francis Bacon (meat)*, 1952

of human skin." In addition, Bacon was well aware of *Documents*, one of the great European magazines of the late 1920s and early '30s; one issue in particular featured photographs of slaughterhouses, which became a recurring motif in several of his paintings.

Even when creating works that referred to other paintings, Bacon preferred to work from photographs. The Velázquez and Bacon exhibition at the National Gallery imparts a sense of reunion that is misleading. Bacon's four studies from Velázquez's portrait of Pope Innocent X all derive from photographs and reproductions of the earlier masterpiece rather than any firsthand experience with the actual painting. Despite traveling to Rome, Bacon never saw the *Innocent X* in the Doria-Pamphilj Collection. He spoke, instead, of "a fear of seeing the reality of the Velázquez after my tampering with it."

Interestingly, Bacon rarely refers specifically to his use of Deakin's portraits. Deakin started photographing in 1939 and continued to work intently if intermittently through the early 1960s. His heyday occurred during the '50s when he was under contract to *Vogue* (where he had the dubious distinction of being the only staff photographer ever fired twice by the same administration). Although his tenure there was short-lived, in a period of approximately four years he produced more work than his contemporaries at *Vogue*, including Norman Parkinson, Clifford Coffin, and Cecil Beaton.

Deakin photographed everything for *Vogue*, including fashion and beauty, but his forte was portraiture. The poet and novelist Elizabeth Smart remarked that Deakin had "tyrannical eyes," and the art critic John Russell wrote that Deakin "rivaled Bacon in his ability to make a likeness in which truth came unwrapped and unpackaged. Deakin's portraits, like Bacon's, had a dead-centered, unrhetorical quality. A complete human being was set before us, without additives." Deakin's portraits were characterized by a monochromatic austerity and raw clarity that wasn't in keeping with the buoyancy of the work done by Parkinson or Beaton; indeed, it precedes the nearest thing to it—the photographs of David Bailey and Richard Avedon—by a decade.

Despite creating a memorable body of work, Deakin remains largely forgotten. His prints were outsized and consequently not easily archived. Deakin himself distrusted their worth. "He really was a member of photography's unhappiest minority whose members, while doubting its status as art, sometimes prove better than anyone else that there is no doubt about it," recalls his friend Bruce Bernard. His greatest undoing, though, is evident in his portraits. Many of his subjects were his friends and drinking companions from the pubs and clubs of Soho; Bacon and Deakin, along with Michael Andrews, Frank Auerbach, and Lucian Freud, comprised a group (vir-

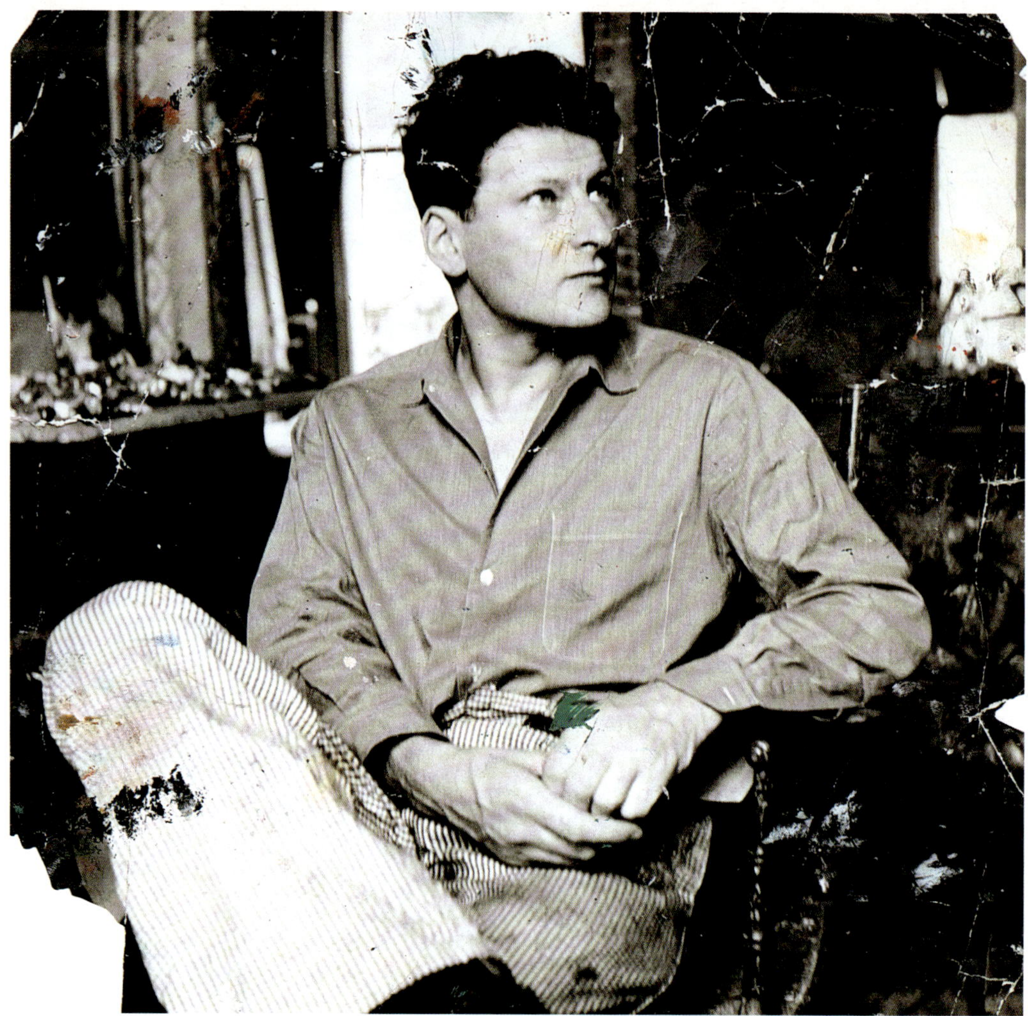

John Deakin, *Lucian Freud (chair)*, n.d.

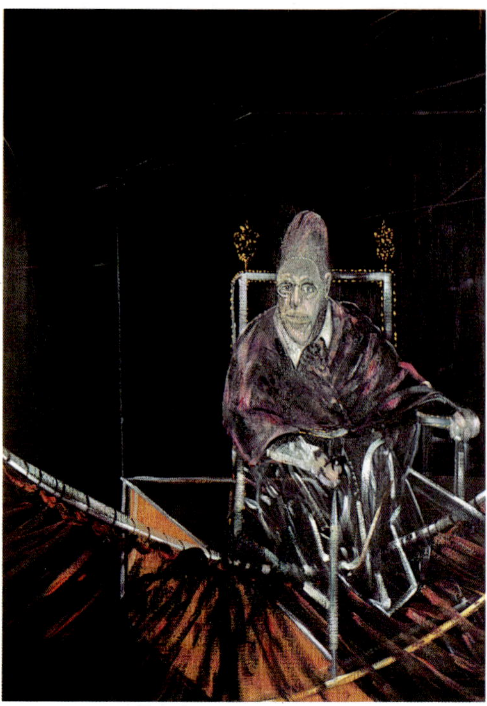

Francis Bacon, *Pope I*, 1951

tually a subset of R. B. Kitaj's "School of London"), that would frequently gather for drinks at Muriel Belcher's club, the Colony Room, a setting described as "a place you could take your grandmother, and possibly your father, but not your mother." But while Bacon would regularly return to his studio from a late night out and religiously put in several hours painting, drinking affected Deakin's work and led to his dismissal from Condé Nast. His career as an independent photographer was not a success and his life devolved into a series of trips abroad.

Deakin's portraits did have a life, albeit largely unacknowledged, in Bacon's paintings. Bacon commissioned many of Deakin's portraits as reference points for his own work. "Even in the case of friends who will come and pose," Bacon said, "I've had photographs taken for portraits because I very much prefer working from the photographs than from them. I think that, if I have the presence of the image there, I am not able to drift so freely as I am able to through the photographic image."

Bacon's studio was notoriously chaotic and cluttered. "My photographs are very damaged by people walking over them and crumpling them and everything else, and this does add other implications to an image," he stated. To see the exhibition of Deakin prints from Bacon's estate consequently becomes an experience in watching the figure deconstruct according to the state of destruction in which the print has settled, much as the figures in Bacon's painting appear tortured, convoluted, and deconstructed. While Bacon spoke about the ways in which he used photography, he rarely specifically cited Deakin's photography by name. Nor did he comment on the inspiration he drew from these torn and crumpled prints. However, in the same manner in which photographs of Velázquez's portrait of Innocent X had an object quality and presence for Bacon above and beyond that of the work itself, it is not inconceivable that Deakin's photographs, transformed by the damage sustained while in his studio, came to represent much more than simple aide-mémoire for him.

As Robin Muir notes, Bacon once commented that "[Deakin's] work is so little known when one thinks of all the well-known and famous names in photography—his portraits to me are the best since Nadar and Julia Margaret Cameron." Deakin's photographic output essentially ended in 1961, yet he and Bacon retained some semblance of a friendship. It was Bacon who was listed as Deakin's next of kin during his last hospital stay and it was Bacon who paid for his convalescence in Brighton where Deakin died of heart failure in 1972. But the kinship seems strongest in the work. The prints of Deakin's photographs which Bacon held in his studio, set alongside Bacon's painted portraits, are evidence of the influence and inspiration photography provided for Bacon. Deakin could have been speaking for Bacon as well when he said, "Being fatally drawn to the human race, what I want to do when I photograph it is to make a revelation about it. So my sitters turn into my victims."

1. *Francis Bacon* (London: Phaidon, 1993).

2. *Interviews with Francis Bacon* (New York: Thames and Hudson, 1987).

PICTURES FROM THE EDGE

by Nick Waplington

Fuck You Heroes: Glen E. Friedman Photographs 1976–1991. *New York: Burning Flags Press, 1994, $29.95 hardcover.*

In order to talk about Glen E. Friedman's photographs in *Fuck You Heroes*, I first need to contextualize them within my own experience as a child in England in the seventies. Back then in the rainy U.K., my gang and I tried to live out a pseudo–California Dream. We went skateboarding every day, surfed when there were waves to surf on, listened to thrash punk, and smoked pot. As this was in the pre-video era, we invented our life-style based on what we saw in skateboarding and thrasher magazines—looking at photos by Glen Friedman, the man who chronicled my teenage-fantasy utopia.

Looking at those same pictures today brings up strangely mixed emotions in me: part fifteen-year-old Nick—"Wow, man, check out that air!"—and part grown-up Nick, trying to deconstruct the photos' cultural reference points.

The first pictures in *Fuck You Heroes* were shot in empty backyard swimming pools in Los Angeles, when Friedman was about thirteen. The images overflow with chlorine charm: they are somehow reminiscent of the great child-photographer Jacques-Henri Lartigue, both in their sense of fun and the joys of being outside, but also in the sense we can feel of the photographer being a participant in the picture's action. Friedman caught skateboarding in its infancy, when, for a few brief summers, all that mattered was skating. While Friedman skated, he documented the scene. It's this clear sense of his own participation, found throughout the book, that makes these pictures work, and gives them their edge.

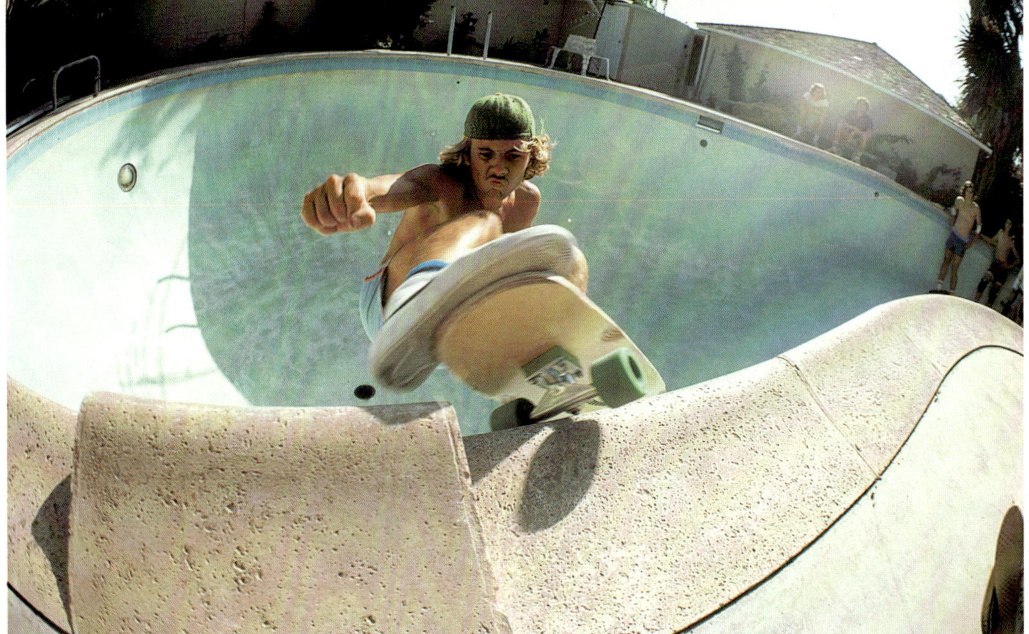

Glen E. Friedman, *Jay Adams, Unnamed Backyard Pool*, West Los Angeles, California, 1978

Friedman's images are loaded with the colors of optimism—they look toward a glowing future that, when it arrived, was just too bright. When the West Coast punk scene (the last of the first generation of punks) came along, Friedman was there, recording an important component of America's new cultural experience. He managed to capture such hugely influential bands as Black Flag and Minor Threat in their first bloom. In his images of these bands and others, you sense the energy and feel the heat of the place.

The values of youth culture as shown in hip-hop and rap music have certainly affected the lives of young African-Americans. Here, too, Friedman was on the scene from the very beginning. In *Fuck You Heroes*, we see images of Run DMC, L.L. Cool J., and Public Enemy during the shoot for the cover of their stunning "Rebel Without a Pause" single.

Public Enemy's hard-hitting music gave them unparalleled access to black youth, and they used that access as a political forum. Preaching Afrocentric politics, the band fought back against Reaganomics and what they saw as its betrayal of the civil-rights movement. Public Enemy were at the vanguard of the hard-edge rap movement. And Friedman's pictures were an intrinsic part of the whole package.

While *Fuck You Heroes* is a powerful book, there is a central flaw in its almost total lack of images of women. Neither skating nor music is or was a solely male domain, and yet there is only one woman in the book. And that one woman, Ice-T's girlfriend Darlene, is dressed up in what is known in the rap industry as "Gangsta Bitch" style—she faces the camera defiantly, in a very tiny swimsuit, carrying a big gun. Is this meant to be ironic? In his notes Friedman defends the shot, saying, "I do not consider myself a sexist for shooting this," and explaining that he and Ice-T were out to show the reality of "the power of a good looking woman in this society." But next to Friedman's other intimate, gritty photographs—which are much more compelling—this image lowers the tone of the work as a whole. It is simply unnecessary: Friedman obviously knows how to make boys look sexy without looking cheap or idiotic, I'm sure he could have done the same for the girls on the scene.

If it weren't for this important gap, *Fuck You Heroes* might have been a better overview of this era. Even as it is, though, the book stands as a powerful testimonial: skaters, rappers, punks, are caught in the bright, charged moments of their youth, and presented to us as a new legacy of heroes. Youth culture, like any art form, takes from the past to build a future. Because Friedman was always hanging out at the right place at the right moments, *Fuck You Heroes* might function as part of an authoritative history for my own generation, and could help to provide the generation kicking at our heels with something to build on.

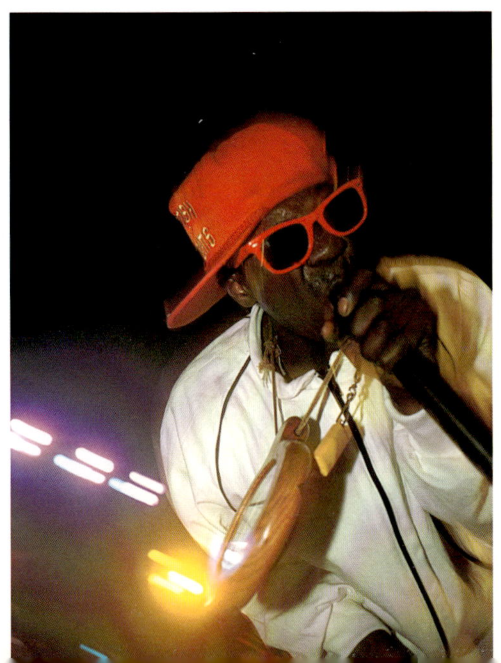

Glen E. Friedman, *Flavor Flav of Public Enemy*, Nassau Coliseum, Long Island, New York, 1988

CHRISTENBERRY'S SOUTHERN DISCOMFORT

William Christenberry's Klan Room *provokes controversy in his current major retrospective.*

by Mark Muro

"Reconstruction: The Art of William Christenberry" at the Center for Creative Photography, Tucson, Arizona.

William Christenberry may be a collector's classic, a curator's dream, but in truth he has rarely been seen whole. Instead, he has been truncated. Reductive labels have distorted his career, designating the artist, by turns, a "regionalist," "Walker Evans in color," or merely a great photographer.

At the same time, those who arbitrate taste have tended to pigeonhole Christenberry's multifarious meditation on his Alabama roots, slighting the artist's almost protean facility with the entire twentieth-century Babel of techniques and media.

As a result, an overfocused, oddly partial light has brought acclaim to Christenberry's immaculate color photographs of vacated rural houses and weathered facades, relegating to narrower connoisseurship the Alabaman's early paintings, his reconstructions of vernacular buildings, his recent series of geometric sculptures, and the provocative installation known as *The Klan Room*. Given this selective illumination, an ironic fate has befallen the artist. Though committed to William Faulkner's project of finding the universal in the Southern provincial, he has found his reception—if not his accomplishment—constrained by his red-dirt subject matter and the occasional myopia of the art world.

"Sometimes it is frustrating—I admit," acknowledges the fifty-nine-year-old Washington D.C.–based artist. "Even today I get people who say, 'Oh, I didn't know you made sculptures,' or 'I didn't know you painted.'"

Only now comes redress—in the form of an extraordinary new traveling retrospective and 208-page book of Christenberry's varied art. Mounted by the Center for Creative Photography in Tucson, Arizona, "Reconstruction: The Art of William Christenberry" tenders the most substantial appreciation to date of this imperfectly understood artist. Consisting of 153 works in a dozen media, as well as the largest version ever seen of *The Klan Room*, "Reconstruction" presents a more complete Christenberry than has been seen before. But what makes the show powerful more than its size is the challenge it poses to narrower accounts.

Trudy Wilner Stack, the exhibition's curator, suggests, "The point was to show this work as the artist creates it—all of a piece—rather than the way it often gets presented, which usually assumes he is primarily important as a photographer. This way the individual works and mediums can resonate with each other as they can't otherwise."

What is the effect of this show?

The first thing it conveys, of course, is new appreciation for the reach of Christenberry's obsession with the forms and mysteries of his vanishing Alabama. Even those who know Christenberry's work may have to jettison views of his career as modest in scale, or "regional." No way, in terms of sheer volume of production, can Christenberry any longer be regarded as a modest Southern gentleman tending a minor-league postagrarian garden.

But the show also explodes other categorizations of the Christenberry career. For one thing, it obliterates once and for all segregations of the artist as "merely," or even primarily, a photographer. Instead, it shows Christenberry as an energetic "crossover" specialist, a title the artist himself embraces. Not content with photo-work, Christenberry turns out to have materialized his preoccupation with the look and feel of the receding past using whatever came to hand: painting, Pop Art assemblage, surrealistic constructions, expressionist drawing, tabletop sculpture, doll making.

In this respect, Christenberry appears to function as what Wilner Stack calls a "modernist beast," employing a multitude of critical and formal strategies in most major art media. The show demonstrates once and for all how photography interested Christenberry at first only as a tool for recording the colors of the Alabama landscape—specifically for use in early Abstract Expressionist paintings such as *Tenant House I*, which in turn revealed to him his signature iconography of fading rural buildings positioned and sized as monumental geometric presences.

This alone forces recognition of Christenberry's nonphotographic energies. But they are made even more apparent by the show's repeated juxtaposition of more or less simultaneous, interreferential works in different media. In one room, for example, a 1981 photograph, *Windows of Palmist Building, Havana Junction, Alabama*, 1981 (February), cohabitates with a 1975 model of that building festooned with a Grapette soda sign, which connects to a Rauschenberg-inflected col-

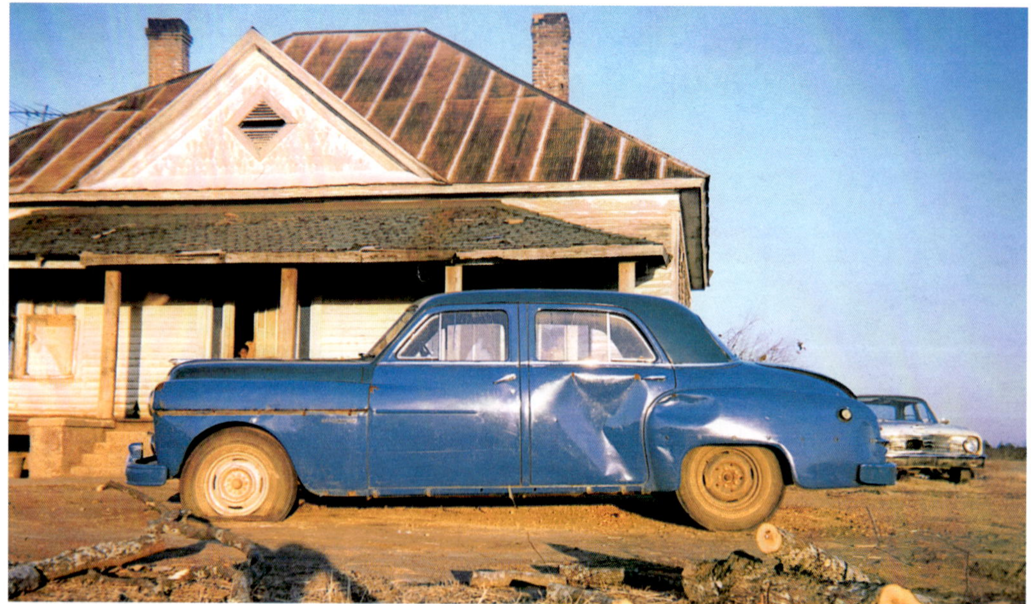

William Christenberry, *House and Car, near Akron, Alabama*, 1978

lage entitled *Advertisement* (1964), which in turn links to an adjacent wall-sized line of rusted Royal Crown Cola signs (*Royal Crown Wall*, 1973–80).

Such a display—privileging no single work or practice but collating and juxtaposing them all—goes a long way toward establishing Christenberry's photography as but one expression of a thirty-five-year attempt to make sense of roots. This revelation makes more poignant the artist's attentions to the icons of his home place. By showing how the Christenberry lexicon of broken-down houses, gravestones, churches, ladders, cones, cubes, and cannon balls recurs and recurs, the Center for Creative Photography's exhibition gives new bite to Christenberry's determination to mine the universal in the rural/local.

"Getting it all together like this makes sense because I as the artist never saw these projects as separate," remarks Christenberry. "In this book and exhibition you can see that painting affects everything I do, that photography changed my painting, how sign collecting fed into the sculpture, and how sculpture is now affecting the photography."

But another essential refiguring comes with the inclusion in "Reconstruction" of the controversial tableau *The Klan Room*, which has been publicly displayed only twice before. This addition—the product of thirty-five years' steady indignation and accumulation—restores to Christenberry's oeuvre the edginess and social commentary overlooked by typecastings that patronize his work as romantic, humanistic, or simply documentary.

In this context, *The Klan Room* functions as a rebuke to any facile nostalgia for home places summoned by the rest of the work, gathering into a claustrophobic, closetlike installation some three hundred of Christenberry's responses to the dark side of his Alabama birthright—the Ku Klux Klan. The effect is intense. From floor to ceiling, and on every square foot of wall space, an unholy klavern of satin-clad G.I. Joe dolls, harshly drawn specters, hooded forms, and treated gun ads invoke the KKK's historical campaign of bigotry. Some of the ghost-dolls congregate in Plexiglas boxes. Others clump together confined by a circular metallic railing or the walls of a Christenberry vernacular structure. But all have the unnerving power, in their luxurious theatricality,

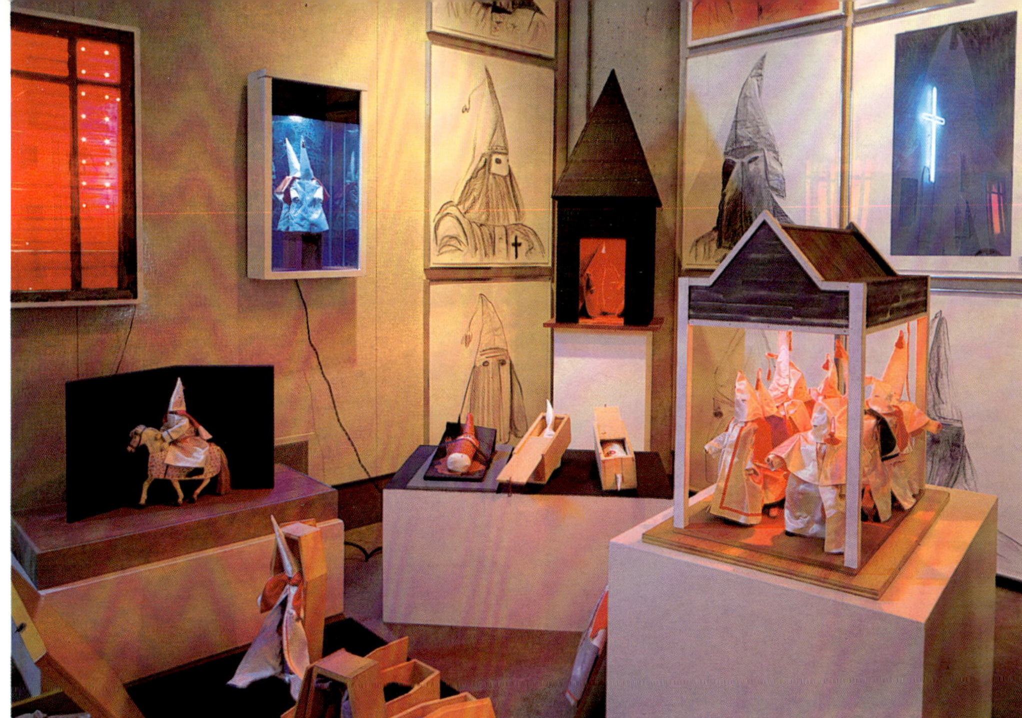

William Christenberry, *The Klan Room*, 1962–present

of luring the viewer into unsettling intimacy with a half-lit secret ceremony that Christenberry reveals as inseparable from the sunlit daydreams of his other work.

"The room is a closet, a vessel for evil, but it's not just put out as 'The Other': It's connected to the show, and implicates it all," observes Wilner Stack. This suggests the manifold tensions *The Klan Room* insinuates into all that surrounds it. Some of the ghosts that seem to populate Christenberry's worn landscapes, for example, are undoubtedly implied here to ride with the Klan. Christenberry himself is revealed to dwell on a birthright tainted by organized hatred. Even the exhibition-goer, drifting into rural nostalgia, realizes he or she had best guard against complacency.

Such insinuations tighten the entire show with a challenging, self-reflexive current that forces just the unease and "perplexity" the artist says he desires to provoke. "Isn't it the responsibility of art and institutions to clarify, to inquire, to reveal the most difficult issues?" Christenberry asks. "Certainly it is. And walking into that room you become part of it—implicated—and that can be disturbing, even when you walk out. You get swept up. But having to respond also makes you think."

Given the category-exploding tenor of this show, it may well be precisely its strengths that have so far precluded its wide reception. In this regard, it appears that a number of troubling rigidities and prejudices and reflexes toward self-censorship in the art world and elsewhere have helped to restrict "Reconstruction" to a limited tour of mostly Southern venues. Evidence exists that fears of controversy over *The Klan Room*—which did surface briefly among local "human rights activists" prior to the show's spring opening in Tucson—cost the show at least one booking at a major national art museum. This suggests to Christenberry and many others in Tucson the threat to all culture that continues given the highly charged—and increasingly toxic—political atmosphere enveloping the arts and museums today.

"You see, that some people—and worse, some museums—seem not to want the Klan material shown raises very serious issues for me of what an art institution is supposed to be doing," says Christenberry. "These museums have to keep these issues on the table, yet we're at a position now where places are afraid of displaying anything—*anything*—that will create the least controversy or possibly endanger their funding. That surely raises very scary questions."

It may also be that the reception of Christenberry's art still bears the burden of its Southern ground, which reads to an international-cosmopolitan art hierarchy as "provincial," "folky," "without buzz." Then again, "Reconstruction" could demonstrate that the art world sometimes doesn't know what to do with a truly multimedia artist who, by doing everything, doesn't quite fit in anywhere. At any rate, it prompts reflection that Christenberry's way has at times been complicated by his identity as a white, Southern, male artist whose practice looks always to transcend

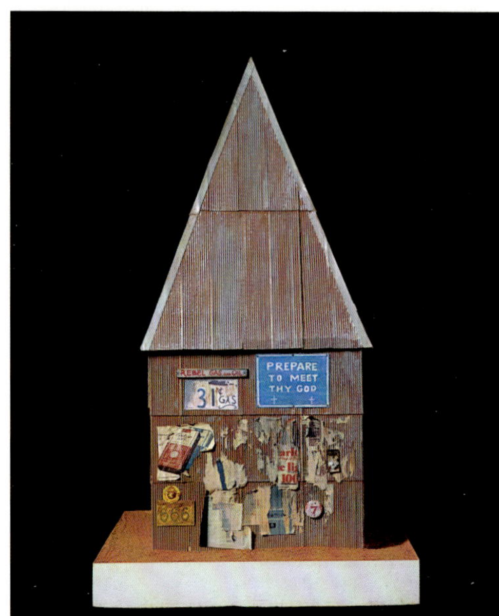

William Christenberry,
Dream Building I, 1979

the rubrics of gender, sexual preference, medium, or skin color.

Still, by every indication William Christenberry continues to flourish and grow as he worries on and on about that Alabama postage-stamp of home ground that he has made into his Greece, his Arles, his Yoknapatawpha.

In this way, "Reconstruction: The Art of William Christenberry" has, like all important shows, thrown a revealing light on both a provocative career and the imperfect ways the art world has hitherto perceived it.

"Reconstruction: The Art of William Christenberry" was shown as a combined venture of the Center for Creative Photography and the University of Arizona Museum of Art from April 21 to June 30, 1996. The exhibition will appear at the Contemporary Arts Center in New Orleans, Louisiana, February 1 to March 16, 1997, as well as at the Museum of American Art at the Pennsylvania Academy of the Fine Arts in Philadelphia, June 20 to August 21, 1997, and the Southeastern Center for Contemporary Art in Winston-Salem, North Carolina, October 25, 1997, to January 11, 1998.

The book Christenberry—Reconstruction: The Art of William Christenberry *was published in May 1996 by the University Press of Mississippi and the Center for Creative Photography, and contains essays by Allen Tullos and Trudy Wilner Stack.*

HELEN CHADWICK 1954–1996

by Mark Haworth-Booth

The extraordinary work of the British artist Helen Chadwick is internationally admired. She showed all over Europe and across the world from São Paulo to Tokyo. Her work appeared in On the Art of Fixing a Shadow: 150 Years of Photography *in 1989 and her first book,* Enfleshings, *was published by Aperture the same year. She showed at the Houston FotoFest in 1990 and the Museum of Modern Art, New York, exhibited "Bad Blooms" in 1995.*

I saw Helen at the opening of an exhibition at the Whitechapel Art Gallery in London one evening in March. She was her spirited, striking self, enjoying the seductive finesse of Jeff Wall's color transparencies—a medium she, of course, used with great success. Helen told me about the exhibition "Feminin-Masculin," at the Centre Georges Pompidou in Paris, in which her notoriously named but elegant and ethereal *Piss Flowers* were prominently displayed. They were positioned in such a way, she gleefully explained, that their phallic protuberances appeared to penetrate Courbet's even more notorious erotic masterpiece *L'origine du monde*. We hadn't met since last summer. Helen was keen to see the rococo silk designs of Anna Maria Garthwaite in the V&A Print Room—which also holds the largest collection in the world of Helen's own photographic works. We arranged for a visit and lunch on the Friday. As it happened, a child's illness kept me from our appointment that day, but Helen studied the marvelous Garthwaite floral designs—made for clothing as a serious art form—before she went on to a meeting to finalize the layout and proofs for her next show, at the Barbican Art Gallery. On the Saturday morning the artist Christopher Bucklow rang me. Helen had collapsed the previous evening, apparently from a heart attack. Within minutes she had died. Shock spread across London's studios and galleries. Late that evening the art critic William Feaver was asked for a comment by his paper. The next morning's *Observer* carried a paragraph on the death at forty-two on Friday 15 March of Helen Chadwick. "She was the most eminent woman artist of her generation." The sentence was terrible in its finality.

Over the weekend two of Helen's closest friends heroically wrote fine obituaries which appeared in daily newspapers on the Monday—Louisa Buck in *The Independent* and Marina Warner in the *Guardian*. Other long appreciations appeared during the week in major newspapers and on radio. Helen—"with her smooth, light, bendy epicene body and her signature Louise Brooks haircut" (Marina Warner)—was more important to more people than perhaps she ever knew. Many knew her from the wonderful film she made with the BBC on Frida Kahlo in the series "Artists' Journeys," in 1992. She broke through to a large gallery audience for the first time with her exhibition (and lavishly illustrated catalog) *Effluvia* at the Serpentine Gallery, which set a new attendance record for a contemporary solo show in London's most attractive art space. Over 54,000 saw her well-known chocolate foundation, *Cacao*, her *Bad Blooms*, *Viral Landscapes*, and *Piss Flowers*. Out on the lawn was another work, which was almost impossible to see—*All Flesh is Grass*. Two of her students had painstakingly

She made her Gesamtkunstwerk *with an office photocopying machine that had a toning device, a computer, some photobooth self-portraits—and with her intense powers of concentration. She manipulated improbable materials until they answered the vision with which she had dared to set out.*

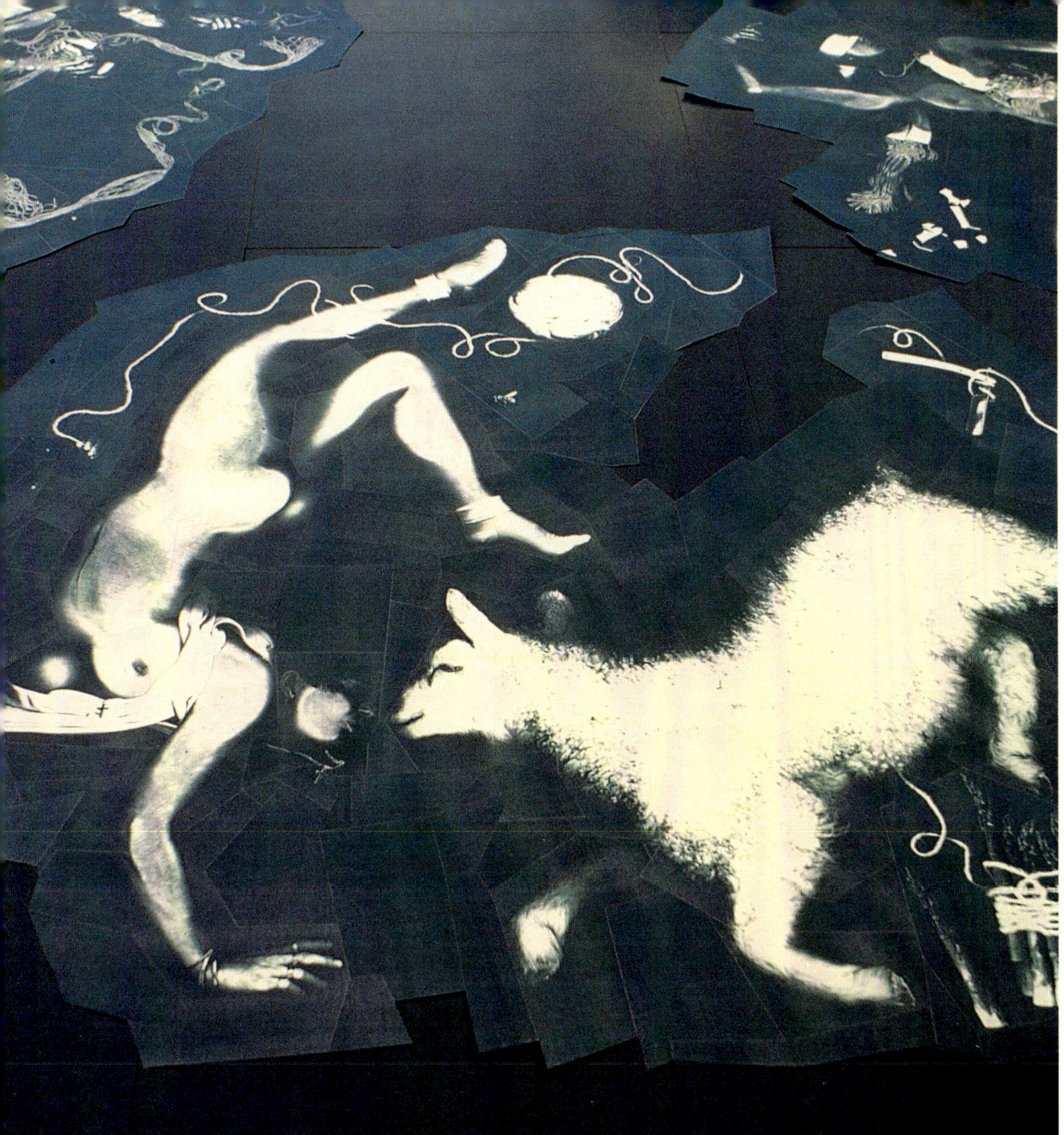

Helen Chadwick, *The Oval Court* (detail), 1986

dotted the yellow faces of daisies with black felt-tip. The work was hard to see in the first place, but Helen found that her fans were removing the daisies as Chadwick originals. "And who says the English won't collect contemporary art?" she joked.

In retrospect there is an astonishing preoccupation with transience and mortality in her work—the feathers, bubbles, mirrors and flowers. It is especially true of her most ambitious and inventive installation *The Oval Court*—the cycle of swirling blue figures and animal attributes—shown at London's Institute of Contemporary Art in 1986 and bought by the V&A two years later. Helen began the piece when her head was filled with the rococo splendors of the pilgrimage churches of Bavaria. She made her *Gesamtkunstwerk* with an office photocopying machine that had a toning device, a computer, some photo-booth self-portraits—and with her intense powers of concentration. She manipulated improbable materials until they answered the vision with which she had dared to set out. Her *Self Portrait* from 1991 is a human brain held—and held together—by the artist's hands. Her unconscious spoke through her fingers, from the self-portraits made of sweets in her Fluxus period in the seventies to the gorgeous floral confections of the nineties. I taped a four-and-a-half-hour life-story interview with Helen for the National Sound Archive in summer 1994. She spoke of early repeated dreams of flying and changing sex. She sketched a life filled with projects which I wanted to see or see again. She spoke captivatingly, like the star she was, but she sometimes looked worn out in the studio light. Her death was recorded as from unknown causes—but perhaps the cause was years of incredible overwork.

CREDITS

TEXT CREDITS: Pages 29–33 excerpted with permission from "Polkography," by Paul Schimmel, copyright © 1996 The Museum of Contemporary Art, Los Angeles; pp. 36–39 copyright © 1996 Rosalind Krauss; p. 40 excerpt from *The Daily Practice of Painting: Writings and Interviews 1962–1993*, by Gerhard Richter, New York, MIT Press, 1995, p. 66; p. 42 excerpts from *The Daily Practice of Painting*, pp. 259–260; p. 44 excerpt from *The Daily Practice of Painting*, p. 232; pp. 60–65 a longer version of this essay on Marker will be published in a forthcoming book by Jan-Christopher Horak, entitled *Making Images Move: Photographers and Avant-Garde Cinema*, to be published by Smithsonian Press; pp. 67–71 text by Wim Wenders from *EINMAL: Bilder und Geschichten*, Verlag der Autoren, Frankfurt/Main, 1994. Translation copyright © 1996 by Joachim Neugroschel.

PHOTOGRAPHY CREDITS: Unless otherwise noted, all photographs are courtesy of, and copyright by, the artists: front cover image Cibachrome, crystal, and felt, courtesy of Metro Pictures, New York City; pp. 2–5 courtesy of Metro Pictures, New York City; pp. 6–11 copyright © 1996 Estate of Pablo Picasso/Artists Rights Society (ARS), New York City; pp. 12–17 copyright © Oslo Kommunes Kunstsamlinger, Munch Museum, Oslo; pp. 18, 20–21, and 24–25 courtesy of PaceWildensteinMacGill, New York City; pp. 19, 22–23, and 26 copyright © 1996 Artists Rights Society (ARS), New York City/ADAGP, Paris; pp. 28–29 and 31, bottom, gelatin-silver prints with paint; all photographs pp. 28–33 courtesy of The Museum of Contemporary Art, Los Angeles; pp. 34–35, Type-C prints, images from the series "Aachener Strasse," 1995, photographed by David Janecek and courtesy of The Museum of Contemporary Art, Los Angeles; pp. 36–37 installation photograph courtesy of Metro Pictures, New York City; pp. 38–39 Cibachrome, crystal and felt, courtesy of Metro Pictures, New York City; pp. 40 and 44 courtesy of Städtische Galerie im Lenbachhaus, Munich; pp. 41–43 courtesy of Marian Goodman Gallery, New York City; p. 45 courtesy of Luhring Augustine Gallery, New York City; p. 46 courtesy of Jack Shainman Gallery, New York City; pp. 47–49 courtesy of Laurence Miller Gallery, New York City; pp. 52–59 gelatin-silver photographs, copyright © Estate of Richard Pousette-Dart and courtesy of Zabriskie Gallery, New York City; p. 54 right, oil on linen, courtesy of Knoedler and Company, New York City; p. 57 left, oil on linen, courtesy of Knoedler & Company, New York City; p. 58 right, oil on linen, courtesy of Knoedler & Company, New York City; pp. 60–65 courtesy of Landeshauptstadt Munchen, Münchner Stadtmuseum, Munich; pp. 67–71 from *EINMAL: Bilder und Geschichten*, Verlag der Autoren, Frankfurt/Main, 1994; p. 72 courtesy of the Francis Bacon Estate; p. 73, left, courtesy of The Board of Trustees of the Victoria & Albert Museum, London, right, courtesy of *Vogue*, The Condé Nast Publications Ltd.; p. 74, left, courtesy of the Francis Bacon Estate, right, courtesy of The City of Aberdeen Art Gallery and Museums Collections; pp. 76–78 all photographs courtesy of the Center for Creative Photography, Tucson, Arizona. Installation of *The Klan Room* photographed by Dianne Nilsen; *Dream Building I* photographed by Keith Schreiber; p. 79 photograph of Helen Chadwick's *Oval Court* courtesy of Edward Woodman.

CONTRIBUTORS

A curator at the Picasso Museum in Paris, ANNE BALDASSARI is organizing a cycle of three exhibitions between 1994 and 1997 devoted to different aspects of Picasso's relationship with photography. She is the author of the catalog *Picasso photographe, 1901–1916* and *Picasso et la photographie, À plus grande vitesse que les images* (Picasso and Photography, faster than images), and of an article entitled "Heads, Faces and Bodies: Picasso's Uses of Portrait Photographs," which was published in the catalog for the exhibition "Picasso and Portraiture, Representation and Transformation" at the Museum of Modern Art, New York, 1996.

DAVID FRANKEL is an editor in the publications department of the Museum of Modern Art, New York. He is also a contributing editor at *Artforum* magazine, where he was for many years a senior editor. He is the author of the recent book *Masterpieces: The Best Loved Paintings from American Museums* (Simon & Schuster).

CHARLES HAGEN is a writer and photographer who teaches at Bard College in Annandale-on-Hudson, New York. He has written about photography and art for many publications, including the *New York Times*, *Artforum*, and *ARTnews*. He was editor of *Aperture* from 1988 to 1991.

PETER HAY HALPERT is an independent writer and curator based in New York City. He is an editor for *American Photo* magazine and a correspondent for *ARTnews* and the *ARTnewspaper*. In addition, he writes for *The Photo Review*, *Popular Photography*, *Elle*, *Mirabella*, *Art & Antiques*, *Creative Camera*, and *Art Press International*. He has published a book on Hiroshi Sugimoto's photographs, and is at work on a book about Dieter Appelt's work.

MARK HAWORTH-BOOTH is Curator of Photographs at the Victoria and Albert Museum in London. He is the author of *Photography Now*, published by Dirk Nishen/V & A in 1989, and *Camille Silvy's "River Scene, France"*, published by The J. Paul Getty Museum in 1992.

JAN-CHRISTOPHER HORAK has been the director of Munich's film museums since 1994. Prior to that, Horak spent ten years as the senior curator of film collections at the George Eastman House in Rochester, New York, and as a professor of film studies at the University of Rochester. His books include *Lovers of Cinema: The First American Film Avant-Garde 1919–1945* (1995), *The Dream Merchants: Making and Selling Films in Hollywood's Golden Age* (1989), and *Film und Foto der zwanziger Jahre* (1979).

MARK MURO is a Tucson, Arizona-based writer and critic. He wrote on the arts for a decade at the *Boston Globe*, and is now a member of the editorial board of the *Arizona Daily Star*.

ROSALIND KRAUSS is Meyer Schapiro Professor of Modern Art and Theory at Columbia University and a founding editor of *October* magazine. Author of *Passages in Modern Sculpture* (1977) and *The Originality of the Avant-Garde* (1985, both MIT Press), her most recent books are *The Optical Unconscious* (MIT Press, 1993) and *Cindy Sherman* (Rizzoli, 1993). She served as curator for the Guggenheim Museum's retrospective "Robert Morris: The Mind/Body Problem" (1994), and "L'Informe: A User's Guide" (1996) for the Centre Georges Pompidou in Paris.

PAUL SCHIMMEL has been the chief curator of The Museum of Contemporary Art in Los Angeles since 1990. From 1981 to 1989 he served as chief curator at the Newport Harbor Art Museum, in Newport Beach, California, and from 1975 to 1978 as curator of The Contemporary Arts Museum in Houston, Texas. Schimmel has curated several major exhibitions, including "Sigmar Polke Photoworks: When Pictures Vanish"; "Hand-Painted Pop: American Art in Transition, 1955–1962"; and "Helter Skelter: Los Angeles Art in the 1990s," all of which were accompanied by publications.

NICK WAPLINGTON is an accomplished skateboarder and an internationally acclaimed photographer. Books of his photographs include *Living Room*, *Other Edens*, and *The Wedding*, all published by Aperture.